Boy, Girl, Fruitcake, Flower

ANTHONY BUNKO

Copyright © 2006 Anthony Bunko

The right of Anthony Bunko to be identified as the
Author of the work has been asserted by him in
accordance with the Copyright, Designs and Patent Act,
1988

All the characters in this book are fictitious *(Honest....cross my arse and hope to die)* and any resemblance to actual people, living, dead or kinetically frozen and stored in a fridge in ASDA at Dowlais Top, is purely coincidental.

All rights reserved. No part of this publication may be
reproduced, stored in a retrieval system, or transmitted, in any
form or by any means without the prior written
permission of the publisher, nor be otherwise circulated
in any form of binding or cover other than that in which
it is published and without similar conditions being
imposed on the subsequent purchaser.

ISBN 0-9547273-3-9

First published 2006 by A. Bunko, 17 Cyfarthfa Gardens, Merthyr. CF48 2SE

Printed and Bound by:- Gomer Press, Wales

www.anthonybunko.co.uk
Email:- anthony@bunko.freeserve.co.uk

Dedicated to:-

"To all the girls in the world like Lois who wear their hearts on their sleeves and Pink G-strings pulled up as far as possible"

Other titles by Anthony Bunko

The Tale of the Shagging Monkeys - 2003

The Tale of Two Shagging Monkeys:-
    The Siege of El Rancho - 2004

The Belt of Kings - 2005

Next project 2007 :-

'Working up to the Slaughterhouse.'

Books available from:-
All good book shops
Amazon.co.uk
gwales.co.uk
and a bloke called Neville

Boy, Girl, Fruitcake, Flower

Part 1

Before TV

Chapter 1

Bump

Amanda tried to move her arms. Unfortunately they had been firmly, but not painfully, secured to the post of the large wooden bed. A blindfold, fashioned from some kind of silk material, wrapped around her eyes made the situation appear just a little exciting, but with a hint of danger. Way down in her chest her heart beat like a bass drum that provided the opening note to a 'Frankie Goes to Hollywood' song. The induced darkness caused shivers to explode all over her semi-naked body. She bit her lip, both in fear and excitement which engulfed her in equal measures.

'How the hell have I got myself in this situation in the first place?' she quietly asked herself.

Vulnerability wrapped itself around her similar to a blanket covering a new born baby. She felt totally exposed in her apparent nakedness. She heard someone moving in the room. There was the distinctive rustling of clothes being removed. It was easy for her to make out the sound of a zipper being undone. What Amanda assumed to be a pair of trousers fell to the carpeted floor. A coin escaped from one of the pockets. It rolled and clattered into the door, piercing the silence. The metal object spun and fluttered then stopped.

Who was it?

She tried to talk but she found that avenue of communication had also been denied to her by the use of some masking tape.

'What are they going to do to me?' Questions bounced about in her mind in quick succession.

She tensed as she suddenly felt a breath of warm air travelling up her body to her neck. It made her jump and gasp for air. Her lower body automatically arched up towards the ceiling as if it was getting systematically sucked up by some kind of large fanny-magnet which had somehow been attached to the light shade. Amanda wondered if she could actually purchase 'Fanny-magnet light shades' at any department store in the High Street.

'IKEA will probably sell them,' she giggled at the thought, for the moment forgetting the predicament she found herself in.

Was she in danger?

She wasn't sure of the answer but what she did know was that she was very damp down below. She didn't know if she should have been or not, but she was. Her juices trickled down the smooth skin of her thighs as she squirmed about in pleasure. The sexual tension in the room was on maximum alert.

Her captive lightly stroked her breasts before gently focusing his attention on her erect nipples. Inwardly she was glad he had noticed them. She had always been very proud of her nipples. The way they pointed to the heavens when aroused was a pleasure to behold. Her husband always commented that she could poke someone's eye out with them. In fact, unknown to him, during a back seat romance while she was in her teens, she had accidentally (but fortunately, temporarily) blinded poor Tommy Harris in his left eye when the rather nervous third former had reached across to unclip her bra. He had had to wear an eye-patch for a while and even to this day he was still known as Lord Nelson. Tommy never forgave Amanda for that.

Back in the heat of the room, a disturbing thought entered her head. She stiffened, afraid to struggle or move a muscle.

'What if it was the weird bloke from the office?' She cringed at the thought. 'Oh shit... it can't be the creepy thirty-something man with the dirty fingernails and the strange stains on his trousers; the one who letches at all the girls.'

Unfortunately for her the weird bloke did have an obsessive crush when she had first started work. He would leave her flowers on her desk everyday and once he even wrote a poem for her (which was rather spooky.) At first Amanda thought it was quite sweet, and would smile at him, until she found out he had pinched the flowers from the local cemetery.

'Oh no!' she thought, 'perhaps he drugged me during the 11 am tea-break and now he's dragged me to his home in the sticks. He's most likely slipped a date-rape tablet into a chocolate digestive biscuit.' She became nervous. 'Shit.... I've just eaten half the bloody pack, I will be like this for a month, and I bet he's even got his dead mother sitting watching in an armchair with the stuffing protruding out of it.'

She pictured both the chair and the mother in urgent need of repair.

Having a vivid and active imagination was a gift (and sometimes an unwanted present) that she had possessed since a child. She developed the technique of seeing life through a strange set of lenses after spending long periods of time in her own room while growing up. She had been painfully shy, mainly caused by her being a little chubby around the cheeks in her early years, plus her mother's insistence on her wearing her hair short. Her mother told her she looked lovely; Amanda thought she looked like a tom-boy. During these years she spent most of her time alone in her room, either drawing, reading or talking to imaginary people. It was an art form she took into her later life, but thankfully she had lost her chubby cheeks and always wore her brown hair long and curly since then.

Just as a set of lips kissed her ear her thought process instantly switched from being turned on to turned off at the image of the weird bloke slobbering all over her body.

'No, it can't be him.' She suddenly realised, partially because whoever the mystery person was smelled clean. She knew that the bloke in her office, whatever his name was, always smelt of ginger beer and embalming fluid. She breathed a deep sigh of relief and relaxed again.

Another thought crossed her mind. What if her captive wasn't a man? Her brain-cells were cart-wheeling out of control.

To be truthful, the person could have been any gender. Up until this point in the proceedings there had been no real clues. The sexless person was now slowly using his, or her, tongue to discover some more hidden places that she had almost forgotten existed on her body.

She wondered if the underneath of her armpits should actually be so sensitive, considering the situation she found herself in.

'Who can it possibly be?'

'What if it is a woman?'

Of course, like most females, Amanda had had the odd fantasy about getting intimate with someone of the same sex when she was growing up. She had been told that it was quite normal for every teenager at one stage in their developing life to tiptoe down the street named 'Lesbian Lane'. In later years, she had quickly abandoned the idea of turning the fantasy into reality after getting food poisoning from eating a prawn and mayo sandwich which she had bought in a Little Chef near Bath. From that day on, anything that reminded her of fish (in any form) was strictly off the menu.

She again felt a jet of hot breath on her neck. She prayed that the person licking it was a man. She began to struggle violently for the first time.

'Cool down, just relax. I'm here for your pleasure,' a man's voice drifted softly into her ear. His large hands tenderly engulfed hers. He nibbled her earlobe.

She breathed out with relief. 'Thank God. It is a man and not some big butch lesbian with short hair and wearing a Ben Sherman shirt. And it's definitely not the old letch with the dirty nails from the office'.

She closed her eyes under the blindfold. After twenty seconds she realised it was pointless, so she opened them again. Deep down inside she hoped the person making love to her could somehow be George Clooney, or, at a push, Brad Pitt, but of the two superstars it was grey-haired George, with the silky voice and the mischievous eyes, that always made her pop her cork. Her imagination went into overdrive.

He touched her. She felt the sheer size of the stranger's hands. They were real man's hands; big, strong, and yet tender. She melted under the touch.

'You know what they say about men with big strong hands?' her best friend Lois always reminded her when they saw someone she fancied who had large hands.

'No, Lois, why don't you remind me?' Amanda would always play along.

'Large hands, massive weapon.' Lois always made Amanda smile (even when Amanda didn't feel much like smiling).

Her mate always had an uncanny knack of bringing every day situations back to the 'S' for sex word. Last week when they were both in Tesco, she saw this young, attractive boy with a bunch of bananas in his trolley. 'Thought so,' Lois declared proudly, 'You know what they say... 'Bunch of bananas, massive weapon.... and probably.... big, seedy balls.'

Amanda had giggled to herself all day over that one. She couldn't help but continually picture a large, black gorilla swinging through the jungle, holding a bunch of bananas, with its naughty bits dangling freely between its legs.

Back in the room, Amanda could now taste the person's breath. She again racked her brain to try to identify who had suddenly, and tenderly, started to use their tongue to discover concealed places which had lain dormant on her anatomy for many a year. She inhaled with pleasure, sucking in the moment.

A little devil appeared on her shoulder and muttered into her ear, 'I wonder if he's got a large pecker on him?'

Amanda could feel herself going red. 'I don't care how big his pecker is, I'm a decent woman!' she snapped back at the little, mischievous, sprite figure.

She was well aware that most women she knew would often pretend to scoff, scorn and pull a face when the word 'penis' was dropped into a conversation. Most would shake their heads in disgust as if it was some kind of taboo subject. On the other hand, Lois would actually pride herself with being a 'Full Penis Protagonist' who loved to chuck the man genitalia word into any opportunity possible. Amanda recalled her friend had once used the 'Cock' word, seventeen times in less than ten minutes. If they had been in a pub and Lois was telling a rude joke, it may have been acceptable, but the fact that they were in church, attending Amanda's Aunty Lizzie's funeral at the time was slightly concerning to everyone who sat in the front three pews.

Secretly, Amanda couldn't wait to feel what the man of mystery was packing in his trousers. Thankfully for her she didn't have to wait long.

He slowly released the tape from her mouth. Before she had a chance to utter a sound, his lips pressed against hers. His tongue flicked out lightly. He kissed her neck again.

She should have let go of a thousand words that had been previously held back by the tape around her mouth, but all that escaped was a soft moaning noise that drifted up to nestle on the headboard.

Then she felt it. It touched her thigh. It was rock hard. It must have been the size of an American traffic cop's truncheon, but with the added bonus of having a bell-end like a coal miner's helmet. She imagined it, shiny bright as it lowered itself deep into the dark depths of her love shaft.

She hadn't thought such dirty thoughts for a very long time, especially about some other man (anyway, not since she had been married.) But recently, it was all 'Wham, bam, the footballs on Mam', type of sex with her husband. He couldn't even be bothered to tune into Nipple AM during their love making. Nowadays she counted herself lucky if he actually rolled off before he fell asleep (often leaving her to manoeuvre her unsatisfied body around the damp patch).

So, to have someone turning her gently around and kissing the nape of her neck was a new adventure for her. It was an exciting experience to savour and enjoy.

The fanny magnet on the ceiling had been cranked up to maximum power and she found herself bucking wildly like a black stallion at a rodeo trying to dismount a cocksure cowboy, whose name happened to be Todd, and who was really a press operator working in a plant making car parts in Ashtabula. On times like this she cursed her fertile imagination for going off onto tangents for no reason.

Amanda tried hard to concentrate and to get it back on track. 'Who are you?' she whispered, nails squeezed softly into his strong broad shoulders.

'You know who I am,' came the reply.

'Is it you?' She was amazed; she left a gap before adding hopefully, 'Is it…. George?'

There was a pause. Then he spoke 'Of course. Who did you think it was? Brad or that weirdo from your office?' It was followed by a laugh, then an affectionate kiss on her pouting lips.

She took a deep breath; she noticed the room stank of sex. Amanda realised that 'stank' was not a very nice way to describe what was happening to her, but it did. She was sure she would have to get the carpets fumigated at this rate. It smelt like a downtown, Bangkok, whore house in the height of summertime.

Amanda felt overjoyed. She was over the moon with a silver spoon in her drooling mouth. 'Great! Wait until I tell Lois,' she thought, 'Who says that you can't pull a Hollywood superstar at the age of 39 years, four months,

14 days and 11 hours, to be exact?' She smiled to herself before kissing him passionately with all her might and an extra helping of tongue.

She knew that reaching the unwanted age of the big Four Zero, was a milestone that everyone at some time in their life must cross, and most people were not looking forward to it at all. But to be truthful, at that moment she felt seventeen and high on life. She thought she had died and gone to heaven.

'Please enter me….. I just need to feel you deep inside of me,' she whispered, saliva dripping from the corner of her mouth.

She knew that her parents wouldn't approve. They had brought her up never to beg for anything. They were very strict, especially her father. He had grown up during the Second World War, when times were tough and food was scarce.

'But it taught me to look after myself…. never to rely on anyone. Nothing, or no-one, is worth begging for,' her father, wearing checked slippers, would often pipe-up from his permanent spot in front of the gas fire. 'If you're to get on in this world my girl….. You need to do it yourself. Take the bull by the horns, ride the horse to market.' She hated him when he dictated to her. He showed little emotion towards Amanda. He didn't even like her to cry, thinking it was a sign of weakness.

She had taken her parents advice to heart. It had made her quite self sufficient and very hard-working. She had gone through most of her life not asking for anything, never begging, stealing or borrowing. Not even when she found herself in situations where she needed help. Like the time she found herself stuck on the side of the motorway in the pouring rain with a flat tyre. She hadn't tried to flag someone down or phone for assistance. She struggled to do it herself. She had blisters the size of baked-bean cans on her hands and spent a week in bed with the flu. Her father was proud; she secretly joined the A.A. the next day.

So her strict upbringing may have been character building, but at that precise moment, while she lay under the powerful, muscular frame of gorgeous George, she would have sold her favourite grandmother into a life of debauchery and slavery to a blind camel herder, with a scabby eye and a hook for a hand, just to feel George's rocket enter her inner space.

'Ding Dong'

She suddenly heard a noise far off in the distance. She wisely chose to ignore it. She ripped the blindfold off her eyes. She pulled him closer, pleading for him to put her out of her misery.

'Come on George…if I was a dog you would have bloody shot me by now….take me….quick…do it.'

'Ding Dong'

'What was that?' George looked up, one of her pubes appeared to be lodged in his teeth.

'God I wish I had a camera with me,' Amanda thought to herself. 'Imagine how jealous the girls in work would be if they saw that the actor had her pube in his handsome mouth.'

'Ding Dong….Ding Dong.'

'What is that?' the Hollywood stud asked again.

Amanda reached between her legs for the superstar's head. She pulled it towards her violently. 'It was nothing baby….quick, I'm wetter than the water chute at Alton Towers.' She cursed and wished she had something a little more romantic to say. But what the hell, she was having the time of her life and she could say anything she wanted. She was participating in pure raw, sweat-dripping sex.....in her front room with none-other than George fuckin' Clooney. Now it doesn't come better than that.

The ding donging turned into a vicious bang banging on a window pane. It was followed by a gruff voice. 'Amanda...Amanda....it's me...open the door....it's fucking freezing....my nipples are about to poke through my blouse.'

Amanda wasn't sure what the hell was happening; George was slowly disintegrating into thin air in front of her.

'Where are you going?' she screamed desperately.

Amanda decided that she had come too close to humping the world famous actor to give in without a fight. In a last ditch attempt, she spread her legs wide open in the faint hope that she could possibly suck him into her, like a vacuum cleaner sucking up dirt, or the way a genie gets put back into a bottle in a Disney film.

'I'm melting....I'm melting!' George shrieked as he finally disappeared in a giant puff of smoke. A black cloak lay smouldering on the fake Egyptian rug.

'Come back....come back.' Amanda's arms clutched at thin air.

'Bang Bang.' The noise again rose up from a different part of the house.

'Amanda, for fuck's sake!...stop squirming around on that settee and open the fucking door...I'm dying for a slash.'

She again bellowed out his name. 'George!'

'Amanda ... Amanda, who are you talking to? Look by the window... It's me... Lois...your best friend.'

Amanda finally looked up to see a face at the lounge window, surrounded by wild, dyed-blonde hair, with black roots growing out of her scalp and laced with split ends. This was Lois, Amanda's best friend in the entire world, or at least from the roundabout by Asda to the self-service garage at the bottom of town. Those three miles or so were the extent of Amanda's entire universe.

She double-checked hoping she had made a mistake. Unfortunately she knew no one other than her mate would plaster that much fake tan all over their face on a Monday afternoon. From where Amanda was sitting Lois resembled a tangerine that had been placed under a grill on gas mark 4 for much too long.

The face at the window waved at her frantically.

Lois was the self-proclaimed queen of Slutsville (and she didn't just mean in the bedroom). Where some girls have a knack for cooking, sewing, or decorating cakes, Lois had a God-given gift for making herself look common. It was like she had worked on it down to the very last detail. The clothes she wore were always too tight and way too short, no matter what the weather was like outside. Her white stilettos were nearly as famous up on the estate as the Wicked Witch's sparkling red slippers in the Wizard of Oz. Even her gravelly voice had been trained to have just the right pitch of commonness. She swore as if it was going out of fashion, but amusingly, sometimes, she just spelled the word out instead of saying it. She believed that if she did this it wouldn't count in the eyes of God and be used against her when she finally went to meet her maker in heaven. She was also counting on God being a bad speller.

'Oh no... don't say I was dreaming,' Amanda alerted herself, before regretfully asking, 'Hang on.... maybe I'm actually dreaming about Lois. Perhaps George has just slipped out to the bathroom to freshen himself up.' The smile returned to her face.

Amanda clambered off the settee. She rushed towards the bathroom on top of the stairs. She kicked open the door. Of course there was no sign of George; just a messy room covered in wet towels, bras and yesterday's used underwear. She came down to earth with a bump. But just to make sure, she doubled-checked in the airing cupboard and behind the cistern. Dejectedly, she shook her head and stared into the mirror.

'Bollocks….it was George who was the dream and bloody Lois is real. I'll kill her.' Amanda splashed cold water onto her face to try to hide the redness of her flushed cheeks. She trooped back down the stairs, alone and very frustrated. She reluctantly let her friend in.

'You took your bastard time. What the hell were you doing on that settee any-road? You looked like a slug that had been sprinkled with salt.' She pushed past into the warmth of the house.

'I think I was having a nightmare,' Amanda lied.

Lois parked herself down at the kitchen table. 'A nightmare…. Yeah! Pull the other one. More like you were having the famous 'George Clooney blindfolded me on the bed' fantasy.'

Amanda could feel her cheeks get even redder than they already were. She thought her head would explode. 'Don't be so stupid…. It was a nightmare…. And by the way, you came in the nick of time and saved me from being bludgeoned to death by some… bloke!'

Lois gave her mate 'The Look'. It was 'The Look' that needed no words. Lois had mastered it into an art form over many years. Worse was to follow. Lois folded her arms and waited for the truth to come tumbling out. Amanda knew she had been rumbled. Lois could have easily made a decent living working as a human lie detector. She could read people like a book, and she normally knew the ending long before the last chapter.

After the compulsory pause that as a rule followed 'The Look', Amanda finally cracked. 'Well Ok Miss Marple... perhaps it wasn't exactly a nightmare.'

'Arrgggh! I knew it. Amanda, its Lois you are trying to deceive. Never forget. Never bullshit a bullshitter, especially one with a GCSE in a Shitty Life and a certificate in Hard Knocks.' Lois reached into her tan handbag that unintentionally didn't match anything she was wearing and pulled out a pack of twenty cigarettes.

A handbag to Lois was just a devise to carry around her fags, condoms and sometimes a set of handcuffs. Her last casual boyfriend had been as frisky as they come; only problem was he couldn't cum unless it was very kinky. She continued talking to Amanda while striking a match. 'Look girl, there is only one fantasy, and only one man that can make someone gyrate that aggressively. That man is King George.' Lois smirked in triumph.

Amanda didn't know where to look.

'Did you get to the part where he slapped his piece of meat onto your thigh,' Lois asked while sucking all the life out of her poor, defenceless cigarette.

She stubbed it out and lit another. Lois didn't class herself as a chain smoker. She really saw smoking as her way to provide a service to keep the cigarette manufacturers from making working-class employees redundant. Her philosophy was the more she could puff at, the more people stayed in a job. It was her simple logic in a down-to-earth, uncomplicated mind.

Amanda filled the kettle up to the maximum level and sat opposite her friend on the new vinyl stools that had transformed the pokey old kitchen into a plush, but still a pokey, old kitchenette, but with a built-in breakfast bar.

'He's got a great cock on him, mind…. fuckin' King Kong would have been proud of it. Did you see the way it lights up on the end?' Lois laid out the cheese in her trap.

Amanda took the bait, hook, line, sinker, mouth wide open. 'I knew it was going to light up on the end…. I just knew it!'

'Hahhhh Hahhhh…. So it was George…. You dirty bitch.' Lois expertly flicked the ash from her fag into the ashtray. The glass container was already lined with the bodies of lots of dead fag nips. 'You were lucky… it could have been your old man at the window watching you wrestling with your fantasies.' The smoke from the fag made a ring which climbed up to the ceiling. It danced about wildly before disappearing.

'You are amazing.' Amanda reached across and pulled a nicotine stick from out of its snug bed.

Lois kicked off her white stilettos and said, 'Don't forget…I invented that fantasy. I wish I had bloody copyrighted it, I would easily have been a millionaire by now.'

Amanda was flabbergasted and completely speechless. She launched three tea-bags into the bottom of the teapot and shuffled the mugs back and forth nervously on the Formica work surface. She followed her mate's lead and produced a ring of smoke that sailed away across the kitchen and clawed its way up the nicotine and grease stained walls. 'Anyway, fat chance of Darryl standing by the window…he's working overtime…again.'

'Overtime again…good God girl, you must be minted.' Lois scanned the grimy kitchen. It didn't appear to belong to a couple who had excessive amounts of funds. It replicated most kitchens on the estate, boringly practical and decorated in an urban working-class style of desperation.

Amanda knew exactly what her mate was thinking, so she got her retaliation in first. 'The wages in the foundry aren't that good and we have a car to pay for.'

'Hey,' Lois enquired, 'he's not having an affair, is he? You know that guys his age start to stray.'

'What do you mean his age? He's the same bloody age as us.'

'Ok same as us… but men are designed to have affairs after a certain age. A mid-life crisis they call it. I should know…I've cured, and caused, many mid-life crises down the years in this town. But men can't help themselves….its in their Levis.'

Amanda shook her head in puzzlement.

'It's in their bloody genes…. Like gambling, football and having blow-jobs… and I should bloody know, you don't get lips like this from playing the trumpet.' She puckered out her lips, fag nip balanced on the edge, never in danger of falling to the floor.

'Not all men are like that…especially my Darryl.' Amanda poured the tea.

Sometimes she hated Lois and her facts about bloody men. But she also knew that if anyone should know about the opposite sex it was Lois. She had screwed most of them, and in no particular order. It was a case of first come, first served.

'Listen Amanda, it is as simple as this. Men of a certain age suddenly find themselves unable to play footie or rugby on a Saturday, suddenly they start drinking cheap plonk and listening to middle-of-the-road, crappy music.'

Amanda stared at the bottle of red wine which lay empty in the bin. She glanced at the CD rack. Long gone was the music that made her and her husband dance the night away. No more Thin Lizzy or Whitesnake. It had been replaced by mellow, yellow Coldplay and that other over-hyped band of the moment, whose songs sound all the same. 'Fuck me…. Lois is right again.' She thought sadly.

'I know I'm right,' Lois wrestled the conversation back from out of her friends mind. 'They listen to all that poncey crap and then think it's their divine right to supplement their loss of their thirty-something years by poking their meat stick into a new piece of skirt.'

Amanda stirred the tea hurriedly.

'My ex was a right bastard,' Lois pretended to spit on the floor. 'I swear as soon as he went from a size 32 inch waist to a flabby 38, he was straight on that highway to 'Poking some slag in the back of his car,' and without passing GO. I can't believe that Slut!' Lois lit another cigarette even though her third was only half-way through its journey of self-destruction. She simultaneously puffed on both.

'Have you seen him lately?' Amanda passed Lois her mug of Typhoo.

'Yeah…he came around last week to see his kid.'

'Well how is he?' Amanda asked.

Lois took a sip before hissing, 'He's a no-good drug addict.'

'No, not your boy… how's your ex-husband?'

'Oh him… He's fine… more's the pity. He's still having the physio, but the hospital told him that the skin is finally starting to knit together.' Unbelievably the two fags Lois had been smoking finished their life at exactly the same time. That was another reason why Amanda loved her mate, she was capable of things that no one else could do.

'I still can't believe that you scalded him with that boiling water.' Amanda winced as she mentioned it.

'Look…. If you live by the pork sword… and you get caught…. You must die by the pork sword….and expect to be scalded.'

Amanda remembered the night of the attack quite well. It was an incident that contained a jealous, dyed, blonde-haired wife, a kettle, six black police vans, thirty policemen, two police dogs, three ambulances, a hospital helicopter and twenty-two emergency operations. The hot kettle revenge attack had taken place when Lois had calmly poured the remains from the kettle over the poor man's groin, after she had found a pair of red knickers and a receipt for flowers in the glove compartment of his car.

Everyone knew it was a terrible thing to do, especially since Lois had been no angel herself over the years. In fact it was a bit like the pot calling the kettle black. But her excuse to Amanda was that she only had sex with other blokes, she never bought them flowers, or shit like that; that was taking it too far.

On a positive note, adultery rates up on the estate, which had been the highest in the country, reduced by 95%, as housewives immediately went out and purchased the biggest kettles in Kwiksave they could find and ensured that they were always full.

Lois opened a new packet of fags from her bag. She farted. It was silent, but packed a punch that would have floored Muhammad Ali in his prime.

'Lois! What the hell was that?'

'Chicken tikka massala with three helpings of banana cheesecake. It is quite potent… to be honest; I thought I'd killed my dog this morning. It was under the bed sheets poor thing and caught the full force of the blast. It just rolled off the bed and started coughing.'

Amanda got up and opened a window and searched around under the sink for some air freshener.

'Anyway, enough of you and your husband's sordid love affair,' Lois joked, 'How about something stronger than Typhoo?' Lois got up and rifled through the units of the cupboards. She soon found what she was looking for, an unopened half-bottle of gin. She tipped the remains of the tea into a plant-pot and replaced it with the crystal-clear, liquid nectar. 'You wait until I tell you about what that bastard said to me?'

'What bastard is this then?' Amanda got a clean glass and poured herself a drink. She had a feeling she would need it.

'That big bastard shit-face in my office. You know, I've told you about him.'

Amanda again shook her head.

'You remember...the one who I meet most lunch-times in the stationery room.' Lois's face was set in stone.

'Oh.... him. How silly of me? I thought you were talking about someone serious.'

'Oh it is serious....he's given up playing five-a-side football with his mates in the lunch break...just to back-scuttle me over the photocopier.'

Amanda laughed and added, 'Poor boy...I bet he's devastated. How old is he anyway?'

'He's twenty-three if you must know.... and less of the bloody sarcasm if you will. Don't forget, twenty minutes ago you were on your back waiting for an imaginary George Clooney to march into your town called Alice and plumb your springs.... So top us up and listen.'

Amanda did what she was told.

'Well, today, right...' Lois spurted out her words, leaning back on the stool. 'We had just finished doing the business. I must say.... what a movement on him.... he could knock a fucking eight-inch nail into the side of a house.... He's a sex-crazed human Hilti gun... Best ride I've ever had. Anyway, he was having a bite of the sandwich that I made him....'

Amanda burst out laughing. She couldn't help it. 'Excuse me... Does 'having a bite out of the sandwich I made him' mean something sexual or degrading?'

Lois screwed up her face. 'Of course it doesn't mean anything sexual or bloody degrading. It means I always make him some food. Hey... we only have thirty minutes for lunch break.... And I'm not wasting precious fanny-filling time while he queues up at the bloody sandwich van....so I always prepare a few sardine and gherkin sandwiches for our after show feast.'

'Sorry Lois....I just thought it was a code for something else.'

'Amanda, there's more to life than pure sex.'

This statement amazed Amanda, because ever since she had known her mate, sex had been a massive part of Lois' life. She was reminiscent of a self-employed prostitute who didn't charge and just did it for the pleasure. She was certain that had men paid Lois to use and abuse her she would be living in the lap of luxury rather than the squalid little shack up on the estate. Sex was high on her list and everything else was a poor second.

'Look Amanda...you drag me over to your house and I sit here listening to your marital problems about your husband having an affair...'

'He's not having an affair...he's working overtime.' Amanda felt like kicking her out into the cold street.

There was that 'Look' again. Lois was the master at it, the Van Gogh of the 'Stare,' or the Leonardo Da Vinci of the 'Awkward Glance.' 'Hey... working overtime….that's what the Yorkshire Ripper told his wife.'

Amanda was lost for words. Sometimes Lois's statements never made any sense, but Amanda had given up trying to correct her. Instead, she poured another measure, too exhausted to argue with Lois. At that moment she couldn't care if her husband was screwing the girl who flashed her arse while doing the weather on the evening news, just as long as Lois finished her bloody story.

'Now can I please get on with my story…? You don't realise how upsetting this all is.' Lois pulled a face. 'So he had just taken a bite out of his sandwich…. WHICH I MADE HIM…. and he turned to me and said out straight that I was the worst shag he's ever had… bar none.'

'Are you sure he didn't mean the sandwich? Cold sardine and gherkins are not to everyone's taste.'

'No, he said shag…worst shag, bar none…that's he's ever had. Cheeky jumped up little fucker…. And I'm the one who showed him where his erogenous zone was and he treats me so bad.'

Amanda was careful to choose her words, 'Alright Lois…. what did he say exactly?'

'Amanda, are you listening to a word I'm saying here? This is serious shit. That tiny-dicked wanker…. challenged my sexuality…. and then he had the cheek to finish off the bloody sandwich, photocopy a report and go back to work.'

Amanda knew that she couldn't move her lips anywhere near a smile. Any movement that represented laughter would simply freak Lois out. Amanda ensured the kettle was well out of reach. 'Did he really say that?'

'No…. of course he didn't. You are thick. No wonder your husband is sniffing after every skirt in the town.'

'Lois...stop saying that...he's not...he's working over....'

'I know ... I know...he's working overtime.' Lois' face was enough. 'Don't forget the Yorkshire Ripper.'

'Well what did he say then,' Amanda bit back. 'And please stop mentioning the Yorkshire fuckin' Ripper when you talk about my husband.'

Lois gulped down her drink. 'Ok, he didn't actually say that... but I could tell that he was thinking it. I could tell by his body language.'

'His what? His body language...when have you ever studied body language... now anatomy-language, I would agree.'

'Well, I went on a course last month. It explained how to read people just by observing their movements, expressions and signs. So unfold your arms girl and start taking me seriously, or I'm going home.'

Amanda immediately sprung open her arms, trying to appear concerned. She found this difficult, since she'd just found out that her friend was suddenly this witch-doctor who could decipher hand-signals. Amanda placed her hands under the table and tried hard not to blink.

'Lois, what did he bloody well say?'

'He didn't actually say anything. It was just his attitude. I could sense it in the way he buckled up his belt and he bit into the bread. I could tell exactly what he was thinking.'

Amanda made a mental note to see if there were any more body language courses being run at the local college. Perhaps it would help her to understand the workings of her mother-in-law a bit better. On second thoughts, it would take all of twenty seconds to know exactly what her mother-in-law was thinking.

There was a brief silence which seemed to last a life time. The two women refused to acknowledge one another and they sat there with their arms folded.

Amanda finally cracked and asked another question, 'Well, if he said that, no, sorry, if he was thinking that… what are you going to do about it?'

Lois slowly shook her head. 'Well tomorrow…. I'm definitely not going to give him a blow job during the 11 am coffee break and he can make his own bloody sandwiches for lunch.'

Amanda's face froze. Suddenly Lois let out a loud cackle. The laughter made Amanda's neighbour's dog, Bernie, run up the garden and hide in the shed. The two friends fell about laughing. This was met with the sound of the trickle of gin being poured into two large glasses.

'Lois, you are strange.'

'Hey… I nearly forgot,' Lois piped up. 'Talking about strange, I saw that Desmond bloke about to knock on your door earlier.'

'Are you sure? Desmond coming to my door…that is strange. Wonder why he didn't knock? Maybe he was collecting for the church?' Amanda gestured.

'Hey….maybe he saw you and your invisible pervert dance on the settee and went home for a five finger shuffle.' Lois laughed; it came from way down in her boots.

Amanda slammed her glass on the table. 'Don't be so disgusting Lois, you know that Desmond is not like that.'

Now Desmond was about 53 years old. He still lived with his mother. No one ever remembered his father, not even Lois' grandmother, who was famous for remembering everyone (living or dead).

All in all, Desmond was kind, but an odd bloke. He had been brought up a proper mammy's boy, and since becoming a man, was now known as a mammy's man. He was friendly enough, always said hello, although he rarely made eye contact. Everyone realised he was different but it still came as a massive culture shock to the community when he turned up six months ago at the Spar shop, to get some milk and bread, wearing a dress and high heeled shoes. He was apparently in the final stage of having his sex-change operation. It was the time before they cut his manhood off and folded his bits back.

Lois mused, 'Perhaps he was seeing if you had any old dresses or skirts he could borrow?'

'Lois… Stop that. He can't help it. I blame his creepy mother. I heard that she made him dress up like a girl until he was fourteen.'

Lois was less sympathetic to his cause. 'I don't care…people like that give me the willies.' Lois was blunt in her assessment.

'People like what?'

Lois stubbed her fag out. 'You know people like Desmond… bizarre ones… mixed-up sexes… it's not natural. You can't trust them. Their mental state is balancing on a knife edge …. One thing goes wrong and they snap.'

'What about you and the kettle?'

'That was different. That was in the name of love,' Lois huffed.

'In the name of love… you can't call scalding your husband in THE NAME OF LOVE.'

'Ok…in the name of 'Getting your own back on the bastard,' then…. But I've been told that after Desmond's gone through this stage of wearing a dress for a few months, he can have the operation.' Lois's words painted a picture. It wasn't a pretty one.

'What operation?' Amanda enquired.

'The op to cut his little worm off and throw it away.'

Amanda screwed her face up. 'No way! He's not going all the way is he? Isn't he too old?'

'I think he's paying private.... with those Bopa people.'

'Bupa Lois... not Bopa.'

'Whatever.... But apparently he'll be in and out in a day,' Lois added.

Amanda shook her head. 'God... imagine that... what a shame?'

'A shame.... I think by the way he shuffled out of your garden he may have already had it done,' Lois added, 'That's another thing they taught me in that bloody body language course.'

The two women burst out laughing.

Chapter 2

Snap

The following morning, Amanda and her mate sat in Lois's clapped-out Ford Escort. Outside, the rain bashed noisily against the windscreen. The car leaked in several places. Amanda commented that if it had been a boat it would have sunk by now. The main source of the problem was the body work, which was only being held together by rust. It should have been condemned to a life of recycling. In her defence, Lois claimed that was the main reason why she didn't bother to get it taxed and insured.

They both stared out of the windows. Drops of rain fell onto the glass and obscured their view of the wonder of the caravan site where they were parked up. The area looked like a large refuse tip. It was a place where the council had decided to dump all the caravan people amongst the coal tips, the abandoned washing machines, the old mattresses and the black rubbish bags. A vicious looking mongrel of a dog was chained to an iron railing. Amanda wasn't sure if the dog may have been crossed with a wild boar. It was nasty. It had a head that Mike Tyson would have been proud of.

For no reason, the dog would bark and rush forward until the chain tightened around its neck, ending its movement. They watched with amusement as the mutt would recoil back and somersault in the air. Seconds later it quickly got back on to its paws before attempting to go through the same pointless routine again.

Near a pile of car wrecks, two unkempt men wrestled with pieces of scrap-iron on the back of an open-top pick-up truck. They were making a metal bonfire from the items they had gathered that morning. They stopped momentarily as another car pulled up and waited in a line. The older man shouted something before spitting onto the ground. He laughed. The younger man didn't look up; he just continued hauling the morning's collection onto the ground. Amanda couldn't actually tell if the language they spoke was English, some lost diddycoy dialect, or if he had his tongue cut out in some earlier violent gypsy caravan feud. They intimidated her; men like them always did.

'Hey…that young one is quite sexy,' Lois said, searching in her bag for some lipstick.

'Lois… he looks like he's never seen a bar of soap in his life. Look at his finger nails…..they are black.'

'He's got lovely big hands mind. You know what they say about men with big, dirty, rough hands.'

'Let me guess...? Big dirty rough hands, big, dirty, scabby cock!' Amanda replied sarcastically.

Lois gave her mate a strange stare. 'No… Big hands…. Massive weapon!'

Amanda changed the subject as fast as she could. 'What time is our appointment anyway?'

'It's eleven'

'Eleven?' Amanda stared at the clock on the beaten up dash board. 'But it's only ten thirty. Why are we here so early?'

'Because if we miss our slot, Madam Zelda will refuse to see us, and she'll still insist on us paying and if she's in a real bad pissed-off mood she'll put a curse on us that will last for three years.' She said sternly. 'She's been in great demand ever since she told Mrs Taylor during a session that her husband would get murdered..... Now people come from miles to see her and get their fortunes told'

'Yeah...but hang on a minute,' Amanda commented 'Wasn't it Mrs Taylor who murdered poor Mr Taylor after coming home from having her fortune told by Madam Zelda?'

Amanda recalled the hullabaloo in the local newspaper. Mrs Taylor was found guilty of bludgeoning her husband to death after Madam Zelda hinted that maybe he was holding her back and it was time for a change. She allegedly came home, stuck an axe in his head and then booked a holiday to Greece on Teletext. The police eventually discovered her at the airport buying a bottle of whisky and a large bar of Toblerone in duty-free.

'Exactly.... Madam Zelda is shit hot.... She knows her stuff.'

Amanda let the comment drift over her head. Instead she stared out across the wasteland covering the top of the mountain. The wind was so strong it could bend a tree in half. A hand-written sign pinned to the window boldly stated that 'Madam Zelda was the best Clairvoyant in the County, and was available for business.... Palms read, tarot cards, tea-bags, crystal balls.... Madam Zelda knows exactly what's around the corner.' Underneath it also announced, 'Cash only. No plastic, No bartering with old clothes, or dodgy electrical gear.'

She noticed six cars surrounding the tiny caravan; all were occupied by middle-aged women. Amanda knew that the womenfolk around this area were desperate to cling onto anything that may brighten up their grey-looking lives. It was evident in the lines etched onto their faces and the way their knuckles gripped the steering wheels they needed a glimmer of hope to march behind.

Amanda stared at the bold prediction on the sign. 'If she does know what's around the corner, then why doesn't she use her crystal ball to pick the right lottery numbers in next week's prize draw? She could then afford to pitch her caravan in LA and read the palms of the stars,' she pondered out loud.

Her cynical thought-pattern was disturbed by Lois rolling her eyes and cracking bitterly, 'Don't be so stupid.... Madam Zelda ain't allowed to do the lottery.... All fortune tellers' are banned from doing that stuff... They can't even do the football pools.'

Amanda was stopped from giving her mate a counter-argument by the door of the caravan opening and a well-dressed woman gingerly stepping out. She appeared to have been crying.

'Quick... we're next.' Lois stubbed her fag out and leapt out of the car. The mad dog rushed at them. Teeth glaring. Unfortunately for the canine, the chain stopped its advance in mid-flow. It reeled backwards yet again.

'Thank you Madam Zelda... thank you very much... I will promise to start going to single's bars tomorrow,' the departing woman shouted back.

The two girls knocked on the dilapidated caravan's door and waited. It was cold. The door opened and they entered. The inside of the mobile home was just as small as it appeared from the outside. For some strange reason, Amanda expected it to be like Dr Who's Tardis, with maybe a big camp fire in the middle of the room, a stuffed bear and a plastic waterfall. Amanda shook the thoughts out of her head. But the room was miniature, cramped and very untidy. It smelt of oil-fired heating, vinegar and damp clothing. A serious looking boy, who couldn't have been more than five or six, but who had the weathered appearance of someone much older, pointed at them to sit on a threadbare bench.

'Madam Zelda is busy. She'll be with you soon.' He then whispered to someone behind a curtain. 'Ma…. The next ones' are here.'

The girls' sat opposite the crystal ball. Lois looked around before giving it a quick rub. 'Mirror… Mirror… in the ball….'

'Stop it, Lois.' Amanda slapped her hand.

From behind the greased-spattered, green and white striped curtain they could hear the sound of water being poured into a metal container. After a few seconds, the curtains whooshed open and an elderly woman appeared with a tea-towel wrapped around her head. She was readjusting her skirt.

'When nature calls,' she said before taking her position opposite the girls.

'She's just had a slash,' Lois whispered. Amanda nudged her sharply.

To Amanda, Madam Zelda could easily have been about two hundred years old. She had never seen so many lines on one face before. They were so deep, cavers could easily have got lost in them. She had unnaturally dark skin which was in stark contrast to the pair of ice-blue eyes that pierced into the two ladies who sat nervously in front of her.

'Who wants me to look into their futures, then?'

Both women put their hands up.

'How do you want me to do it?'

The girls hesitated and looked at each other. Madam Zelda handed them an A4 laminated card which listed the options, plus the price list.

Lois studied the card and said, 'If we have the tarot card option…. does that include biscuits and coffee?'

The old woman nodded and snorted, 'Yes, but only plain biscuits. If you go for the full package you could have custard creams, or two jammy dodgers each.' She smiled; her teeth were yellow with spots of green around the edges.

Lois beamed back, 'That's Ok….the tarot card will be good.'

'That will be thirty notes.'

'No problem.' Lois answered back.

'No that WILL be thirty notes each.' The old witch held out her grubby paw.

They handed over the cash. She passed the money onto the little boy who put it in a large red biscuit tin and placed it under the bed.

'Let's see what the cards tell us then?' A pack of tarot cards appeared.

Madam Zelda started to shuffle them. She indicated for Amanda to touch them. Amanda did what she was told to do. The old woman turned the first card onto the tea-stained table cloth.

The first card showed a colourful castle, surrounded by a moat.

'What does that mean?' Amanda asked.

'It means you live in your own house and life is going well.'

Amanda nodded meekly. She wasn't impressed; she imagined that was a typical opening start to the woman's routine.

The next card showed a sad looking woman with her soul floating above her. Amanda and Lois looked on curiously.

Madam Zelda stared at Amanda. 'You are not satisfied.... It's because you are missing something in your life.... The patter of tiny feet, maybe?'

It was as though an arrow had pierced Amanda's heart. She filled up, tears blurred her vision.

'I told you she was good.' Lois jumped in.

Madam Zelda shot dagger-eyes at her. She was aware this was a delicate situation. She tried to recover it. 'Don't worry my girl... maybe one day.... Never give up hope... let's see what else your future holds for you.'

The next image was of a tall dark man. 'You are going to meet a tall, dark, handsome stranger and fall in love.'

'Hey.... she already met him yesterday on her settee,' Lois just couldn't stop herself from joining in.

As quick as a flash, Madam Zelda added 'Oh....you must have had the George Clooney dream.' Both women slumped back on their seats in shock.

'How does she know about George?' Amanda thought, scanning the room to see if she could find a television set. There wasn't one to be seen.

'Maybe she can pick up Sky TV on that crystal ball thing,' Lois said, sounding about four years old. 'I wonder if she needs a TV licence for it?'

The old hag continued, ignoring Lois. 'Was it the dream when he had a tongue like one of those Komodo Dragon lizards?'

'Hey, hang on just a fuckin' minute!' Lois stood up, her cheeks red in anger. 'What fuckin' dream about

George with the tongue like a Komodo dragon lizard? There's no such thing. In my fantasy he's got a cock similar to a policeman's truncheon with a coal miner's helmet on the end, but there's definitely no scaly tongue in sight.'

'That was in dream one. This is in the sequel…. 'George Clooney Fantasy,' part two Haven't you experienced it yet…it's great?' The gyppo knew when she was a couple of steps ahead of her clients and she used it to her advantage.

'What bloody sequel? I invented the dream in the first place and now some cheap tart has hop-scotched onto my patch. Wait until I get my fingernails into the old cow. Who is she? Where does the bitch live?'

Amanda frowned. 'Look, can we continue with the cards, I want to find out more about this tall, dark, handsome stranger who I can't fall in love with because I'm married.'

'But that's what the cards are saying… and the cards are never wrong.' Madam Zelda stated, straightening her head-piece. Lois sat back down.

The next card showed a real ugly old woman.

'We all know who that is,' Lois laughed. 'That's your mother-in-law, even down to the round shoulders and carrying the Lipton's carrier-bag.' Both women laughed. The Physic didn't. She never laughed; she had been trained to show little emotion. She quickly slapped down the fifth card as if she was playing poker in an old cowboy movie.

She moved her hand to reveal the Death card. She stiffened; the young boy momentarily stared opened mouthed at his mother.

'What does that mean?' Amanda said worryingly.

'Hopefully your Mother-in-law is going to snuff it.' Lois cried. They both giggled again, until they felt the cold stare of the diddycoy.

'Don't mock the cards.' Her words were coated with warning.

'Why not?' Lois breathed.

'Something terrible might just happen to you.' Her eyes burned into Lois.

'Like what?' Lois was playing along. The old hag didn't frighten her.

'Maybe your husband will come back and scald you one day.'

Lois smiled, 'Fuckin' hell... she is good.'

'Let's try another.' Madam Zelda turned a card from the top of the pile. Another death card appeared.

'SNAP,' bellowed Lois and pretended to grab the cards.

'Stop it Lois....behave.... look I've just been dealt two bloody death cards...that can't be a good sign.'

Madam Zelda was flustered. 'It's OK. It's only a bad sign if you deal the third and final card.' She gave the pack a good hard shuffle before slowly turning over the next card.

Amanda grabbed Lois' hand and squeezed it tightly. Off in the distance, the mad chained-up dog barked wildly. This time the psychic didn't let the girls see the card. Down the years she had been taught by her mother, who, in turn, had been trained by her mother, to ensure the stupid punters left her caravan happy and believing in the other side, and of course, willing to come back and part with their money at another time.

The gyppo looked at the card and the colour visibly drained from her face. Her fingers shook.

'What card is it?' Lois was afraid to open her eyes. 'It's not another fuckin' death card is it?'

'What's wrong?' Amanda asked the woman. She felt like screaming. 'It is....it is another death card....isn't it?'

'No it's much, much....worse.' The gyppo ripped off her headdress, her face was ashen.

'Fuck me!' Lois cried. 'What the hell can be worse than three death cards?'

The old woman turned it over. It showed a man in a woman's dress holding something that looked like a knitting needle. The woman frantically spread out the rest of the cards and started to thumb manically through them.

'A man in a woman's dress welding a weapon... that's bizarre ... what does that mean?' Amanda asked.

'Well it still can't be worse than having three death cards for Pete's sake,' Lois interjected.

Madam Zelda stood up and started to throw some clothes and china items into a drawer. She pulled an old suitcase from under the bed and put her fortune telling costume into it.

The young boy shook his head. 'This is bad ladies,' he said and started to shoo the pair out of the caravan.

His mother was barking instructions at him.

The two women were baffled; Amanda asked again what the problem was.

'Look...you don't understand. Something is wrong. Something is terribly wrong.' The boy explained.

'Why?' Amanda was perplexed and a little anxious.

'Because, girls,' the woman injected slowly, goose-pimples covering her lower arms, 'there isn't a card with a man wearing a dress wielding a sharp object in the tarot pack. I've been doing this since I was twelve and I have never witnessed anything like it before. I'm off to try and get my job back as a quality inspector in the button factory.' She slammed the caravan door behind them.

'Hey! What about me?' Lois asked banging on the door. 'You haven't told me about my future?'

'Go away.' The woman's voice was lined with nerves.

'No... I wanna know what's in store for me?' Lois protested.

The gyppo stuck her head out of the window, looked her up and down and shouted 'Let's just say that you will not marry into royalty, you wouldn't be remembered for your wit and you will definitely never win a Beauty competition.'

'Well what about telling me something that I don't fucking know? Look you fake, we want our money back!' Lois screamed out. The words sailed down the valley.

The woman was annoyed. 'Look there's no refunds, you should have read the small print,' she pointed to the hand-written sign. 'Now if you don't piss off, I'll put a curse on you.'

'I want my money back,' Lois shouted and banged the side of the caravan.

'That's it. Ronny,' she screamed at the serious looking-boy, 'get me my curse book and quick.'

He searched in a drawer before handing a black book to her. There was a pause as she flicked through the pages.

'Hey...here it is.' She proceeded to spit out some foreign words. The two guys humping the metal stopped to look. One made the sign of the cross.

'What does that mean?' Amanda asked.

'She will be covered in boils and die a painful death... and hopefully very quickly,' Madam Zelda cried.

'That's terrible,' Amanda said.

Lois rolled up her sleeves 'Boils.... that's fuck all. If you had the crabs I had in 1987, you would realise that boils will be like a walk in the park. Now give me my money back or I'll report you and your son to the social.'

There was a brief pause then within a few seconds, thirty pounds landed at Lois' feet and the caravan sped away into the grey morning light and over the top of the mountainside.

Chapter 3

Cracks

Approximately two hours after the experience with the fortune-telling diddycoy with the ice-blue eyes and strange son, the two women had fled the campsite and rushed back to Lois's house. They had locked the front door (just in case) and had nervously downed half a bottle of neat gin. They were now well on their way to polishing-off the other half.

Neither of them had the nerve to mention the incident with the two death cards and the other eccentric card. They both conveniently placed it out of reach somewhere at the back of their minds.

Lois excused herself and headed off to use the little girl's room. Meanwhile, Amanda leant back on the thread-bare brown and green checked armchair and surveyed her host's humble and miserable surroundings.

It wasn't really a house that Amanda would have been proud of inviting anyone back to, (unless the guest was into urban decay style interiors).

The house itself was situated on the worst estate in town. If that wasn't bad enough, Lois's street was the most run-down in that area, and her house was the most run-down in the run-down street. It looked as though it belonged in a war zone next to a bombed-out tank. Amanda was sure that soldiers in the First World War, slumped in trenches while praying for a ceasefire, lived in a cleaner and safer environment than Lois's living room. She guessed that just calling it a 'living room' was breaking some law. She imagined an architect, responsible for designing council houses, turning in his grave at what his masterpiece had become. Housework was never Lois's strong point, but when Amanda thought about it, neither was ironing, cooking or anything to do with household chores. Up until last year Lois honestly believed that Mister Sheen was a magician who performed at kids parties. Come to think of it, Lois's only strong point was men, and how to hunt them down!

On the settee opposite Amanda, Lois's son lay semi-conscious. A set of beaten-up headphones straddled his head. James Dean Crocker, as he had been christened, or Ramone, as he had been nicknamed later on in life, hadn't stirred a muscle since the women had arrived home. She stared at him with a mix of pity and fear. Lois had informed her that he was the type of boy who usually spent all of the daylight hours hidden behind the darkness of thick curtains, caressed by the stupefying effects of some sort of drug, home grown herb, or moonshine alcohol. He only ventured outside of this coffin when the street lights came on, and then only to go in search of houses to burgle, scores to make, or hobnobs to shop-lift when the munchies set in.

That afternoon, he slumped in the chair like a corpse that refused to decompose. A bottle of white-lightening cider lay by his side, snuggled up next to a hypodermic needle, which judging by its appearance, had seen better days. From where she sat, it wasn't hard to make out the injection marks dancing up his arms in between the lines of scabs and homemade tattoos.

Amanda guessed that people classed Lois in the category of 'bad mother.' Amanda knew there couldn't be anything further from the truth. Lois tried hard to raise her boy in the right way, and, in the beginning, everything was fine. Sadly an unhealthy addiction to easily-accessible heroin had turned the boy against the world, not just his family. Lois had spent nights wandering around dead-end streets searching for him. She usually found him out of his head and covered in sick. Amanda felt her mate's pain; she wished she could help.

She suddenly caught sight of a dog the size of a polar bear, roaming around in the background. The creature was aptly named Bostick, after Ramone's glue-sniffing stage which had nearly resulted in him losing his life. Lois went to court on a GBH charge after she had attempted to stab the shopkeeper who had sold the glue to her son on that fateful day. The dog stared through the dirty pane of glass before taking a dump by the side of an overflowing wheelie bin. It trotted off, a lot lighter, looking to pick a fight with some other mongrel in the tough old street.

Amanda positioned herself on the edge of the chair, hoping she wouldn't catch anything that was lurking in the undergrowth of the cushions. She pictured man-eating insects with large teeth ready to pounce on any unsuspecting victims. She shivered at the thought.

Lois finally appeared from the kitchen carrying another bottle of white spirit and a large box of cheap cup-cakes.

'Open them love... I could eat the flies off a camel's back.' She threw the box across the room and plonked herself down on the only remaining empty piece of furniture.

Amanda bolted upright. 'Rat,' she yelled, on seeing a long tailed rodent scurrying behind a pile of empty pizza boxes that fought for floor space with the growing army of cigarette packets.

'Oh don't worry,' Lois ignored her screams. 'It's only his new pet rat, 'Biscuit.' He wouldn't bite you... Ramone took his teeth out with pliers last week after it nibbled on the gas-man's shins.'

Amanda was too afraid to ask why the gummy rat was called Biscuit. Instead, she opted to pick her feet up off the floor quickly.

Over the next few hours the conversation bounced back and forth like a Spanish fly trying to make its evil mind up on which holiday-maker it should bite next. It started quite lightly with a brief rundown of the goings-on in some soap opera on TV; it then progressed to the sale at Asda and, as usual with Lois, it quickly detoured off down the dirt track road towards sex town. Lois was a master at driving all her debates firmly towards that destination; it was all to do with Lois's mind being packed tightly with nothing but dirty thoughts or men's bodies.

Amanda listened as Lois told her about this new boy who had recently moved into the house next door with his parents. The way Lois describe him, he was too good to be true.

'He's absolutely drop dead gorgeous,' Lois said. 'He could curdle milk with his hips.'

'When are you going to bed him, then?' Amanda knew it wasn't worth asking Lois 'if' she was going to bed him. Lois always got what she wanted when it came to sex. She had a skill for wearing-down her prey, until they gave in without a fight, or the courts issued her with a restraining order.

'There's one big snag.'

Amanda was curious. 'What's that…. is he courting?'

'Courting…. no fuck that… I wouldn't care if he was engaged to the Queen. No, it's worse than that…. he's as bent as a five dollar bill.'

'How do you know?' she asked, wondering how the hell a five dollar bill could be bent.

Lois shook her head. 'It's easy…. You can tell by the way he walks. And he's too perfect. Lovely shoes, immaculate hair; he smells nice too! He even gets his nails manicured.'

'Perhaps he's just one of those guys who look after themselves.'

'Yesterday, he commented on how lovely my pink blouse was, and…' Lois got up and strutted around the room, swinging her hips. 'He walks like this!' She mimicked his movements, but exaggerated it to the power of ten.

'Oh…' Amanda laughed, 'he's definitely gay. Don't need a bloody body language course for that…..the pink blouse comment is enough.'

Lois muttered, 'Pity, mind. He's got such a cute, tight arse. I wouldn't mind sinking my teeth into it. That reminds me…I've got to get new batteries for my vibrator and love eggs later on.' She took a felt pen out of her bag and wrote on the back of her hands. 'Duracell extra, extra strength and a loaf of bread.'

'Lois…. what the hell are you going to do with a loaf of bread?'

Lois' face was expressionless. 'What do you mean...? I'm going to make a fuckin' sandwich with it...! What do you think I was going to do with it?'

'Never mind,' Amanda looked embarrassed.

With all the laughter in the room mixed with the large amount of drink sloshing about, Amanda was feeling quite drunk. Lois reached across and stubbed her fag out into the overfilled ashtray. She then expertly released another cigarette from out of the packet and twirled it into her mouth within the blink of an eye.

As Lois slumped back and took an exceptionally long drag on her nicotine stick, Amanda's mind drifted back to the time of her youth and the first time she had laid eyes on Lois 'Bug' (as she was called way back then).

It was at Bishop Hedley High School in 1976. The place was a vast, mixed-gender comprehensive zoo for Catholic children in the borough.

Amanda had noticed this girl who, although it was her first day, strutted about as if she had been there for years. She had an attitude that betrayed her age; a confidence that shone bright above the gloom of the nervousness of the rest of the first formers.

Even back then Amanda sensed that Lois was different. She oozed working-class style, made more apparent in her hand-me-down clothes and scuffed shoes. Every one of the new recruits was kitted out in brand new blazers and satchels. Lois stood out as the exception, leaning on a wall, wearing a jacket with holes in the elbows. A Lipton's carrier bag housing her school stuff was slung nonchalantly over her shoulder.

Later that morning the two girls had found themselves sitting next to each other in class. (Amanda had accidentally on purpose made sure of that). During the first session, the form teacher asked each member of the class to tell everyone about themselves and their family, their pets and other interesting trivia. This was his way for himself, and the rest of the pupils, to get to know each other.

Most of the class rushed through their brief, potted-history, as if in a race to the finish line. Everyone seemed to follow a similar script, including Amanda. She had proudly told everyone her name was Amanda Willis. She lived with her mother and father, but didn't have any brothers or sisters, as though she did have a pet dog called 'Basil.' She finished her spot by telling them all that when she left school she intended to own a flower shop or go to university. She did not come close to achieving either of these dreams.

Then, the pendulum of opportunity swung towards Lois. She stood up, marched to the front of the class and exhibiting zero respect for the teacher, sat on Mr Hill's table. Amanda noticed the poor attempt of a homemade tattoo on the girl's arm and lots of dirt under her fingernails.

Without fear, and a large helping of arrogance, she relayed to her wide-mouthed audience that she was the youngest of a family of six. Her two oldest brothers had just been sent on a three-year holiday to some high security prison for beating a post office worker during an armed robbery. Her father (she spat on the floor after mentioning his name) had left them all to go and live with some saggy-breasted, peroxide blonde slut, who worked down the bookies and who Lois' mother (herself a prescribed Valium and amphetamine slimming-tablet junkie) said couldn't cook chips as long as she had a hole in her arse.

She explained that she wasn't allowed pets because she lived in the flats, before adding that she couldn't wait until she finished school so she could sign on the dole and have a couple of sprogs of her own. During her confession Lois chewed on a live matchstick.

Lois lived a tough existence. Her lack of a normal family life and parental love was combated by being brash and cocky. Otherwise she would have only got lost in her world of desolation. It was a dog-eats-dog type of upbringing, and the bigger, and sharper her teeth, the better her chance of survival.

There was complete and utter silence in the classroom. Mr Hill was flabbergasted. He was, thankfully, saved by the bell, which made everyone jump.

Lois, uncrossed her legs, stood erect and jokily shouted 'The Milkybars are on me.' She strolled passed Mr Hill and winked at him.

The following day Mr Hill resigned. It was rumoured that he'd given up the teaching profession and become a supervisor in a bomb making factory in County Londonderry.

After that open and honest introduction into Lois's world, Amanda had found herself in love with the girl. It wasn't love in a schoolgirl, lesbian crush kind of way, but she couldn't believe how someone could be so cool. And what's more she was sitting next to her in registration. The following night Amanda gave herself a similar tattoo on her arm. She chickened-out of using Indian ink and a needle. She just drew it with biro instead.

Since Amanda found herself skipping merrily down memory lane, she couldn't help but recall a major thing that bugged her during her school years. It was all connected to purple underwear; or, more precisely, why girls in the first year were instructed to wear purple knickers. Purple was the school colour at the time.

She remembered standing in assembly, kitted out exactly as the girl had been in the school uniform brochure, (even down to the pig tails), but with the added frustration of having to wear army issue purple knickers.

These must have been made out of goat's hair and Brillo pads. She wondered why the school had insisted that all new female starters wore them. To her knowledge the boys weren't told to file into line in purple Y fronts (but, strangely enough, she later courted a boy who insisted that he wore purple schoolgirl panties). He actually went on to university and became a judge, or a lawyer, or something to do with the legal system.

So why purple knickers? How sexist was that? And more importantly, who the hell would know if a girl didn't wear them? Did comprehensive schools employ knicker inspectors to visit schools, lifting up young girls' skirts as they played hopscotch in the yard?

Was it politically correct? Would schools get points deducted if it was discovered that some young harlot from the Estate was actually keeping the cold wind off her private parts with a pair of yellow pants?

Amanda's mind went into overdrive.

'Sorry, Headmaster Black...but your school would have easily won the best school in the world award, if we hadn't caught Amanda Willis wearing these.'

In her mind she envisaged a loud gasp from the lines of kids in assembly as the bespectacled knicker inspector pulled a pair of multi-coloured pants from the depth of his grubby pockets with the words 'Wednesday' printed on the front and a sticker on the back proclaiming 'three for one' at Woolworth.

'And it was Friday when we caught her wearing them,' the inspector astonishingly added.

A loud gurgle of anticipation from the audience, as Headmaster Black snapped his cane in anger. Mrs Price, the piano teacher, fainted; her head bounced off the keys of her piano, making a dramatic noise. Pandemonium filled the entire assembly hall. No-one involved in the school could begin to imagine the shame and the deep embarrassment. It was worse than treason; it should have been a hanging offence.

'A girl was hung by the neck today for wearing a multi-coloured pair of knickers during a double period of Home Economics,' one of the presenters from Blue Peter informed the nation. Amanda giggled to herself, picturing a girl swinging from the beams in the assembly hall, the last wriggles of life leaving her body as the caretaker polished the floor below.

Thinking back a little harder, Amanda had some fond memories of the assembly hall, which was also used for school prayers on a Tuesday and a Thursday and often to communicate special events or occasions.

It was those special occasions when the entire school was herded like cattle through long, graffiti-stained corridors, into the large church-like, wooden-tiled hall, to be informed about outlandish and bizarre events, which stuck with her even up to today.

Headmaster Black would always be standing on the stage to deliver the earth shattering, but meaningless, news at the pupils.

'I am proud to announce that the school table tennis team came second in this year's town championship,' he once told the entire school one frosty morning in March.

Every face in the hall (not including the members of the table tennis team) gave the headmaster a 'we couldn't give a fuck... we're freezing' face.

Sadly, the sporting prowess of the school never really rose above the dizzy heights of the table tennis team's achievement, except for the incident when the fourth year rugby team got banned and expelled after they all ran through the estate in the nude after an away match. The local newspaper (which was run by a family of Mormons) was vicious in its biased reporting.

'Pathetic Catholic rugby boys show off their little tackle'

All the boys involved were suspended and thrown out of the rugby team.

On another occasion, Amanda remembered being sent urgently to the assembly hall, where they were met by a very solemn atmosphere. Candles were lit, the large curtains were drawn shut and an overwhelming smell of incense filled the air. It hurt her nostrils and burnt her eyes.

'I have some terrible news to tell you all,' the headmaster spoke again, tears rolling down his enormous face. 'Today, at ten o' clock, the Pope passed away and joined his maker.' He bowed his oversized head. There was silence. Mrs Price fainted (as she always did).

'Hurraahh,' one of the kids from the clay class shouted out. 'The Pope's dead!... the Pope's dead!'

Mr Honeywell, the Geography teacher, quickly dragged the delinquent imbecile out by the hair. Many at the school swore the teacher was descended from a long line of Nazi supply-teachers that had infiltrated the United Kingdom during the mid-sixties, wearing old corduroy jackets with red leather patches on the elbows. The deranged schoolteacher was a merciless brute, amongst a school of merciless brutes. He tortured kids for fun and humiliated them for his own personal recreational pleasure and gratification.

'What's the capital of Peru, Jones....? Come on, come on....!' Amanda recalled Mr Honeywell bellowing across the class at a dozing boy at the back of the class.

'Urrrgggg... Is it….. Lisbon, Mr Honeywell?'

'Lisbon...? Lisbon? I'll give you bloody Lisbon!' He stomped to the back of the room and proceeded to stick a sharpened pencil in the poor boy's thigh, before making him stand in the corner (on one leg, the leg on which he had carried out the attack) for the rest of the afternoon.

This incident had scared Amanda half to death. She made a point of studying Geography every night until she knew, off by heart, every capital, in every country on the planet, the amount of rainfall per region, and how an oxbow lake was formed. But, thankfully, Mr Honeywell never asked her. In fact, he never asked the girls any questions. The teacher had worked out that boys were a lot duller than the female of the species and this meant it was easier to degrade them in public without getting a warning off the authorities.

But the announcement of all announcements that stayed in Amanda's mind more than any other was the time all the girls had been told that a flasher, with a bald head and a grey plastic mac, had 'upset and startled' a girl in the first year called Debra Williams, or Winger, or something beginning with a W. The incident had taken place while the girl had been on her way to school one morning.

Thirty minutes after assembly had ended; eight of the older girls (including Lois and Amanda) had tracked down the young upstart called Debra Whatever, who had been flashed at. While one of the gang stood look-out, the others proceeded to interrogate her in the girl's toilets on the ground floor.

'Right... how big was it?' one of the gang demanded to know.

'Big... how big was what?' the young girl replied, her words shook similar to the branches on a tree on a wet and windy, late October afternoon.

Lois took control of the situation. 'How fuckin' big was his dick? Don't play dumb with me.' She probed some more, 'Was it this big?' Lois spread her fingers about four inches apart.

The girl shook her head. 'No, much bigger.'

Lois extended her fingers by another two inches. The girl shook her head again and took hold of Lois's fingers and moved them apart by at least another three inches. Amanda, who was still a virgin, wasn't sure how big a man's penis should be. She'd seen her dad's in the bath and had assumed the water had been cold.

'Fuckin' hell... you lucky, jammy bastard.' Lois screamed. The words caused the poor girl to burst out crying.

'Stop crying, you stupid bitch... do you realise that you have seen a real man's cock. A real cock and not a little wiener like the boys in third year. No... you've seen an honest to God, real man's weapon.... Did he have big hands?'

Amanda could see Lois physically and emotionally, changing into some kind of sex-monster. She started drooling from the corners of her lip-glossed mouth and her hands shook. Lois turned to the girl who was cowering in the corner. 'I can't believe you've seen that lovely thing and you ran to teacher like a tell-tale tit. I know what I would have done. I would have whipped my knickers off and rode the arse off him.'

She proceeded to make strange rotation movements with her hips. The rest of the gang inched back towards the exit, while pretending to laugh weakly. They thought that Lois was messing about, but Amanda could see in her eyes that her mate wasn't in the mood to pull anyone's leg.

The next morning after the interrogation in the bogs, Lois had got up early, put on little white ankle socks and prostituted herself by the tree where the flasher had previously struck. Each day she waited to catch a glimpse of the man who had put the willies up poor Debra what's-her-face. This went on for two months until the bunking officer and the park warden complained to her family and school. She was sent to see a psychiatrist, and, incredibly, ended up giving the shrink a blow-job while advising him on his marital problems. It was then Lois realised she had a gift. Not a gift wrapped up in expensive paper, with a big red bow on the top. Her gift came in a plain brown envelope covered in stains and sealed with old, crinkly Sellotape and a piece of string.

Unbelievably, when the police announced that they had arrested a man who confessed to being the Park Flasher, Lois was inconsolable. She cried all week. She even sent him love letters everyday for a month with rough sketches of a school girl giving someone felatio behind the trees. He never replied.

It was later that year, around March time, that Amanda really became blood-sister with Lois Bug. They were in a lesson with one of the older dinosaur teachers, Mr Mansfield, the school's biggest pervert, who weakly disguised himself as an English teacher.

He was a 60-year-old 'Mr Mainwaring' from Dad's Army type of person. Bald head, big pot and he continually sweated like a pig on a spit-roast. Everyone knew that old baldy had set up a devious way of achieving his ultimate thrill of looking up the skirts of innocent girls. He would lay a piece of mirror on the floor by his desk, and when the girls came up to read for him, he would peep up to the private regions of his victims.

The more he saw, the better grades the girl got. This pissed the boys off immensely.

Amanda had nearly thrown up as she recalled the day he made her read almost four chapters of bloody 'Great Expectations' because she had worn her first pair of silk, black panties to school by mistake.

'The bastard,' Amanda later told Lois. 'I'm reading this crap, you lot are fast asleep and Mr. Fucking Pervert fingers is sitting there with a tent pole and damp patch in his trousers and a smirk on his face. He made me read four bastard chapters! In the end, I thought about giving him a wank just so he would let me sit down again. And he only gave me a B+.'

It was the following day that Lois hatched a plan to give Mr Mansfield a day to remember and maybe improve her overall yearly grade.

'Watch this,' Lois winked at her mate, as he called her up to the front to read. In one swift moment, she stepped out of her knickers and strolled, commando style, to his little sordid desk of mirrors.

'Hello Mr Mansfield, what is it you would like me to read for you on this fine winter's day?'

Most of the other kids were either fast asleep, playing cards, or too busy thinking about their first fag break to be bothered to hear the mischief in Lois's voice. Amanda was transfixed. She knew her mate was mental and she wouldn't think twice about boldly going to places where others refused to go. She was a mixture of Star Trek's Mr Spock, Captain Kirk and the pretty black woman with the enormous tits rolled into one.

'The Klingons would be fucked if Lois was ever beamed up,' Amanda giggled to herself, realising that while most of the girls of their age in the school weren't brave enough to ask some poor boy for a snog, here was

Lois, smirking, knickerless and on a one-way mission for a gold star.

Mansfield cleaned the rim of his glasses with a dirty, stained handkerchief. Lois slowly opened her legs, an inch at a time. Amanda could see old pervey glance slyly down at the mirror under the desk. Sweat ran down his forehead, dripped off his nose and fell onto the wooden desk. His eyes opened wider. 'Read from page 57,' he commanded, wiping his forehead and dabbing the pool of salty liquid before him.

She started slowly. '*My fairy lord....* Hey he sounds gay!' she cried.

Some of the kids laughed.

'Carry on Lois.... and I don't want anymore of your wise cracks.... right?'

'Are you sure, Sir?' she muttered, winking at Amanda.

'Just read.' All this interference was disrupting his pimping routine.

Lois started again. *'This must.... Be done with...haaaaste..... For night's swift dragon's cut the cloud.... Full fast....* This is shite sir!'

'Read.'

Lois breathed in, building up the courage to carry out her plan. *'And Au...Au.... Auror.... Aurora's hamburgers.'*

'What....? It's not hamburgers....! It's harbinger....! Aurora's harbinger!'

'Sorry Sir... it must be because I'm starving.'

After turning the second page, she slowly parted her red sea further and further. His body language suggested he'd hit the jackpot. He immediately became erect, his shoulder's slumped down, his breathing began to get heavy.

'At whose... approach... ghost wandering here..... And the troops... Home to churchyard.... Damned spirits all....' she whispered in his ear.

He saw the nakedness of her thighs in the reflection of the hidden mirror. In all his forty years of teaching (and perving) he had dreamed and waited for this day.

Lois knew she had him. She knew he wasn't listening to a word she was saying. She decided to test her position of strength.

'Puck sucks cocks in hell,' she said confidently.

He was too engrossed in his private lap-dance to notice. Some of the kids in class looked up but quickly carried on doing whatever else they were doing.

She stood there, legs wide apart. His tongue dropped out of his mouth. He coughed and spluttered. She used her lower muscle lips to wink at him, drawing him in closer. His glasses steamed up. She smiled at Amanda. Suddenly he clutched his heart and kneeled over. His head hit the desk, at exactly the same time as the break time bell sounded. All the children reached into their satchels for half-smoked fag nips and raced out.

So, as Mr Mansfield breathed his last breath, most of the children escaped into the fresh air, still not realising (or caring) what had happened to him.

'Who the hell was the guy in that Shakespeare play with a donkey's head?' some girl asked while they huddled together in the wind and the rain behind the sports hall, sharing the delights of a single woodbine. Amanda had always been amazed just how many fag-crazed teenagers that one woodbine could satisfy. It was like Jesus feeding the masses with five loaves and fishes.

'Yeah... a donkey's head...what the hell is that all about?' Lois piped up. 'Boring or what?.... Now if he had wrote that Fuck, or was it Puck, had a knob like a donkey, then everyone in the class would have read it from cover to cover,' Lois summed up the classic book with another of her priceless sentences. 'What a good editor could have done for that Shakespeare bloke?' she added.

Later, Mr Mansfield was declared DOA at the medical room and he was buried along with his sordid past. On that day, Amanda and Lois became the closest of friends and to mark the occasion, every March 11th (even to this day), the two girls would go and dance on Mr Mansfield's grave, completely bladdered. They wore no knickers and read lines from Shakespeare, substituting 'Fuck' for 'Puck'.

The end of an old pervert's life started the beginning of a great relationship. Amanda joked that maybe Shakespeare could have written a play, or a book about it.

It was a couple of years later, in youth club, where Amanda, Lois and a posse of well selected, handpicked girlfriends leant on a wall. They were giving it some serious posing, lip puckering and breast pouting. They were in the middle of a short-lived Punk Rock phase of their lives. The girls weren't quite old enough to have caught the full storm of the punk revolution but were surfing around on the end ripples of the early eighties.

It was more like a mid-teenage crisis time for Amanda. She hated following the fashions of the day, or the fads of the moment. She hadn't minded the disco glamour stuff of 'Saturday Night Fever' era, but then came along this horrible thing that swept the country and turned innocent fifteen-year-olds into Frankenstein figures, with black eye liner and the sex appeal of a loaf of stale bread.

Unluckily for Amanda, Lois's older brother had got into the punk craze and because Lois fancied some of his friends, she thought it would be a great way of attracting their undivided attention. Lois even went as far as giving herself a punk persona and became known as Venus Flytrap.

'Venus Flytrap,' her step Dad screamed with laughter on hearing her new name. 'Fuckin' Penis Cocktrap, more like.' He continued laughing all the way to the bookies, where he frequently lost all his Giro money and ended up having a blow-job in the alley at the back from the peroxide blonde with the saggy tits.

One night Lois ventured into the big city to watch a band called The Lurkers, or The Shirkers, or something like that. She informed her gang the following morning that she'd had a great night. She told them that she had ended up making love to the drummer of the support band, who was the spitting image of Billy Idol from Generation X. Lois even showed them a photograph, but it was an actual picture of the original Billy Idol out of Smash Hits. Even Amanda had to admit that the lead singer was quite cute, in an urban-gangster type of way.

But the truth behind the story was that Lois had in fact got completely shit-faced on cider and had a three minute knee-trembler in some piss-smelling alleyway, with a Mohican, who had 'Sham 69' tattooed on his neck and 11 hole Doc Martins. She also forgot to mention that he had given her a serious dose of crabs. The creatures had burrowed into her groin and refused to depart even after she shaved all her pubic hair off. Sitting in a bowl of Dettol every morning and night for three weeks eventually cleared the infestation.

Anyway, back in the heat of the youth club, the gang of plastic punk girls had vacated their position on the wall by the changing rooms and were now leaning by the main notice board, still pretending to look bored and pretty at the same time. It wasn't an easy thing to do, especially for Lois who was trying desperately to control the army of crabs that seemed to be marching up and down from her arse to her belly button.

It was then that Amanda saw two boys walking past. One was tall, blond and well built. He had a huge love bite on his neck that could have been made by a ravenous King Kong. He seemed to blush when he spied Lois.

'Who's that?' Amanda asked 'and why is he scratching himself so much... he looks like he's got fleas.'

'He's called Daryl. They're in the next form up,' Lois replied.

To be honest, Amanda had been paying more attention to the blond boy's friend. He was dark and handsome. She had seen him around the school. The girls all thought that he was arrogant. Amanda thought that he maybe shy and mysterious. While most of the boys wore their hair short and spiky, he wore his shoulder length. He intimidated but intrigued her. He rarely spoke. He just listened and sometimes smiled. He was the silent type who made girls go weak at the knees and dig each other in the ribs when he sauntered past. She let go a little moan of approval to herself.

The blond boy quickly marched up to Lois and pulled her violently to one side. He started pointing and whispering at her. Amanda found herself in an awkward silence with the dark haired boy. Now she was the one who couldn't think of anything to say.

'Have you heard the new single by 'The Crash'?' she finally stuttered.

'I think you mean 'The Clash,'' he answered back and smiled.

She was thinking desperately for something else to say, as the blond boy returned, still scratching his nuts. He informed his mate that they were off to the local chemist to pinch some detergent.

Amanda felt so stupid. She wanted to chase after the quiet boy and tell him that she knew it was 'The Clash,' but was joking with him.

'I'll see him tomorrow,' she promised herself. 'I'll let him know that I ain't as dull as I look.'

Sadly, tomorrow never came, because the handsome dark-haired boy, who was named Jacob, never came back to school. Rumours spread as fast as flames on dried grass.

'Hey, have you heard... Jacob's killed his parents and his younger half-brother and run off with his sister. He's now in prison,' someone muttered during assembly.

'Yes... I heard he'd slaughtered his step-mother with a garden fork,' someone else joined in.

'No... It wasn't a garden fork... it was a machete' Lois stated, 'and he was hooked on drugs.... You could see it in his eyes.'

'But he's only fifteen,' Amanda snapped-back against the tide of unjust gossip that was engulfing the school.

'It's always the quiet ones you need to watch! I should know... I'm a music teacher,' Mrs Price added while belting out 'Ave Maria' on the piano in C minor.

It wasn't until years later that Amanda found out where the mystery boy had really disappeared to. Daryl (the blond boy with the crabs, who Amanda ended up marrying) told her on their first date that he had been told that Jacob had left to go to South Africa with his dad and sister, leaving his step-mother and step-brother in Britain. Jacob's parents had finally decided to get divorced and had gone their separate ways.

Amanda suddenly snapped out of her day-dream. There was movement from the settee as Lois' boy woke up. He stretched out his arms, reached for the cider bottle and took a long swig of the warm, flat contents. Amanda's memories of school days faded as she came back to the present with a jolt.

'Ma... got any cash.... I need a fix?' he shouted, a shiver the size of a dumper truck ran down his spine.

'Fuck off,' Lois cried. 'Get your own money for a fix, you fuckin' junkie.'

'Come on Ma...you bastard.' He lobbed the plastic cider bottle at her.

Lois sprang on the boy, fists clenched, arms pumping. Amanda knew better than to get involved in domestics. She made her excuses and left.

Chapter 4

Spite

Amanda was worn out from cleaning. She was thoroughly knackered. She had decided to retire for an early night, with a cup of hot chocolate and a magazine. During the day she had scaled great heights, sunk to greater depths and had even attempted to get the inside of the cooker to resemble a germ-free place where you could actually cook food. She did the best she could but finally gave up, coming to the conclusion that she would need to hire a pneumatic drill and an industrial steam cleaner, just to begin to peel away the layers of grease.

The reason for the frantic cleaning activity was that her mother-in-law would be honouring them with her half-yearly visit tomorrow.

Daryl insisted everything must be spick and span for her arrival. The fuss he made to ensure Amanda got everything perfect every time she visited was just as if the Queen herself was coming to stay. The way he went on suggested she was expecting guards in red tunics to be standing by the front door and corgis to be shitting all over the garden.

The whole experience was a nightmare for Amanda. The last time the old witch came, she marched about the house with a score card giving her marks out of ten. She couldn't believe it. Sadly for Amanda, who had slaved away tirelessly for over three days, with a duster and several large cans of Pledge and Mr Muscle kitchen cleaner, she still only achieved two out of ten in the cleanliness audit and faired even worse for the meal she had sweated over.

Of course, Daryl didn't actually participate in the clean-up operation himself. As usual he was out with his mates, probably getting shit-faced, playing brag and arguing about how to put the world to rights, or who scored the best goal in some pointless football match. Men were so predictable when it came to real life.

She often recalled the urban myth which many of the women folk talked about. It told the tale of a new type of man, who lived far away from her town, in a land of hope and honey. Legend had it that this strange new man was tall, dark and handsome; he liked soap operas and never farted in bed. It went as far as to say that this breed was sexier, more understanding and extremely more reliable than the usual model she was used to. In car terms it was like comparing a Toyota against a Rover 600, and not just any Rover 600. No, this Rover 600 had been quickly bolted together in the last hour, of the last shift, on the last Friday afternoon before the summer holidays.

Like the rest of the desperate women up on the estate, Amanda hoped that these supermen actually existed. But over the years she had found out the hard way that it was just a fable, a lie, a downright sham. These men didn't exist at all. In fact, in working class slums in Milan and Madrid, there were housewives who were told that, across the sea in Britain, men were called gentlemen and walked around in bowler hats while opening doors for ladies. It was all bollocks. Amanda knew that when you neutralised their accents, peeled away their suntan, they were all exactly the same, shaped from the same mould. All blokes were obsessed by football and ruled by the little thing in their trousers, or was it ruled by football and obsessed by the little thing in their trousers? Whatever the case, unless it was a sport-free Monday night, women all over the world came a long way down the priority list.

Back in bed, Amanda must have dozed off and gone into a deep sleep because she was suddenly awoken by the sound of running water. She had been dreaming she had been travelling on a large ocean liner which was about to crash into a titanic Dairylea cheese triangle in the car park in ASDA. She held her breath, waiting for the collision into the soft cheese substance. Thankfully, she realised quickly that she was actually safe in the familiar surroundings of her own bedroom. The cheese and car park dream had again been a recurring nightmare. Lois had told her it was a sexual thing and had gone into great depths to explain why. She reckoned it was all to do with the ship symbolising a penis and the cheese triangle signified women's struggle to get away from it. The rest of the explanation was a blur; Amanda was to busy trying to figure out the penis and ship significance to catch any more of it.

It was pitch black in the room. In the corner the light from the bathroom dramatically cut the space in two reminiscent of the top of a box of light and dark chocolates. After several confused moments, she finally realised what the sound was. No, it wasn't the noise of the ship in her dream about to sink and it wasn't the drip of a burst water main. It was her husband using the toilet facilities. Well she hoped it was him anyway, unless of course, George Clooney had finally come back to ravage her (she decided not to go back down that route again.)

Sadly and more predictably she knew it was Daryl. He had finally found time in his diary to return home from the pub, or wherever he had been, and at such an unsociable hour. From the noise he was making, he was in the process of attempting to remove from his bladder some of the gallon of beer that he had consumed down at the social club.

She knew it had to be done and was thankful he took time out to perform the peeing operation before coming to bed. It could be worse; a woman in Bingo had once told her (and the rest of the crowd) that her husband had pissed the bed every night, without fail, since he was twenty-eight. (He was now fifty six). She enlightened Amanda that over the years she had gone through fifteen mattresses, ten bed frames and about four hundred nightdresses.

So, all things considered, Amanda was grateful for small mercies. Though she still didn't understand why he needed to wake her up in the process.

Why didn't he just close the door?

Why didn't he just use the toilet downstairs?

That's what the bloody thing was designed for. She hated him every time. If the truth was known she was beginning to hate him most of the time.

What bugged her more than anything was during his 'waking up the street,' drunken peeing session, there would be sudden silences. During the ceasefire, she hoped and prayed that he had actually finished but she knew from bitter experience that he hadn't. She knew he had missed the bloody target again and was soaking her orange rug, leaving a mark like an oasis in an orange desert.

'Bloody dogs are easier to house train than men,' she snapped out in the darkness.

She couldn't for the life of her understand why men didn't sit down when performing nature's bladder emptying procedure. She knew that if all men agreed to do it that way, it would have saved a million, trillion arguments from ever starting up in every household in the world.

Why did men do it?

Was it a genetic thing? Or did they just do it for the devilry?

Maybe they enjoyed winding women up, just like women did by pretending not to understand sport or having no road sense. She remembered her father had it sussed when it came to strange toilet routines. He always sat down when on the pan, even when he was only doing a number one.

'Why stand up when you can sit down,' he often asked her when she was growing up.

At first Amanda thought her old man was some kind of working class Confucius; a true eighth wonder of the world and way ahead of his time. She often sat looking at him waiting for the great one to utter some more words of wisdom. When she became older and a little wiser herself, she realised her Dad was in fact a typical warehouse manager who always took the easy way out and often delegated any manual work to someone else, if he could.

But lazy Dad or not, it was the way to do it. All men should adopt the 'sit down not splash about' approach. Of course it would have a positive knock-on effect on other 'Men verses Women' arguments especially involving the 'Should the toilet seat be left up or down?' debate. The expression killing two birds with one stone sprung to her mind.

But Amanda also knew that if loving couples weren't fighting over which way the bog seat should be positioned, or 'who peed over the rug inquiry?', they would be pulling their eyes out over some other mundane thing like who put the wrong cutlery in the wrong spaces in the kitchen drawer or who had misplaced the cars key?

Her mother had told her that, apparently, her grandmother had chopped her Granddad's little finger off, after he'd accidentally put a spoon in the knife compartment, whilst wiping the cutlery on Boxing Day. It may have been a bit harsh, but, to be fair to the old woman, she was going through 'the change,' and little things like that can cause people to do crazy, nasty little things. On a more constructive note, she remembered that her forgetful Granddad never made that mistake ever again. So maybe the bog seat debate was God's way of keeping the status quo; his holinesses way of steadying the ship of life by providing a few icebergs here and there to break up the boredom. He may have been a cleverer God than we made him out to be and not as stupid as we made him look in the movies.

She realised the great bog seat debate could wait until another time. There were more pressing matters on her mind, mainly concerning her and Daryl's frayed relationship. There were more specific questions that needed addressing; questions like why they didn't really kiss anymore or, in fact, had stopped communicating at all? Why they didn't cuddle up in each others arms on a stormy night while the rain lashed against the windows?

They used to love to do that when they first got married. They would find themselves lying naked in a warm bed, watching the lightening fork through the sky. Old Mother Nature's show of power and strength always seemed to act as an aphrodisiac for Daryl. He would physically alter into some great sexual beast, with the passion of a thousand Latin lovers and the stamina of a wolf. Ok, so Amanda knew it had been a long time ago, and maybe her emotion had clouded her judgement a little concerning the wolf and Latin lover descriptions, but, to be fair to her husband, he had been pretty good between the sheets during that period of their lives. He could usually press the right buttons to start up her engine, even though sometimes he wasn't quite so efficient at switching her back off when she was still in gear.

Amanda still loved stormy nights.

Tonight, she felt as though she could burst out crying when she recalled those happy days in her life, when everything appeared so fresh and exciting. Looking back, it felt as though she had predominantly reached the peak of Love Mountain, and all before the tender age of twenty-four. Ever since those days, she had been unknowingly slipping down the icy slope towards ground camp Reality, with its steep, bumpy path, with lots of hidden crevasses and not a soft landing in sight.

She wasn't sure if love had deserted them over time, or simply overnight. Had it fallen down like someone stepping off the edge of a cliff or had it been more gradual than that? These days their relationship seemed a million miles away from those heady days of love bites, passionate kisses, oral sex and holding each other tight, long into the night.

She prayed for those times to come back. She closed her eyes.

Eventually the bathroom light went off, a sure sign that he'd finally emptied what seemed akin to a large section of the Indian Ocean from his bladder. He clambered into bed. He proceeded to go through his normal yeti impersonation. It consisted of several disgusting traits that started with grunting, continued with feet shuffling and ended with a bout of extremely loud farting, before he settled down and fell off to sleep. Curry nights at the Labour Club were the worst. The air was so thick with fumes of Carlsberg, poppadoms, lime pickle and Jalfrezi, she couldn't breathe.

As usual, Amanda was now wide awake. She poked him hard in his ribs. It didn't do much good; he just grunted a bit more before farting again. He was like a machine. A top German engineer couldn't have designed an automobile which could have been more reliable than her husband after a few beers. She lay back in the unpleasant knowledge that it was the same routine, same husband, same bed, but just a different day. She wondered if things would change.

She stared at him as the light from the neon clock lit up one half of his face. He resembled a baby; a forty-year old, beer smelling baby, but still his mother's pride and joy.

'The old witch,' Amanda cursed whenever she mentioned her name. 'And, God forbid... she's bloody coming tomorrow.'

Amanda studied his features once more. To be honest, she had never really found Daryl drop-dead gorgeous, not even before they got hitched. After a while, he had more or less grown on her, rather than sweeping her off her feet with a single glance. Like most girls, she had always dreamed of meeting her Mr. Right as he charged up to save her from a fire-breathing dragon, on a fine Arab charger, with a single red rose in his mouth. Sadly, real life was slightly less romantic. First off, fire breathing dragons were quite rare to come by, even in Wales (unless you included her mother-in-law). There weren't too many Mister Rights riding around her housing estate on the backs of large stallions either. There was probably more chance of seeing a flying pig in platform boots floating above Argos.

Regrettably she had met plenty of Mr. Wrongs in the time since she had left school, usually driving around the streets in rusty Ford Escorts with furry dice and heavy metal music blasting out from the sunroof. Life up on the estate was a bit more realistic, a bit less of a fairy tale and a lot more warts and all. It was a place where council estate princes found more contentment in a four-pack of lager, while watching the footie on the box, rather than bothering to rescue a damsel in distress.

Funnily enough, she had met Daryl years after leaving school, while she was on the rebound from a long-term, nine month relationship with the original King of the Mr. Wrongs. He was a leather-clad loser who had introduced himself as a musician on a mission to conquer the world. His name was Robin or Rob for short, or Mr. Complete Arsehole to give him his full title.

They had met while she was with friends on a weekend at the seaside. She had fallen head-over-heels in lust with him, from his long greasy hair, to his odd-shaped toes. It may have had something to do with his bad boy image, or his slim, taught muscular frame, or the stories he told her about how he was going to be the next big thing.; the second King of Rock and Roll; the next Jon Bon Jovi of South Street; the Ozzy Osborne of the Chemical works. She believed every last word that tumbled out of his thick, pouting lips.

Several months later, it came as little surprise when her lust for him dissolved as quickly as sugar in hot tea. She got bored of his talking; she got tired of his boasting about what he was going to do. She didn't really like people who bragged about what they had done, never mind droning on about things they hadn't done. It had taken her nine long months to finally realise that Robin, the wonderful musician, was in fact full of his own shit and importance. Nine long months of giving him head while he gave her nothing but anger and genital warts. She later heard that he couldn't even tune his instrument without the aid of a black box; it was the same story with their sex life.

So one sunny day, she confronted him, told him he was a fraud before walking out of his smelly bedroom. Amanda said goodbye to his mother and skipped home on a jet of warm air for the first time in ages. She was finally free of the fake rock star and her aim was to enjoy herself again. As expected, he bombarded her daily with phone calls and even threatened to write the world's greatest love song about her. Fortunately, the world was also spared that pleasure.

Days later, as Amanda waited at a set of traffic lights in her car; Robin leaped on the bonnet and tried to serenade her with his homemade love song. The song was so pitiful that Amanda didn't wait for the lights to change. She drove away; leaving him sprawled on the pavement, the neck of his guitar snapped in two. She never saw or heard from him again or his dreadful love song.

She met Daryl (her husband-in-waiting) two weeks after the incident at the traffic lights. They had bumped into each other as they queued at the fruit and vegetable stall in the market. She recognised him instantly. They spent several minutes passing pleasantries. He warned her about the unripe bananas. She told him that the plums were absolutely delicious. They seemed to have a fruit-thing in common.

He offered her his phone number. She took it, just to please him and she promised to call. He knew she'd lied;

she had no intention of contacting her old school pal. From what she had remembered about him, he wasn't her type, (Lois had been the one who had given him crabs), and his knowledge of erotic fruit unnerved her a little.

But, for some reason, a week later, in a moment of weakness and in need of company, she pulled his number out of her handbag and dialled it. A new chapter in her life began the following Friday night.

The mother-in-law from hell arrived at eleven a.m. on the dot. In Amanda's fertile mind, the clock in the lounge stopped ticking; birds flew out of the trees and the dog next door howled and bolted. Amanda was sure she could see bats circling around the eves of the house, even though it was daylight. She wondered if she should go to the local church to get some holy water, a crucifix and some garlic.

The old woman didn't walk as you would expect a 70 year old person to. This one glided, floating, as if being moved by a magnet hidden under the floorboards. Sadly for Amanda, the old lady was extremely well and fit for a woman of her age.

'More's the pity,' thought Amanda, wondering if she could accidentally poison her with a chicken breast marinated in a sweet and sour arsenic sauce and get away with it.

Daryl took her coat from her and hung it on a peg in the hallway. As soon as their eyes locked, Amanda was introduced to the famous mother-in-law stare. It was not like Lois's look which she had encountered earlier that week. No, this was an evil stare, packed with contempt and lined with hatred. It was the type of gib that was often seen on the faces of murderers on the front cover of Criminal Monthly, or on mad dictators on a mission to destroy the world. The stare didn't need words to tell her what the hag was thinking. The silence alone screamed out in a loud voice, 'You are not good enough for my little boy.... Never have been, never will. Even when I'm six feet under and getting eaten by bloody maggots.... I'll still be his favourite girl.'

Amanda could tell it was going to be a long day. They still hadn't got past the hallway and the old hag had tutted fifty-seven times about everything.

'Are you still bothering with that trollop?' she asked Amanda about her best friend.

'Her name is Lois and she's not a tr....' Amanda didn't bother to finish the sentence. She knew she was on a loser to start with. Lois was indeed a trollop, with a capital T. Even Lois called herself a Trollop. She was proud of it.

In fact, if there had been a qualification given out while they were at school for the person most likely to 'Become the town's biggest common or garden slut,' Lois would have won it hands down (or legs apart). She could easily have had a master's degree in the subject. Even Lois's son had once bought her a mug which stated in large red letters on the side *'To the best mum and greatest slag in the world.'* Lois placed the cup in her glass cabinet like it was a lifetime achievement award handed out at the Oscar ceremony.

'Are you still washing Daryl's clothes at a regular temperature...? He's looking thin... are you feeding him proper food?' Before Amanda could retaliate, the mother-in-law, who was a master black-belt in chopping people down to size with the use of a sharp word placed strategically into a sentence, had added dryly, 'Hope you are not going to give me that muck you regurgitated up for me the last time I came. I wouldn't have served that to my cats.'

'Cheeky bastard. They were pork chops cooked in a Sharwood's mushroom sauce. Fucking cats…. I hope they smothered the old bitch,' she hissed at Daryl while they hid in the kitchen.

'Are you getting out enough Daryl? It's no good being stuck in this house…. Looking at that face day in, day out,' she meowed from the living room. 'I allowed your father to go out every night, without fail…. Every night.'

Amanda felt like emptying the contents of the saucepan over the woman's head and screaming, 'Yeah and he ran off with the bloody barmaid…. Lucky bastard!' But she bit her lip in anger, punching Daryl in the arm in spite.

'Oh, and by the way, Amanda I may as well be the one to tell you… I think it's time you smartened yourself up a bit…. or he'll be looking around for a younger model…. Have you considered joining a gym or maybe weight watchers…? What about a face lift...? You know what I mean. Flowers don't always stay fresh in water.'

Daryl shook his head and placed his hand on his wife's arm, but that wasn't enough to quench the volcano which boiled and bubbled below Amanda's fragile interior.

'Don't be silly, Mam, Amanda is all I ever wanted,' Daryl tried to smooth out the situation while placing a plate of bread on the table.

'Look, I'm just saying,' the old woman knew exactly when she was on top. She was just setting the bait and waiting for Amanda to bite. 'You can't let yourself slip… especially at your age and with such a handsome looking sophisticated man under your roof.'

'That's it.' Amanda slammed her knife down hard onto the table top. The words tumbled out of her mouth with a force. 'A handsome sophisticated man…. if it hadn't been for me he'd still be tucking his shirt into his underpants and eating his own ear wax.'

There was a brief hush within the room.

'Bit early for the menopause ain't it dear?' The woman dismissed the outburst and carried on chewing on some meat. 'Is this meat supposed to be this tough?' She exaggerated her jaw movements.

Amanda was livid, she turned to her husband. 'Daryl. Are you going to stick up for me for a change?'

He looked at her, then at his mother, then back at his wife. 'Now come on love…. Mam doesn't mean anything by it…. Do you Mother?' His question didn't really need a reply.

The old woman knew she was near victory. It was all a game to her, but a game she was going to play to the death. She took the meat out of her mouth and said, 'I can't possibility eat this stuff… I will have to buy you a decent cook book for Christmas this year.' She smirked victoriously.

That was it. The final straw. Amanda rose to her feet. Her blood was boiling.

'Hope you fuckin' choke on it you old hag,' she could hear herself saying the words without realising the consequences. She glanced pitifully at her husband, grabbed her coat and rushed out of the house.

She didn't know where she was going. She didn't really care. She just needed to get away from the mother-in-law from hell and her yellow bellied excuse for a husband.

It was Sunday afternoon. It was drizzling. The streets were all but empty; the odd taxi cab whizzed past. She imagined similar arguments taking place behind all the closed doors in the street.

She walked passed a sign that announced there was a circus in town until Thursday.

'A circus in town.... This place is a bloody circus... we don't need any other clowns,' she screamed aloud, her words filling every corner of the empty street.

She needed two things at that moment. Firstly, someone to talk to and secondly a stiff drink. She knew where to go. She found herself banging on Lois's door. It took her mate a while to answer. When she did appear, her hair looked like a bomb had exploded in it. Her eyes were wide open and had a slightly scary glint to them. She had small scratch marks on her neck.

'Hey, what's this... having the George Clooney dream are you?' Amanda joked confidently.

'No! It's actually better than that.' She lowered her voice. 'I'm having hot Moulin Rouge sex with two dwarves from the travelling circus.'

'You are having what with whom?' Amanda looked puzzled.

'Hot Moulin Rouge sex.... You know the thing when you are sandwiched between two blokes.... little blokes.'

'Lois, that's Ménage á trois..... not bloody Moulin Rouge. You're amazing and your dreams are getting worse... you should go and get some help'

Lois positioned her finger to her lips. 'Schhhh... It's not a dream. I met them down the pub last night. I felt so sorry for the little men...look at these,' she opened the door and Amanda saw two pairs of little shoes neatly positioned by the stairwell. One pair was red, the other yellow.

Amanda laughed. 'You can't be serious?'

'Of course I'm serious... I wouldn't joke about a thing like that.' Amanda knew her friend well enough to realise she was telling the truth.

'I thought you were the Pizza man. We ordered some grub before we start round three. You can join us if you like. They maybe small in stature but they are both hung like stallions on Viagra,' Lois thought about what she had said and added, 'maybe not stallions... but definitely little pit ponies and they can do some right weird tricks.'

A picture of Lois laying flat on the bed with a midget, in the nude, getting shot from a cannon by another small person from the hallway popped into her head. Amanda felt like being sick. She actually heaved. She shook her head before running off aimlessly down the street towards the canal.

'What type of place am I living in? My husband doesn't care about me, my mother-in-law is the devil in disguise and now I find my best friend entertaining two men whose combined height is less than six foot.... What next?'

She felt as though she was starring in a film. And it wasn't some romantic comedy with a happy ending in sight. No...this film was a right weird one, probably one of those arty French flicks, written and directed by a student in a polo-neck sweater and little round glasses. The same student who in later years would end up imprisoned for performing indecent acts on various kinds of animals.

Amanda headed for the park to cool down and have a good cry before heading home to say sorry.

Chapter 5

Angel

He stared long and hard into the cracked shaving mirror while standing partially naked in the freezing cold bathroom. Two, large, swollen bags positioned under his eyes were a sign that he'd been crying for far too long.

He studied his features, wondering what it was about him that made people afraid of him. He knew the town in which he lived (or survived) was full to the brim with small minded individuals who refused to tolerate anyone who was a little different.

But he was a decent sort of person. He would help anyone if only they gave him the opportunity, instead of pre-judging him. It seemed that all of his life he had been surrounded by some invisible force-field, a barrier, which prevented others from connecting with him.

He glanced at his reflection again. It wasn't as if he had the shocking appearance of an elephant man type of character that could make small children scream out in horror. It was just that there was something about him that persuaded people to keep their distance.

He knew he was different. But he would rather describe himself as misunderstood and he definitely wouldn't class himself as abnormal.

He got angry; it made his blood boil and bubble when he was faced with their prejudices. The scars of his hurt ran deep. He'd had a lifetime of being constantly battered with cat-calls from the faceless masses. The masses who believed it was their god-given right to shout insults at him at the tops of their voices. They were small time losers living in a small time town.

He couldn't help who, or what he was. He was trapped in this confused state, and there seemed no way out of his maze. His only crime in this unfair world had been to be born into a body that didn't walk correctly along the pavements of so called, 'Normal Street.'

People had always treated him like a misfit. While he was growing up they would find it amusing to gang up on him and call him names. Some would even pelt him with stones or throw pieces of earth at him in the street. He was never invited to other children's houses or their birthday parties. He invited all of them to his party every year, but no one ever showed up. It was just left to him and his mother to cut the cake, unwrap the presents and play a game of musical chairs. (It was the shortest game of musical chairs in history). So growing up was hard and lonely. He didn't have any friends. His mother would tell him that the others were the peculiar ones, with their perfect bodies and sickening angelic smiles. He was her little angel. 'Mammies little angel,' she would sing to him each night.

Back in the bathroom he flushed the toilet, moved back to the bedroom and shuffled across the floor. The yellow sodium light from the street lamp crept through the net curtains and flooded onto the wall like some modern art painting. It was full of right angles and squares.

Out in the darkness of the alleyway that adjoined his house, he could make out the distinctive noise and shape of a teenage couple making out in the shadows. He peeked out from his window, careful to hide his face behind the safety of the net curtains. He wondered why he had been robbed of this the most basic pleasure in life? He'd always longed for some kind of love.

As each year rolled off the calendar and he grew older and stronger, people still avoided him like a bad smell. Even when he had found himself a half decent job, it was he who spent most of his lunchtimes sitting alone eating banana sandwiches which his mother had prepared. He was never asked to go for a drink with the gang after work; they never invited him to share his opinion on current issues, or comment on the weather. What made it worse was every Christmas some mystery person (or persons) would always leave him a big bottle of cheap aftershave on his desk. It was as if they were trying to tell him he smelled. He bathed every morning and every night, but the aftershave was the only present he received each year.

Outside, under the streetlight, the amorous couple were locked in a firm embrace, legs entwined, tongues sword-fencing in the darkness. The noise they made reminded him of farmyard animals, grunting, snorting and squelching.

He wanted to open the window and chuck a saucepan of icy cold water all over Mister Pig and his slaggy, piggy whore. He lay on his bed, tears rolling down his face. He fiddled under the pillow, searching around for his little ray of sunshine. He carefully held the Polaroid photograph in his fingers; the photo of the person who had come into his life and changed it forever.

He stared at it with tender love and smiled. He brushed his hand across the image on the colour picture, whispering sweet nothings while softly kissing the face of the person half-smiling back at him. It made him feel so alive.

It was then that he came to a life-changing decision. Tomorrow, he would go and see her and tell her the truth. He couldn't carry on like this. Tomorrow, he would tell her everything. Tomorrow would be the start of his brand new day.

Suddenly, from the depth of the alleyway, the moans and groans from the youngsters reached fever pitch. He listened to their lovemaking as he had done a thousand times. He switched off the lamp and reached between his legs for his groin.

Chapter 6

Trolley

It was exactly a week to the very day that Amanda's mother-in-law had climbed back onto her broomstick and disappeared into the night sky. Amanda had decided to celebrate the occasion by doing a spot of relaxation shopping in town.

She stood in the entrance to her favourite department store and watched with fascination, as some little brat from the estate, in short trousers and with a green, runny nose, unwrapped a chocolate bar with such speed and agility that in later years, the evil little five-year-old would definitely be employed in the SAS, or at least, become a full-time shoplifter. Within seconds, and with a mouth full of Hazelnut delight, the brat threw the wrapper to the floor and slalomed in and out of the legs of grown-ups, as the mother chased him desperately around the shop.

'Get back here you little bastard…. Or I'll stop you watching the Disney Channel,' the mother screamed at the top of her voice; to the great delight of all the other shoppers in the store.

Amanda smiled to herself as the rascal was finally cornered in the lingerie section, but still refused to give up without one last defiant fight for freedom. He somehow managed to push over a stack of promotional stockings and suspenders which toppled helplessly to the floor. His mother grabbed him by the throat and proceeded to belt nine lumps of shit out of the sobbing boy, before chucking him into the shopping trolley head first. Luckily, he landed on two large bras that his mother had bought for a special occasion.

Around the store, older women shook their heads and tutted in disgust. Some took exception to the mother's heavy handedness, while others were shocked at the ghastly behaviour of the infant. Amanda looked on in sadness. The incident caused a sharp emptiness to pinprick a hole in her already punctured heart.

To be honest she would have given anything in the world to have chased her own little brat through the aisles at Morgan's. She would have let him munch on a thousand bars of chocolate until he was sick and then she would have given him some more if he'd wanted them. But hers and Daryl's attempts at having a baby of their own had been unsuccessful. They were the unfortunate one-in-a-hundred couple who were unable to produce their own bundle of joy. And, up to now, they'd spent all of their lives smiling weakly when people asked them how many kids they had. They found themselves grinning politely through clenched teeth and changing the conversation as quickly as they could.

They had been too scared to find out which one of them couldn't conceive. They had discussed it and decided that it wouldn't be fair. So, like most working class couples, they just hid their heads in the sand, choosing to ignore and never mention the 'C' word.

Deep down, Amanda's heart lay broken in bits. She felt incomplete. Her marriage was incomplete. There was a major piece missing from the jigsaw box and she would have given anything to have found it.

She had always wanted children. Two or three would have been wonderful. Again she had used her vivid imagination to try and compensate for the situation. She invented kids of her own, pretending they were real. She had pictured them growing up, two girls, and the youngest, a cute little boy. She had even christened them and given them colourful personalities.

The oldest, Sarah Jane, was a very outgoing type, extremely self-sufficient, and, of course, very beautiful. She was a cross between a princess and a wild Romany gypsy. Her other daughter, Marie, named after her obsession with Marie biscuits, was more reserved, very shy, but very well-educated, and, of course, very beautiful. Amanda dreamed of her entire family and the rest of the village catching a train up to Oxford, or Cambridge, to see Marie receiving top honours from one of the old Universities.

Then there was Joshua, or Josh for short. She couldn't make her mind up if he was a sports star, or a famous actor, or maybe both. But, of course, he was extremely talented, handsome beyond belief, with millions of adoring females following his every movement.

Some days, Amanda would fast forward her little fantasy to a time where she could surround herself with the many grand-children her own children would have given to her in return. There would be hundreds and hundreds of them wandering around her garden, similar to the puppies from the film '101 Dalmatians,' all filling her life and home with sounds of laughter and joy. In her mind they would have been a fitting end to her reasonably good (but quite uneventful) life; her icing on top of a nice, but plain, raspberry-cake existence, covered with lashings of artificial cream.

The fake family portrait which stood proud in the far-romantic corners of her mind was sadly losing its colour and focus. As the years rolled on, she came to appreciate that her dream of kids was fading fast, along with most of her other hopes and ambitions that had once lit up her life. Regretfully they were now all boxed-up and stored forever in a little room way back behind her left eardrum; a place that was in danger of being locked forever.

Back in the crowded department store, she winked at the little tearaway as he was dragged kicking and screaming towards the check-outs, while still in his trolley-prison. She wondered if it would be the first of many jail cells that the youngster would see in his life. She hoped, for his sake, that it was the last time he would be surrounded by bars. Unfortunately, around here, the chances of kids growing up trouble-free were becoming less realistic each day. She guessed he had about as much chance of becoming the next Pope as he did of not getting into trouble with the law. Most of the poor kid's future was already mapped out for him in big bold letters. It simply stated; born, school, dole, addiction to drugs, short walk to death, and all before the tender old age of twenty (if they were lucky). Apparently in school, English teachers asked their pupils to write essays on 'what they wanted to be if they grew up?'

'Maybe it's a good thing I can't have a child,' she told herself, as tears welled up in her eyes.

She got ready to begin her quest for hunting in the food hall of the vast store. She prepared to close her eyes. She had once read in some women's magazine that an experiment was carried out in America, where they blindfolded housewives to see if they could wander around their local convenience stores and do the shopping at the same time. Unbelievably, it stated that nine times out of ten, the women tested would not only put the correct items into their shopping trolley, but hold conversations with other similar women when they passed in the aisles. It concluded that women had an ability to do this because they suffered from a genetic disorder named Zombieitus, which became more acute, especially when faced with familiar surroundings. In the test, the women scored higher than a bunch of thoroughly-trained laboratory white mice. On finishing the column, Amanda thought it must be a poor reflection of the life of an American housewife, if this was true.

Of course, the day after reading the article, Amanda decided to try and validate the research herself. Maybe it stemmed back to her father's influence. She closed her eyes on that first morning (her maiden blind-shopping voyage) and sauntered about slowly. At first she found it a little strange. She took baby steps and within no time she got the hang of it. Amazingly, she found she had moved around the store without once opening her eyes until the checkout and not bumping into anything, or anyone. She was hooked. From that day on she instantly carried out all her shopping like this. It soon became a nation craze with bored housewives without the land.

Today she stopped pushing her trolley and took a deep breath. From the smell of the fresh bread dancing about in her nostrils, she must have been close to aisle nine. She counted ten paces, before reaching out to gather her normal bottle of washing up liquid. Strangely, she felt a cardboard box where plastic should have been. She frantically rummaged around on the shelf for the correct item (her eyes still firmly shut.)

Had she made a mistake? Was she still in row seven, not nine? She questioned her judgment. She was stuck, unable to move. She knew it was bad luck to peek before the wine and spirit section. The drink aisles were out of bounds. They had been made into 'open-eye' aisles only, after one inexperienced blind shopper smashed into the shelf stacked with expensive Chilean wines. The red grape liquid had flooded the area, closing the store for two hours. The management had warned shoppers that they would be sentenced to a life-long ban if they were caught wandering down that aisle with their eyes closed. They even installed hidden cameras as a precaution. The camera system was flawed because, unbelievably, the crafty women bought fake glasses with a pair of open eyes drawn on the lenses. It was becoming a war between shop owner and shopper.

Finally Amanda gave in and opened her eyes. She saw another lady standing staring at the shelf, completely bewildered.

Amanda had a knack of being able to always judge people by the contents of their shopping trolley. If she saw a woman with a trolley full of frozen items, she was quite obviously a poor mother who was more concerned with going out on the pull, than ensuring that her children had proper, healthy food on the table. Many mothers up on the estate were in this camp. When they did actually venture to the shops, they would only bother to go to the frozen counter unless they were on a fag and alcohol run. On the other hand, Amanda took great care when placing items in her trolley. She never went for any of the store's dreadful, cheap, own brand; there were always lots of fresh vegetables and a decent bottle of red wine.

She may have grown-up living on a council estate, but she was determined to drag herself out of the 'pie and chips' culture that had taken root in the town.

Once, she remembered going shopping with Lois and nearly dying of embarrassment when the check-out girl scanned through a Barry White CD, 48 ribbed and flavoured condoms, some KY Jelly (the 82g tube), a bottle of extra virgin olive oil, a punnet of strawberries and a bottle of cheap champagne. Lois had just seen 'Pretty Woman' and had thought that she would get prepared in case Richard Gere would turn up looking to shag with the town's best hooker. When asked 'why the olive oil?' Lois claimed that one of her men friends didn't like the taste of KY Jelly and would only go down on her if she smothered herself in the Italian lubricant.

Back in aisle nine, she noticed the other woman's trolley was full of good gear; organic beans, wholemeal bread and lots of fresh fish. 'She must be a teacher or something like that,' Amanda said to herself.

After a while the lady eventually said 'What the hell is this...? Where's my usual detergent gone?' The woman looked cross.

'It must have been a man who stacked the shelf,' Amanda tried to comfort the woman at her side with a bit of an 'in' joke about how useless men were, especially when it came to the serious matter of blind shopping.

'Well, I'm off to see the manager.... I've never been so humiliated in my life.... I've been blind shopping now for three months and I never opened my eyes until the check-outs.... Never... It's disgusting....You wouldn't get this treatment in Marks and Spencer's.'

Amanda watched her storm-off in a giant huff, smoke coming out of her ears

Amanda shrugged and proceeded to carry on, eyes shut. During her journey she suddenly felt abnormally uncomfortable. She sensed someone was staring at her. She opened her eyes again and looked around. At first she could only see other women in her aisle, all with their eyes closed, busy scanning the shelves, reading the tin labels with their fingers like blind beggars on a picnic.

She glanced behind her and she was surprised to see Desmond looking straight at her. His eyes were following her every movement. He was dressed in a long black evening grown and he was pushing his mother in her wheelchair. His slightly deranged and totally insane mother, was, as usual, beating people out of the way with her cane as Desmond pushed her towards the direction of Amanda.

Desmond arrived by her side. He was still staring intently at her.

'Doing a bit of shopping are you?' Amanda said to the strange man, with the stranger mother. He nodded his head, looking down at the floor in the vein of a naughty schoolboy caught smoking behind the sports hall.

She automatically glanced into his metal trolley. She was lost for words as she saw that most of the basket was empty except for twelve tins of cat food, a container of sparkly lip-gloss, and a copy of 'Hello' magazine.

Amanda searched for something else to say to the man in front of her; any crumb of conversation to help her get away.

'It's raining again, Desmond,' she eventually said, as she noticed that he had a brown hair-clip positioned behind his ear. She was dying to laugh, until the pain from the cane on her leg caused her to move back sharply.

'Mother, there's no need for that,' Desmond apologised, turning brusquely to berate the old woman.

'Well, Desmond. Stop talking to that whore… I need pile cream…. I need pile cream,' his mother bellowed out, before wheeling herself to the shelf where the ointments were displayed.

Amanda commented, while glaring at the old woman. 'Well I must be going. It's been great having a chat Desmond.'

She went to walk past. In the background the mother pulled items manically off the shelf while searching for the cream. He fixed his stare at the floor deliberately blocking her path,

'What's wrong Desmond? What is it?' she enquired.

'Ummmm… Well Mrs Grey… I need to tell you something.'

Amanda looked puzzled. 'What?'

A loud yell from the direction of his mother broke his concentration. 'Desmond….' She was holding up a small tube.

'Mother… You can't do it here.' Desmond turned to grab the container off her. 'I'll do it for you when we get home… After your bath.' He wrestled to get the tube out of her vice-like grip.

The comical tug-of-war between mother and son gave Amanda enough time and space to shuffle past and to the safety of the frozen-goods aisle. She had her eyes fully opened now. There was no time for messing about. She needed to get away and fast. He gave her the willies. She laughed at her own pun. If Lois was right about Desmond's operation he could actually give her his Willy within the next few weeks, probably wrapped up in a brown paper bag, or in a jar. It was a terrible and sickening thought to have crossed her mind. She cursed herself for thinking it. She just knew it would stick in there all day like humming an annoying tune that she'd heard on the radio.

She quickly threw in some small items and rushed to the check-out.

As she nervously waited she heard a woman complaining to the manager that she'd just witnessed some bizarre incident over by the fresh bread roll section.

'Look,' the woman explained to the young manager, 'I'm telling you now, there's an old woman in a wheelchair trying to apply some substance down her knickers... Right there next to the crumpets and scones. It's unhygienic... I'll be reporting this shop to someone at the council.'

The manager was pissed-off. He'd already had an ear bashing off some school teacher about changing items on the shelves. He quickly summoned several part-time assistants, armed with broom handles and bar coding guns. They all went scampering gingerly off into the department store.

Amanda didn't hang about. She paid for her goods and raced out into the drizzle and the cold wind. She put them in the boot before getting in her car. She wondered what Desmond was trying to tell her. What surprised her more was the fact that he knew her name in the first place? She didn't realise he knew anything about her.

'Perhaps he's going through hormone treatment and it's starting to affect him,' she told herself.

She took a deep breath and went to start the car. She stopped as she glanced to the right into the next parking space. She looked through the steamed up windows of a clapped out Renault Clio and saw, in the front seats, a teenage couple necking furiously. Their hands were disappearing all over each other and the car was rocking gently. She heard muffled groans.

Amanda didn't know why, but she was jealous for the second time that day. The first was seeing that upstart of a kid running amok in the store, and now it was watching these two lovers making-out in broad daylight. She was in her own private hell whichever way she turned.

She wondered why she and Daryl never kissed like that anymore. The rare occasion their lips did come in contact with each other was when one or the other was leaving the house. It was a little peck on the cheek like kissing a distant, unpleasant relative. All the loving feeling they shared in the past had disappeared.

She recalled how his lips used to be red hot when they first started courting. He would kiss her all over, no place was left untouched. They were probably the best times of her life. They were exciting; mind-blowing. They made love everywhere, in all kind of exciting places; cars, woods, even in amongst the non-fiction section of the local library during a very, wet, August bank holiday.

She would dress-up and make a point of slowly undressing for him. Sometimes, when they were both feeling a little kinky, he would dress-up for her, but it was all done in the best possible taste.

She stared once again at the couple in the car. Even though her eyes were wide open, she was too blind with jealousy to notice the girl disappearing out of sight between the boy's legs.

Amanda was still wondering when and how she and Daryl had lost their passion for each other, their spark for life together. Was it an age thing? Or maybe it was being married for a million years thing? Perhaps people only have a certain amount of love and lust for each other, before it was used up.

She guessed that lots of couples reached a crucial point in their marriage when they just simply ran out of gas.

Maybe she and Daryl's love-tank had automatically switched to empty, without any warning. No red indicator light and no warning bleep to tell them so. She wondered if this was the case. Was there an emergency twenty-four hour love station open with a plentiful supply of high Octane lust fuel and a forecourt that could supply them with all with the essentials they would need to survive through life's dark journey? Or were they just going to be left to rot by the roadside of marriage, by the RAC man of relationships?

She snapped back into focus, just as the boy in the car opposite seemed to be reaching his point of no return. He shrugged his shoulders back and fore and his body jerked wildly. Amanda thought the boy was having some kind of seizure. She was about to go over and offer some assistance when the girl reappeared, brushing her hair from her face and swallowing hard. She reached in the glove compartment and wiped her chin with a dry and crispy, yellow shammy-leather. The boy whispered in her ear and pointed at Amanda. They both waved, the girl smiled and blew a kiss.

Amanda nervously fiddled with the ignition keys.

'What's wrong with this bloody generation?' She asked. 'I blame their parents, or the TV, or maybe the government, or perhaps even bloody Bagpuss... anyone really. We have all made-out in the back of a car, but not in broad daylight in the car park of a department store.... and definitely not while other people were watching....and not in a fucking, clapped out Renault Clio.'

She sped out of the car park, around the roundabout, and just missed an oncoming police van that was racing to the store to try to quell a possible riot taking place in the fresh bread section.

Chapter 7

Rome

It had been over three weeks since the visit to the tarot card reader. In that time Amanda still hadn't come across anyone who resembled a dark, handsome stranger, but she had noticed that Cyril, her fifty eight year old milkman, had, for some reason, started to dye his hair. He reminded her of an overweight Superman driving through the streets on a milk float, or, to be more specific, Superman's granddad.

Amanda was thinking that Madam Zelda was just another old fraud, but, unknown to her, the old hag's spell had begun to work on Lois. She had indeed caught a disease. She had contracted a mild dose of herpes on the lip from a door-to-door salesman who called to demonstrate the sucking supremacy of a bag-less vacuum cleaner. Fortunately for the young representative, Lois had demonstrated to him how her mouth had a much stronger suction than any Dyson or Hoover could ever muster. She was the original bagless cleaner, or was it the original cleanless bag?

The two friends again sat in Amanda's kitchenette on a damp and cold Wednesday evening, chain-smoking cheap fags, which Lois had bought off some Polish lorry driver delivering ingredients to the local chocolate factory. They had run out of all the hard stuff, so Amanda had rummaged at the back of the cupboard for the Christmas sherry that normally didn't see the light of day, unless her aunty visited. Sadly, Amanda's aunt had passed away in the spring, so they unanimously decided that it would be a shame to leave it sitting in the cupboard all alone.

'Hey Amanda... Do you fancy coming to Blackpool to see the lights?' Lois asked, whilst picking at the scab on her lip.

'Blackpool....no way.... Daryl will never allow it. He reckons Blackpool is full of desperate slappers looking to pull young boys before they sign on for their pension books.'

'Yeah... and his point is?' Lois commented sharply. 'Anyway, he's a cheeky fucker... how the hell would he know what Blackpool was like? The furthest he's ever ventured is playing pool with his mates in the next village. Come on... We'll have a great time.... And I'll swear you don't have to pull a young, buck, built like a stallion.... I'll have yours as well.... if you insist.'

Amanda smiled as her mate dunked a chocolate digestive biscuit in her sherry. 'When is it?' she asked.

'October time.... Come on.' Lois dragged on another cigarette, and scratched her swollen lip again. 'Fuckin' door-to-door salesmen... you can't trust them nowadays.'

Amanda grinned. 'What door-to-door salesman? What was he selling?' She reached across and topped up her glass.

'He sold bad news.' Lois picked up her bag and headed for the toilet. 'Oh! Never mind.... Have a think about

Blackpool. Let's go for it! Just the two of us and the tower ballroom full of hot, horny, young, fit men. I'll have to overdose on Zovirax first, mind.'

Amanda's mind drifted off. She was doing a grand job of picturing the young studs gyrating about in tight blue jeans and Calvin Klein underpants, six packs rippling and glistening with sweat, when there was a gentle tap on the front door that broke her concentration. She extinguished the fag. She always thought it was slightly common to open a door puffing away on a cigarette. She glanced in the mirror, puckered her lips and headed off to see who threatened to darken her entrance.

'Hello Desmond,' Amanda was taken aback at the sight of the strange man standing in the doorway, as large as life and as weird as they come.

He looked sheepish as he rocked nervously back and forth, resplendent in a pastel flowery dress.

'Hello Mrs Grey. May I have a word with you please?' he asked politely.

'Of course you can, Desmond.' Amanda stood blocking the entrance, sub-consciously preventing him from crossing the threshold. She wondered if his mother was out of jail yet.

'It's a rather delicate matter, Mrs Grey…. It needs to be in private.' Desmond looked past her shoulder and into the lounge.

Amanda shook her head as if she was shaking away some cobwebs. 'Oh, sorry Desmond, I was miles away…. Do come on in.' She led the way.

He shuffled behind, as if his two feet were chained together. Amanda offered him the settee. He slowly sat down, but kept his back up straight. He looked in pain. Amanda wondered if it was something to do with the story Lois had told her about him having his chopper chopped off. Amanda shivered in her skin at the thought and decided to take the safety of the chair facing the television set, nearest to the door.

The silence was pronounced and all-engulfing. Amanda was searching around every corner of her mind for something meaningful to say to break the ice that had automatically formed between them. Desmond glanced around the room, taking in every detail, but he refused to make eye contact with her.

'How's your mother, Desmond? Have the police released her yet?'

He rolled his eyes towards the heavens. 'Why does everyone always ask me about my mother?' he thought inwardly. 'Why doesn't anyone ask how I am?' but he politely replied that she was fine and the police had only given her a warning about the incident in the store. He told her that the store manager had dropped the charges after the doctors' informed him that he wouldn't go blind from having a dollop of pile cream squirted in his eyeball, and he was grateful that the cyst, that had been threatening to erupt, had miraculously faded away.

Desmond also mentioned that someone from the 'Home Help' was over at his house at that very moment, filing the top off her verrucas and shaving her back. Desmond looked at the floor again, fiddling with his thumbs.

'I heard that you are having your winkle hacked off soon,' Amanda was dying to state, but she couldn't force herself to utter the words. Instead, she opted for safe ground and said 'Are you making those lovely scones and Welsh Cakes for the school fete this year? And Desmond, by the way, there's no need to call me Mrs Grey.... Please call me Amanda.'

'I don't know about the cakes…. My mother hasn't decided yet. She was thinking that this year I could make fairy cakes instead. Ones with the silver balls on.'

Amanda was dying to laugh. Again, there was a silence from the Transvestite on the sofa that was so deafening it pierced Amanda's eardrums.

'Bloody hell,' Amanda whispered, 'it's like being in the doctor's waiting room with a mute Danny La Rue.' Now she wished she hadn't let him through her door.

Suddenly, he spoke softly. 'Amanda….I'm in love!'

This news knocked Amanda backwards. She slumped back in the chair, flabbergasted by the revelation. Then it hit her. Why the hell was he telling her this information? Did he think she was some kind of agony aunt who needed to sanction it?

She concluded that maybe he was making personal house visits; it could have been his way of breaking the news to people instead of putting a piece in the local paper or waiting for the gossip to begin.

'Local weirdo transvestite to marry man of his/her dreams in big white ceremony in community centre…. Sir Elton John is to play the organ.'

Amanda could see the headline in fine bold print in the local newspaper. She wiped the thought clean and continued. 'Desmond, that's wonderful news…. That's truly wonderful news. Who is he….?' She stopped in full flight. She had assumed it was going to be a man. 'Bloody hell,' she thought, 'I hope it is a man…. But it could be anything…. Even some sort of bloody beast wouldn't be out of the question.' She knew Desmond was not what you would call normal, especially when you considered he was sitting opposite her, wearing a frock with matching shoes and handbag. It was her turn to switch on the silent tap.

She stood up, then immediately sat back down. She needed another drink to calm her nerves, and quickly.

He had sensed her discomfort. 'It is a man, Mrs Grey... It's a man...! A gorgeous man!'

'Well, thank Christ for that!' Amanda said without thinking. 'Oh sorry Desmond how rude of me.... Is it anyone I know?'

'Yes...you know him very well.'

'Do I?' She was trying to think who it could possible be.

Desmond stared at her for the first time and spoke quietly, almost too quietly to be audible, 'I'm in love with.... Daryl.' He repeated it twice.

Amanda was so relieved that she had guessed right; she didn't really comprehend what he was actually saying. The content of his words hadn't sunk in.

She asked, 'Oh... that's great news. Where is this Daryl from?'

Desmond stared straight at her. 'He lives here with you.... It's your Daryl... It's your husband who I'm in love with.'

Lots of weird things in life can create a delayed reaction. When the first plane smashed headfirst into the side of one of the Twin Towers in New York, no one moved below. They all stood still, rooted to the spot, just pointing at the amazing sight above them. Minutes later, when the second plane collided, panic set in across the city, people screamed, ran, cried and probably peed themselves. Amanda went through the same emotion, except for the peeing herself part (that would come later).

She hunched her forehead up in confusion. Even when he had muttered Daryl's name, it still hadn't registered who he was talking about (plane number one). It was not until he showed her a photograph of her husband smiling, while sitting in Desmond's house, a wheelchair loomed large in the background, that it finally hit home (plane number two).

'What do you mean Daryl? Not my Daryl?' Her mind was racing. Her heart beat wildly in her chest similar to an idling Harley Davidson on full choke.

'Sorry, Mrs Grey,' Desmond didn't think it was the appropriate time to call her by her first name. 'Daryl and I have been lovers for the past nine months. I love him…. and he loves me.'

Amanda shook her head in disbelief, waiting for the punch-line to kick in, or for her to be woken from some nightmare. This was much worse than the dream she kept having about crashing into the gigantic Dairylea cheese triangle…. and a lot more bizarre.

'We just fell in love…. We never meant it to happen. It just did!' He smiled at her innocently.

Amanda got up, sat back down, and then got straight back up again before pacing up and down the room. She was finding it difficult to engage her brain, never mind actually think about what was happening in front of her. Desmond went to say something else, but she cleared her mind sufficiently enough to jump in before he made the matter worse.

'Hang on… Desmond…. Are you taking drugs or have you been drinking?' she asked in hope. Her sanity needed something tangible to hang onto; a foothold to help her make sense of the situation.

He shook his head, a serious expression fixed on his face.

She stood face to face with him. She could see the bad excuse for blusher caked onto his fat cheeks, stubble clearly visible beneath the cracking layers. He reminded her of a cheap old whore standing down by the blustery dockside in a mini-skirt and 6-inch, white stilettos. She calmed her quaking voice and coolly asked, 'Let me get this straight... you are telling me that you..... And my husband, Daryl... are in love.' She laughed weakly, focusing on his features.

'Yes!' His smile grew even wider on his face. 'As I said... we've been lovers for about nine months.'

'Nine months.'

'Actually it's nine months and two days and a couple of hours ... but who's counting?' He shrugged his shoulders, a smirk formed on his lips.

'Is this a sick joke?' she barked, but before he had time to reply she added bitterly. 'Cos, if it's not, you'd better get that fuckin' grin off your stupid, freaky face before I smack it off. You'll be counting how many front teeth you are missing.' She was in no mood to mince her words.

He backed away before adding, 'It's true...! I'm telling you.... we are even thinking of having a.... having a.... having a baby together!'

'A what....?' her shriek sailed high into the room.

'A baby.... but probably not straight away... we want to enjoy life together first, maybe go on a cruise or go to see Rome.'

'A fuckin' baby! Don't you think that you are a bit old..... And maybe a little bit too much of a man.... for having a baby.' Amanda pinched herself to see if she was in some horrendous nightmare. The pinch hurt and Desmond was still on the settee.

'In six months I will have had my operation... I won't be Desmond anymore.... I'll be Veronica Lace.' It was a name he had seen on a gravestone and thought it was so romantic (even though he didn't realise that the original Veronica Lace had died of the pox in 1843 at the tender age of twenty two.) 'We are going to adopt.... Actually!'

Amanda thought she was going to be sick. It was fightback time. Amanda stormed in, all guns blazing. 'Don't be so stupid... you crazy, mixed-up man, or whatever you are. Daryl is married to me. He's not gay... he's not having an affair...especially with you.' She suddenly remembered Lois's comments earlier of her suspicions about her husband messing about. The reality of the situation then hit her hard. She shook, as if smacked on the side of the head with a baseball bat, as she suddenly realised that her pal was sitting in the kitchen listening to all this.

'Jesus Christ.' Amanda had to think fast, and get the cross-dressing lunatic to shut up so she could check that Lois hadn't heard anything.

'Sorry, Desmond... I've got something cooking in the microwave.' Her mind was scrambled. 'Hang on a minute.... But don't say anything else until I get back.'

He looked around the room, confused, wondering who she thought he would tell in her absence.

She took a deep breath in the hallway, planning what she was going to say to her mate. She opened the kitchen door and said, 'Oh....I'm sure that Desmond has been on the old Bob Hope... or the old magic mushrooms....'

Her prearranged speech was cut short. She stared in horror at the empty table. A half lit cigarette lay burning away in an ashtray. The back door swung about in the wind. She instantly knew this was bad. She needed to get to Lois before she started beating the jungle drums all over town. Amanda rushed out in the garden. The back gate was unbolted and open.

'Ohhhhh, shit!' the words tumbled from her mouth.

She knew her mate was a black-belt master in spreading rumours. Lois could hear a muttering from across town and get it processed and turned into the biggest scandal in history before the secret had time to gather dust. She was deadly, especially when she was loaded with something as juicy and scandalous as this.

'But, she's still my best friend,' Amanda tried to comfort herself, 'She wouldn't say anything?' Sadly, her optimism only lasted a few seconds before Amanda rightly knew that friendship never came into the equation when hot gossip was at stake. Relationships and trust played a very poor second fiddle in the orchestra of tittle tattle. Amanda realised that her life was about to change for good and change very fast.

At that moment a key turning in the front door made her jump. She raced back into the hallway, just as Daryl entered, wearing his dirty overalls.

'Hello baby.... any grub, I'm starving.' He started to take his boots off.

'Yeah...it's in there sitting on the settee dressed in a smock and size nine shoes.' Her face was white and screwed into a ball.

Daryl looked confused. 'Bit early to be on the sauce...ain't it,' he asked, placing his boots under the stairs.

'The day I've had.... I should have pure whisky injected into my veins,' she spat back in anger, her eyes bored into his face.

They walked into the front room. Daryl stiffened on seeing Desmond sitting on the sofa in the dress he had bought him from the catalogue shop for his birthday. The transvestite looked like he had been crying, his mascara streaking down his caked face. Daryl appeared to have seen his past ghosts all at once, wrapped up in a big white sheet (or at least an ill-fitting floral dress).

Amanda immediately knew from her husband's expression that Desmond was telling the truth. She instantly pictured the two men in bed together and then strolling down the High Street, arm-in-arm, pushing a pram. She felt sick in her stomach.

'Daryl...' Desmond cried and held out his arms in desperation. 'I'm so sorry... but I just had to tell your wife about us.... I can't live without you anymore.' He sobbed pitifully.

Daryl was flustered. 'Look you... I don't know what you are talking about. I've never seen you before...who are you?'

'Daryl.... Desmond's lived in the street opposite for the last twenty years...stop fucking lying.... He worked in your factory... What the hell is going on?' She put her face up tight to his. He found it hard to breath. He was claustrophobic from the pressure in the room.

'Tell her, Sweet Pea,' Desmond spoke, 'Tell her about us.'

'Sweet fuckin' Pea...! Sweet fuckin' Pea! Daryl what's happening here? Am I dreaming?' It was Amanda's turn to start crying.

'Look.... Look....I....I.....' Daryl also joined in with his own set of tears.

'Don't you dare fuckin' cry... don't you dare.' She pointed at her husband. She knew men only cried if they lost on horse racing. 'Explain yourself, and quickly. Tell me honestly what's been going on with you and fuckin' Boy George over there.'

'Hey... now, Amanda, there's no need to call people names.' Daryl frowned.

'Call people names? Hang on a minute....You twat! Transvestite Trevor has just shuffled into my front room and told me he's been having an affair with you, my husband..... What the fuckin' hell do you suggest that I do....? Bake a cake....? Throw a party...? Invite the neighbours around?'

Daryl was flustered. He searched around in his mind for a way out, but every exit was locked and bolted. Elvis was truly stuck in the building and left to face the music.

'Oh, and by the way.' She was on a roll. 'Your lover here told me that you may be trying for a baby after you get back from Paris.'

'It was Rome, Mrs Grey?' Desmond corrected her.

'Aaarggghhh....' She screamed out, 'Daryl! Get him out of here before I pull his fuckin' earrings out...with his fuckin' ears still attached to them.'

'Look, Desmond, can you please leave,' he asked quietly.

Desmond looked lost, a puppy in a pet shop left alone over the Christmas period, while all his doggy mates had been picked by the humans and were spending their time eating turkey leftovers and lying by a big roaring fire having their bellies tickled.

Daryl led him to the door. Amanda could hear sobbing and whispers. She was angry. She scanned the room for something heavy with which to bash-in their skulls.

Fortunately, before she found something, her husband reappeared. They stood in silence, two prize-fighters waiting for the other to make the first move.

'Look, love.... It's not what you think.' He tried desperately to put his arm around her shoulders.

She shrugged him off and stood there. She stiffened. 'Well! How is it then, exactly...? Come on...! Tell me...!

I'm dying to fuckin' know what the hell's been going on?' Her blood boiled in her veins.

'It was just an accident!'

'An accident...? Oh, so going to bed with the local weirdo was just an accident was it? I feel sick.'

'It was a mistake... I love you... I've always loved you... you know that.' His crawling made her cringe.

'Was his mother involved?'

'What do you mean, was his mother involved?'

She reached for the glass by the side and threw it across the room in his direction. 'I don't know... I don't know anything anymore. Twenty minutes ago I was married to Daryl Grey, my faithful husband, but that's just been blown out of the water... by a.... by ...a.' She couldn't manage to get her words out.

'Look,' he raised his voice for the first time, 'I need time to think... can I ask you to do me a big favour and don't mention this to anyone... please love... we can work this out... trust me.'

'There's nothing to work out... Lois was right when she said that you were having an affair, but I told her no way... not my Daryl... he's working overtime... I said.'

'It's not an affair.'

'Well what the hell is it then...? You've discovered your feminine side after all these years, or maybe it was 'shag the sicko' week? Tell me, Daryl... Tell me!' The words made Amanda heave. She slumped in the chair, exhausted, stars appearing in front of her eyes.

'I need time to think,' he said again. 'Please keep it to yourself, otherwise we will be a laughing stock.'

She lunged at him and yelled 'We'll be a laughing stock...? You cheeky bastard...! Get out....! Get out before I kill you!' And before he reached the door, she added, menacingly, 'Oh….. And by the way, Lois knows everything… every last detail.'

'What do you mean she knows everything?' In that instant perspiration broke out all over his body.

'She was sitting in the kitchen when your boyfriend called.' Amanda intended her words to cut him to bits. It did the trick.

Worry ran over his face at a thousand miles per hour. He looked stunned. 'Where is she?' He demanded to know. 'Where did she go?'

'Probably down the social club telling all your mates about it…. They are probably having a laugh as we speak.'

She heard the door slam as Daryl raced out into the night.

But she knew whatever he did, he would be too late. Sadly, it hadn't taken long for the rumour mill to start to churn out the gossip. As soon as it began, it burned out of control, like an Australian bush fire with a 100 mph wind behind it, blowing it towards a dry pine-forest, covered in petrol.

Lois had done her womanly duty well. She had left no stone unturned. All possible avenues of communication to set alight the rumour mill had been used. She had started by telephoning friends and family, telling them about what she'd heard while innocently smoking in Amanda's kitchen. Her phone bill quadrupled overnight. She told everyone she could think of and even people she didn't know. An hour after rushing from Amanda's house with her mind loaded with juicy ammunition, she had set about firing gossip-bullets all over the town. Lois even went to confession and spilled the beans to Old Father Wiseman, who immediately happened to mention it in his sermon in mass that evening.

An hour later, Daryl finally came back home. He looked suicidal. He was white with fear. He refused to discuss any more details with his wife. He blanked the incident out completely, just telling her over and over that it was rubbish.

They both separately decided to lock the world out and stay safe inside the four walls of their home. They stayed in different rooms. There was no sleeping or eating taking place, only worry and fear. Outside, the weather had turned chilly but it wasn't half as cold as it felt inside number 42, Gladys Street. Emotional icicles hung from the living room curtains, under a waterfall of tears and a snowfall of frozen cries.

It didn't take Amanda long to know that people had heard all about the news. It was the silence which gave the game away. No one called. The phone lay silent and inactive on the coffee table in the hallway. The postman had stopped walking up the path to their front door to deliver any form of letters, including junk-mail.

Daryl phoned in sick to work. The receptionist, who had taken the call, had burst out laughing when he had unintentionally mentioned that he was feeling a little queer and was going to see the doctor later that day.

'A doctor,' Daryl's supervisor had yelled when he had heard his excuse. 'He doesn't need a doctor... it's a butt-plug he needs.... the dirty bastard,'

The couple kept a very low profile. Each minute alone in the house seemed like an hour. Each hour seemed like a day, and each day was too long to measure. The nights were even longer. It was as though the long night before Christmas and the last hour to welcome in the New Year, had been rolled-up together into one big time zone. It dragged so slowly, that Amanda thought she would end-up losing her mind, as well as her husband. She lay alone in her bed, crying until she had no tears left.

Chapter 8

Out

It seemed like a lifetime since the revelation about the town's newest affair had become common knowledge. Since that time, it was as if Amanda, Daryl and Desmond had flown over some bizarre Bermuda love triangle and had disappeared. Their antics were on everyone's lips. They had become public property overnight. Little kids made up nursery rhymes about them as they skipped in the street. Grown-ups did what grown-ups did best and laughed and sniggered between themselves like little kids.

Amanda wasn't sure why she hadn't kicked Daryl out that very night. It didn't make sense at all. Maybe she was just waiting for the right moment; the right time to show him the door and then change the locks on their life forever. Perhaps she was scared, afraid of being left alone.

It could have been that she needed a friendly face to help her through the pain, a pair of arms to wrap around her and make her feel safe. Since Lois had disappeared without a trace, her husband was the only one left standing. He had come to her and begged her forgiveness, pleading that it wasn't as it had seemed. He told her the story was wildly exaggerated.

She didn't believe him. She screamed and even tried to bite him in rage. But, in a moment of madness or weakness, she agreed to stay until she stopped feeling so confused. She needed time to sort her head out. To be truthful, she felt a little sorry for him. She knew she shouldn't have, but she was made like that. She was also too tired, too exhausted from beating herself up.

It was Saturday evening, as Daryl and Amanda moved as one down the long terraced street flanked by council houses, wheelie bins and cheap, clapped-out cars. Although the couple walked together hand in hand, they couldn't have been further apart.

Amanda was absolutely dreading coming face-to-face with anyone she knew. She saw two teenagers milling around the pavements, playing kerbies with a bright orange football. Thankfully, the youngsters were too interested in winning their game to notice the couple. Halfway down on the left, a gaggle of old women feverishly chatted to each other, while perched on freshly-cleaned doorsteps. They automatically halted their conversation when they saw the couple coming towards them, nudging each other and whispering openly. Then a woman rushed out of her house, picked up her infant, and spat on the pavement before slamming the door shut.

Amanda felt like a Jew being marched through war-torn streets of an occupied Polish city, by a band of expressionless Nazis. She imagined people lined up to spit and swear at them, or throw buckets of urine from upstairs windows, as they shuffled pass with big yellow stars sown onto their chest to indicate that they were evil, cursed, the unclean.

She hated and despised them all. How could they judge her so meanly? But at that moment she hated her husband more for putting her in this predicament; putting her quiet and unassuming life in the spotlight, hanging their dirty washing out to dry.

The couple turned the corner at the end of the road. The haunting figure of the run-down social club came into view. They both stiffened, their stride slowed to a crawl.

'Do we have to do this?' she asked, looking around for a lane or alleyway to escape down.

'Amanda, I don't want to do it either... but we have to do it some time... so it may as well be tonight.' She knew he was right but his reply still didn't make it any easier.

It had been two weeks since Desmond had visited her, with his earth-shattering news. Fourteen days of misery, trying to guess what people were saying, trying to imagine the comments and the stories doing the rounds. Word got around fast on the estate, faster than the speed of light and more accurate than a sniper's bullet.

Amanda disliked going to the bloody social club at the best of times. Each room was masked in clouds of cigarette smoke, which over the years had systematically (and thankfully) discoloured the shocking lime green wallpaper. A million fag burns, beer spills and chewing gum had all but put paid to the once vibrant, patterned carpet. Now it resembled a tar bog, trapping the unwary feet of the casual visitor.

She knew the women from up on the estate would be assembling in rows of long seats feeding like pigs at a trough. Lines of haggard-looking women, attempting to dress ten years younger, which only made them appear twenty years older. Their cheap makeup applied with a trowel, a decade behind the times. Each night they would binge on a vast, unhealthy diet, of warm beer, forty

Benson and Hedges, and helpings of hot gossip, all served up with lashings of cold tongue, stale fags and scampi fries.

They normally spread rumours about everyone and everything. No-one was spared. Spiteful stories about those who weren't there to answer back or protect themselves. In fact they gossiped about anyone, even if they were there, but out of courtesy they waited until the person had stepped out to powder their nose. No-one was safe.

The deep worry-lines that were etched on their faces thinly disguised the hurt and pain that had overtaken their desperate lives. Years spent looking after selfish husbands who only cared about gambling and drinking had taken their toll. On top of that there were the many sleepless nights worrying about their children. Kids who would usually bunk school to go shoplifting, or, more recently had found paradise in the dark pleasures of a shared needle. Little wonder that the mothers appeared like Mrs. Death out on a day trip.

This was their way of life. No-one knew any differently. It was the culture, and it wasn't a particularly pretty one at that. Their halcyon days of love and romance had long since deserted them all, along with their muscle-tone and control, leaving them to try and survive in a goldfish bowl, infested with loan-sharks and hire purchase TV's.

Amanda took a deep breath, tightened the grip on her husband's clammy hand and they walked into the social club. There was a hush as soon as they entered the drab-coloured entrance of the smoky dance hall. Even the bingo caller stopped calling. The entire place stopped in freeze frame, as if some giant person had pressed the pause button on a giant remote control, while he stomped off into the kitchen to get a drink during the commercial break of 'Emmerdale Farm'.

Amanda could feel their eyes fixed on the couple. She wanted to scream out 'Hey! Don't bloody stare at me! It wasn't my fault.... he was the one messing about, not me.'

Selfishly at that moment, she wished that she was amongst the crowd and giving some other poor couple the daggers. She knew it was spiteful and shallow, but it was a label she would have been more than willing to wear. She felt as though she was walking the plank on a pirate ship with bloodthirsty sharks circling below in bright red lipstick and badly applied mascara.

She and Daryl finally reached the bar.

Daryl took control. Amanda was pleased with that. 'A pint of lager and a white wine and soda for the wife please, Ronny,' he instructed the barman.

Still no-one uttered a word. The only sound was the bingo balls going mental as they bounced and banged against the inside of the plastic bingo machine.

Then, without warning, an old woman of about eighty, who had been marking five bingo cards in the other room while listening to the game on the Tannoy system, opened the lounge door and shouted out 'Hey Eugene - are you going to call the next bastard number, or have I got time to go and empty my colostomy bag.... It's leaking out of the edges.'

There was a loud groan, followed by a laughter that surprisingly brought the room back to life. It magically filled up again with noise and activity. Swearing, coughing and belching rose up and collided with each other. This gave Amanda and her husband some well-needed breathing space. It took the pressure off for a short time.

'OK… let's get this show back on the dusty road,' Eugene the bingo caller commanded, 'we are still waiting for a line…. next number, 3 and 2…. 32.'

'House,' shouted a woman sitting by the toilet, in a headscarf and Wellington boots.

'Jammy bastard,' cried Father John, who sat by the fruit machine stroking his lucky black rabbit's foot. 'I only wanted one number…. Bloody 69!'

'We could all do with a 69, Father,' a man's voice rose high above the commotion.

The priest went red and pulled out his rosary beads. The laughter grew more intense by the second.

'Great,' the old woman appeared again and shouted above the bustle, 'Eugene… Don't start the next card until I've emptied my bag.'

After the bingo the atmosphere calmed down, but Amanda still felt uncomfortable. Music started up from the direction of the stage. People eventually began to talk to Amanda, but she could see in their eyes that they wanted to ask her all about the affair. They wanted to know the ins-and-outs of the cat's arse. They unconsciously wanted to know every detail, so they could exaggerate it and add on their own bits. That was the way it was up on the estate. Anything could be stretched and bent out of shape and then tweaked some more.

Amanda looked around to see if see could see Lois. Her so-called best buddy; her pal who had immediately left her house on that day; the day when Desmond had called; and the chum who had blabbed to every living soul in the town within five minutes. She was nowhere to be seen.

'Probably shagging someone,' Amanda thought. 'Hope she dies of syphilis.'

She took a sip of her drink. It was going down in clumps. She couldn't wait until closing time to get back home and away from their stares. She wondered how Daryl was doing. She looked across where the men were congregating. They were laughing; Daryl was trying his best to join in. She felt sorry for him; it was as though he was a new kid in school waiting for the opportunity to join in with the 'Cool' kids. She stared at the floor fiddling with a beer mat. The local DJ changed the mood and slipped on a smoochy record.

'Fancy a dance,' He came up behind her. His voice was friendly.

'Won't everyone stare at us?' Amanda replied to her husband's request.

'They are doing that anyway... so fuck 'em,' Amanda could tell he was well on his way to Drunktown. She could sense the hatred in his words. She didn't want the scene to get any uglier than it was already, and it was already damn ugly... a right double-bloody-bagger.

She took his hand. They were both sweating as they wandered onto the dance floor. Again she felt the eyes, sharp as knives, sticking into her back. The whispering tongues cut into her exposed skin. It broke her heart and played on her mind.

They held each other close. It was closer than he had held her in many a year. They experienced solidarity in the face of the enemy.

'I'm so sorry, love,' he pushed his words into her ear, pulling her tighter. She couldn't breathe. 'Please forgive me... I do love you... I've always loved you... always will.'

'Well you've got a bloody strange way of showing it,' she hissed back through clenched teeth, while keeping the smile planted firmly on her face.

He stared at his feet before adding, 'Love, we can get through this...we can... please forgive me.... please.'

She looked long and hard into his eyes. She saw a glimmer of hope. But before she had time to answer, the record on the turntable had finished its three-minute musical journey.

The DJ instantly introduced the next song. 'Ladies and Gentlemen and other strange people on the dance floor, the next song is dedicated to Daryl Grey.'

Amanda's heart missed a beat. Everyone stared, firstly at the DJ, then at the couple who found themselves alone in the middle of the tiny dance floor. Coloured lights shot across their bodies and blinded their view.

There were several seconds as the needle hissed its way through the grooves of the vinyl. The anticipation was unbearable. The DJ gave an evil smirk from behind his twin deck. Suddenly, the beat to the song *'YMCA'* belted out from the second-hand Marshall PA speakers.

'Bastard... the fuckin' bastard.' Daryl yelled and stormed towards the stage.

'Leave it Daryl...! Leave it!' Amanda knew her words were lost somewhere in-between his anger and his feeling of humiliation which was bouncing about in his unstable mind.

As the chorus belted out, Daryl leapt like a salmon onto the stage. The old woman with the colostomy bag came dancing into the room, singing at the top of her voice. 'YMCA.... Come on down to the YMCA.'

Daryl caught the DJ by the throat and launched him backwards into the collection of electrical equipment and the defenceless bingo machine. Sparks and coloured bingo balls rained down onto the wooden floor tiles.

The scene was greeted with silence from a stunned audience.

'You queer lovin' freak,' the DJ yelled, hiding behind the safety of the amplifier.

Daryl went for him again, fists clenched.

'No Daryl...! No....! He's not worth it,' Amanda bellowed, tears rolling down her cheeks. 'None of them are worth it.... Leave it.... Let's go home'

Daryl stopped and glanced around the room at all the faces. No one looked him in the eye. He jumped off the stage.

'Fuck you all.... You bunch of hypocrites.' He ran past Amanda and out through the fire door. It slammed open with a crash and closed shut with an equally big bang.

In the centre of the room, Amanda stood silent. Her knees were shaking, her mouth was dry. She stood tall for what seemed like an age, unable to move. She finally collapsed under the weight of the stress of the bizarre situation. She sobbed, her head spun round causing everything to become a blur. She lay on the shiny wooden floor. No one else moved, except the old woman with the colostomy bag, who was still jigging about in the corner.

Someone held out their hand to help her off the floor.

'Amanda... I'm so sorry... I really am.' Amanda recognised Lois's voice instantly. She was so glad, even though she had been the catalyst that had caused this; she was pleased she was there for her. The two, long-lost friends walked out into the bitterly cold night, arm in arm. At that moment they were closer than they had ever been.

Later that same night, Daryl sat with his legs dangling over the edge of Stonewall Bridge. He stared down into the blackness. His mind raced around, confused. Thoughts bashed into the side of his brain causing him to wince in mental pain and anguish.

He lobbed the empty whisky bottle into the dark abyss below. It took several long seconds before the smash of glass echoed back up towards the spot where he was perched.

It had been four hours since he'd stormed out of the social club. He needed to get away from the madness. He required time to think, time to make a plan.

He'd been crying. His knuckles on both sides bled after pummelling a wooden door in the high street with his bare fists. He needed something inanimate to take his anger out on. The door had been in the wrong place at the wrong time.

The alcohol made his head muzzy, but it was still clear enough to realise that his once quiet, comfortable, working-class existence had now changed forever and would never be the same again.

He knew exactly what the town and its small-minded inhabitants could do with a rumour about a closely guarded secret. They would cling on to it like leeches feeding on a blood clot, parasites sucking every last drop of life out of the situation, lapping up every gruesome detail until it was their turn to twist the knife in deeper.

It was a town that loved to see the weak suffer. It prided itself on causing pain and hurt. It won medals in competitions for grinding poor people into dirt and kicking them in the goolies when they were down. It would then proceed to stamp on the individual's head until he or she was unrecognisable.

Over the years the town excelled at it. It had got it down to a fine art. The perpetrators could informally convict and sentence someone to a lifetime of shame and embarrassments over just a simple, throw away comment.

He recalled how they had stripped the former Catholic priest, Father Clancy (the very loyal and moral servant of the community), down to the bone after someone, somewhere, mentioned that his nose was a bit red and maybe he was drinking too much of the communal wine.

It was a harmless throwaway comment which went badly wrong.

Within 48 hours, Father Clancy's life was devastated, ground into the dust.

'Father Wino,' kids were encouraged to shout at the priest, as he walked by.

'I saw him drinking a cocktail of mentholated spirits,' someone lied to the local newspaper, in an exclusive interview about the priest's wayward life.

'After a heavy session on the weekends... his nose glows in the dark... like one of them flashing beacons,' someone else chipped in, making the actions of a Belisha-Beacon with his hand.

Within a week, letters were sent to the Archbishop. Father Clancy was dismissed for gross misconduct and several years later he killed himself by jumping under a tube train in London. What no one cared about was that Father Clancy had been strictly teetotal, and had suffered from terrible sinus trouble that made his nose go red. For the record, he didn't even drink wine during the services; he would use Vimto as a substitute instead.

So Daryl knew full well the power of the town and its ability to drown a person in a sea of accusations.

Not for the first time that night, his mind thought about Amanda. Daryl wished his wife was sitting with him, so he could talk to her and explain why he'd got involved with Desmond; why he had found refuge in the arms of another.

'She'd understand,' he told himself, 'If only she knew why.' But, to be truthful, he himself didn't know why, so it would have been hard to start from the beginning.

Meeting Desmond had been a pure accident. He'd had no intention of ever doing something with someone of the same sex. He never dreamt of it in a million years.

But one night it just happened. He recalled walking home alone, slightly drunk. He'd been having a stressful time at work. He heard sobbing coming from the alleyway by Thomas Street. He stopped for a minute. He actually walked on, but something dragged him back to see if he could be of any assistance. Looking back it was a stupid thing to do, but hindsight is a great thing to have in one's pocket after the event.

He slowly walked into the alleyway. There slumped up against a wall was the figure of Desmond. He was crying uncontrollably. Apparently, early that morning, he'd had a letter to say that his sex-change application had been rejected.

Daryl felt uncomfortable trying to comfort the man. He eventually placed his arm around his shoulders. Desmond was shivering. Then out of the blue, Desmond grabbed Daryl's head and kissed him full force on the lips. He was stunned, too shocked to react. Daryl just stood still. The light from the lamp reflected off his face.

Then Desmond kissed the younger man again. This time Daryl didn't pull away, and, for some unknown reason, he moved in closer, attaching his hands to Desmond's hips. They kissed long and hard. Daryl was lost in the moment, he could sense the older man getting physically aroused in his trousers (it was in the days before he had switched to dresses).

Surprisingly Daryl also found himself getting hard. He was bursting in his pants. He couldn't help himself even though he knew it was wrong. Desmond fumbled with the belt on Daryl's trouser. He located his manhood and released it into the night air. Daryl came almost immediately, dropping to his knees.

It was then the guilt kicked in. He quickly gathered his thoughts, buckled up his jeans and rushed out of the lane leaving Desmond alone again.

Daryl stopped by someone's gate and was sick. It took him five minutes to empty all the contents of his stomach.

He swore on the Holy Bible he'd never do it again. He went home immediately and showered, trying to wash the memory out of his mind and off of his skin. The next morning, he convinced himself it was all a dream, but he refused to look at himself in the mirror, afraid in case he came face-to-face with the truth.

A week later, Daryl went searching for Desmond, basically to tell him he was sorry and it had all been a drunken mistake. He knew where Desmond would be. He often sat in the lounge of the social club reading cookery books, or sowing sequins onto dresses.

Daryl waited for the man to head home. He approached him by the same alleyway. He had his speech prepared; he had even considered using violence if Desmond tried to be funny. But like all great plans, it went wrong. Within a few minutes, they were locked in an embrace in the darkness yet again. This time it lasted longer, this time Daryl played a more active role. On this occasion, he didn't rush off to spew his heart out, he stayed, and he enjoyed it.

It had started so innocently. Once a week he would pop in to see Desmond, mainly for some uncomplicated sex, which, as time went on, became more and more complicated.

Back on the bridge that night, Daryl stared down into the darkness again. As he sat pondering the right thing to do, he hadn't noticed a dark figure walking across the bridge. Way off in the distance a police car siren pierced the night sky. The other person coughed politely, Daryl swung his head around.

'W... W... Watch yourself there.... o...o...or you might fall over,' the man's voice was shaky. 'It's....it's a long way down!'

'Not long enough for me,' replied Daryl, as he watched the blue flashing lights from the cop car as it raced off towards the estate.

'Joyriders,' the person spoke again.

'What'

'The police car...... probably chasing after joyriders.'

Daryl thought they were more likely off to break up some domestic argument that had broken out. Saturday night was domestic fight night up on the estate; especially after they started selling scrumpy cider in the social club; domestic disturbances and violence had increased by 35% and husband kettle scalding by 83%.

'Yeah.... Probably,' Daryl looked back into the darkness of the night.

'You're upset... N... n.... nothing can be that bad,' the man said, while shuffling a little closer.

'It is...' Daryl's voice was soft in its tone. 'But I know what I'm gong to do.... I know exactly.... I'm going to... fig.... 'He didn't finish the sentence. He plunged into the darkness, arms swaying, legs kicking. He tried to reach for safety. His world went silent as the darkness sailed past.

At that moment he realised he was going to die. He closed his eyes, waiting to see if his life would shoot passed him in slow motion like it did in the movies. It didn't. Instead he envisaged Boy George singing 'Do you really wanna hurt me?' on the Christmas Top of the Pops special.

Daryl didn't know if this was God's way of expressing irony, or the devil's way of just taking the piss. He giggled at the thought. As he fell backwards, he looked up at the face of the stranger peering over the rock-clad bridge. Daryl thought he could make out a wide smile on the man's face.

'That's strange,' he thought before the thud caused the lights to go out.

Chapter 9

Needle

A few days after poor Daryl's crumbled body was found at the base of the bridge, innuendos and snide remarks floated on the breeze like paper blowing around on the cold breath of the wind. Without mercy, spiteful accusations were thrown at Amanda from all directions.

'She drove him to it. She was FRIGID you see,' the old ladies brigade, heads covered with scarves, would tell each other in bus-stops, at the bingo or while lined-up on the saw-dust covered floor of the local butcher shop.

'I heard,' Butcher James merrily joined in during one of the many conversations about the incident, while wiping his two large hands full of ox-blood onto his already crimson-stained overalls, 'she knew all along that he was going out with that TV.'

'Going out with a TV,' an elderly customer muttered, looking confused at the other punters. 'What the hell as his television set to do with it, Mr James?'

Another OAP, who was rotating his false teeth around the inside of his mouth, said, 'I was told that she threw the poor man's TV out of her house.... She smashed it to smithereens with a hammer.'

'Someone stole my bloody TV last week,' cursed a partially deaf woman standing at the front of the queue, before adding, 'I still haven't paid the hire purchase on it. Only another 48 weeks at £5.24 a week to go. Anyway, Mr James have you got any faggots? My husband just loves the taste of faggots.'

'Mrs Herbert.... Don't bloody start now... Will you.' The butcher laughed, 'There's already one man dead and another man, or half-man, gone mad and is hiding in the woods like some kind of Robin Hood figure because someone liked the bloody taste of faggots.'

Everyone laughed, except the woman who still wanted to know about the television set. She was still mystified, 'Did it have surround sound? I bet it was the same gang that stole my bastard TV..... Hope they rot in hell.'

Unknown to the people sharing the joke in the shop, Lois had been standing in the queue, way back by the door. She had heard enough of all this mickey-taking and back-stabbing concerning her friend. She put her best, white, stiletto foot forward and stormed into the centre of the room, eyeballing each and every one of them in turn.

'Oy...! You lot....! And what about the poor widow left sitting all alone in that house over there,' her voice rose up, sharp and direct. She pointed across towards Amanda's house, which was several gardens over.

Everyone stopped talking to look at her.

She paused before continuing, 'You should all be ashamed of yourselves. There's only one victim in this mess.... And that's Amanda .... Not bloody Daryl... and definitely not Lily bloody Savage'

'Who's this Lily Savage woman?' the partially deaf woman asked again. 'Did she get her television pinched as well... the place is going to the dogs... I blame the black people... always pinching stuff that doesn't belong to them.... They can't afford to buy stuff.... Foreign you see.... Like that guy in the programme 'Roots,' about those black slaves who pinched stuff.... What was his name?... oh yeah... Kevin Keegan.'

The rest of the people in the shop, including Lois, shuffled about embarrassed as they all turned en-mass towards Jack the Black, the town's first ever black bus driver who had just entered the shop.

'It was Kunta Kinteh.... and actually I've got three TV's if you must know, madam,' Jack the Black replied, obviously offended.

But as quick as a flash, the partially deaf old woman added 'Yeah! We know you have... mine, that bloke who's just topped himself and that Lily Savage woman that they have just mentioned..... It's in your blood.'

'Will you all shut up?' Lois yelled. 'This is serious shit!'

The butcher's shop went quiet for the first time since it opened in 1965. Old women, with a long history of gossiping and peeling the skin off innocent people with their tongues, were left staring anxiously at the floor. The old guy, who earlier had mentioned the TV set, watched in horror as his teeth popped out of his mouth and landed in the sawdust on the floor. Lois could see that, for some bizarre reason, the false teeth had a set of braces on them. Someone accidentally kicked the dentures under the counter.

'I pity you lot' Lois glanced at them, while inching herself to the front of the queue.

They all stared at the floor, embarrassed, afraid to catch her eye.

'I really do... It's pathetic. It makes me ashamed to know you.' She shook her head slowly, before adding 'I thought you would have known better, Mr James especially in your position as the main meat supplier in the town.' Again she left a small space to gather her thoughts. 'By the way.... While I'm here... can I have four lamb's hearts and 1lb of mince-meat?'

No one complained about her queue hopping. The butcher processed her order in double-quick time. He packed them up in newspaper and handed them over the counter to her.

Mr James felt guilty, which was extremely rare for someone who spent most of his working life slaughtering animals and the rest of his spare time gutting fish. Lois's speech had the desired effect; it had touched a nerve.

'We're sorry Lois.... really sorry.' He waved his hand to indicate that there would be no charge for her order of meat.

'Bastard' thought Lois, 'I should have asked for some pork chops and a couple of slices of sirloin steak....fuck it... trust my luck.' She took the plastic bag and turned to leave. She was accompanied by the distinctive sound of the clip-clopping of her high heels as she exited the shop.

Out in the fresh air, she realised that she had more to say. Who the hell were that lot to call her best mate over? She was bubbling with anger. They weren't getting off that lightly and maybe Mr James might just lob a few spare ribs in a bag to shut her up. She strutted back inside, deciding to make her final point. 'Hey.... You lot! What did that bloke with the beard once say?'

The other customers looked at each other in utter confusion. The old guy was down on his hands and knees searching desperately for his teeth.

'What bloke with a beard, Lois?' someone was finally brave enough to ask.

'You know that bloke with the beard who was always springing surprises and shit like that.' She closed her eyes to see if it would assist her to remember. It didn't help.

'Oh... Was it Jeremy Beadle?' the butcher said, confidently.

'Yes... it must be Jeremy fuckin' Beadle,' the rest of her audience grinned, laughing at Lois's observation, but they weren't sure where the hell it was leading to.

'No.... not Jeremy fuckin' Beadle.' Lois was bouncing. She paced the shop like Mike Tyson in the ring before a fight. 'No.... Jesus H Christ.... Hey hang on a minute... that's him... that's the bloke I was trying to think of.... Jesus Christ... now what did he always use to say to those Samaritans or the Osmonds, or whoever marched up that hill with him to eat bread and scampi?'

The people in the shop were now completely lost. Lois could have just parted the waves of the Red Sea for them and still they wouldn't know what to do. They stood there silent, afraid to utter another word.

'Look! Didn't he once say.... "He who's never fucked about should throw the first punch... or dinner plate..." or something like that?' Lois turned smugly away, safe in the knowledge that she had got her point across.

Before she began to strut purposefully away towards the direction of the garages, she turned to the man by the entrance and whispered, but loud enough so everyone could hear, 'And you call yourself a Catholic, Father.' She winked at the priest who was laden down with four tins of Homepride cooking sauces, while waiting to purchase some pork chops for his tea.

The priest immediately looked at the butcher and spluttered 'I don't remember Jesus saying that..... I don't.' He could feel their eyes burning into his skin. He opened his portable bible and hurriedly flicked through the pages.

The gang of old ladies and the black bus driver stared at the priest with disdain.

'What type of Holy man of God is he?' one old pensioner muttered under her breath. 'He doesn't even know the bible.' She then turned to the woman by her side and added 'Mavis, put Father John's name in the book. We'll see what Archbishop Tadpole thinks of this heathen tomorrow, and by the way, also put down that I saw him eating a bacon and sausage sandwich last Friday in the park.'

Meanwhile, Lois walked up to the gate of Amanda's house and let herself in. Inside Amanda's front room, the darkness created by the closed curtains hugged the walls tight and ensured that any spilled emotions were firmly locked in.

Lois sat down, next to her friend. The entire contents of the room appeared to have been designed in the style of pain, with large extracts of hurt splattered here and there. Various shades of black appeared everywhere. Everything which had ever been housed in the room with a hint of colour had been banished to a small cupboard upstairs. The living room looked like it had been designed by the guru of death himself, the grim reaper with maybe a little help from his trusty, arrogant and incredibly annoying side-kick, Handy Andy.

Amanda found it impossible to look anyone in the eye, including her mate. Lois could see that her pal had been crying. That was not unexpected or uncommon considering the circumstances.

'What have you got there?' Amanda nodded towards the white carrier-bags in her hand.

'Just some stuff from the butchers'

'Oh.' Amanda looked sad.

'Do you fancy me knocking something up for you?' asked Lois cheeringly.

Amanda declined, not because she wasn't hungry (in fact, she was starving) but she wasn't ready to face one of Lois's infamous concoctions. Her mate could ruin a Pot Noodle without even trying.

Instead, she asked 'What are they saying about me and this situation?'

'Who?' Lois knew exactly who she was talking about, but she played dumb.

'That lot…. The crowd in the butchers… The rumour mongers and their mates…. the jungle drum-beaters'

'Oh them…. Nothing really… They are more concerned with some Jeremy Beadle fellow and lots of break-ins that have occurred around the area, to bother themselves with talking about you.' She fibbed the best she could, without her features giving the real plot away.

But Lois's smoke screen didn't stop Amanda bursting out in a flood of snot and tears. Lois hugged her tightly. She still blamed the tragic events on her own, big, bloody mouth. If only she had kept the secret to herself, and not told everyone in the town then maybe things would have turned out for the best. But on the other hand it was Daryl and his passion for kinkiness that should take most of the responsibility. He was the one who couldn't keep his trouser snake inside his boxers.

'Look girl… You'll get over it. Come on… Cheer up… just think of all the fun we can have picking up young lads in the weeks ahead.'

'Lois…' Amanda appeared disgusted. 'Daryl is lying in there, still cold.' She motioned towards the small sitting room. Behind the glass doors a coffin took centre stage.

Amanda added, 'And you're talking to me about meeting other men.'

'Well relax... He can't hear you!'

'That's not very funny.' Her stare burned into the side of Lois' face.

'Oh ok.... That was insensitive of me, maybe after two or three months... But look Amanda, life goes on.' She lit a fag. 'So, after we put him into the ground, the world's our ostrich'.

'Oyster,' Amanda giggled pitifully. Lois still had a knack of putting a little ray of sunshine into any dark and gloomy room.

'Look... I'll put the kettle on while you have a look at these holiday brochures that I just happened to have lying around. Cuba looks fantastic and the men....Wow! You could eat grapes from the cheeks of their arses.' The wild woman with the tattoo sauntered into the kitchen whistling *'I should be so lucky.'*

The sudden activation of the doorbell reverberated around the house. Both women jumped. Lois stuck her head around the door. For some reason they both quickly looked to the room where Daryl lay in his pine box.

'Well...He's not going to fucking open it... Is he?' Lois joked, walking into the hallway to see who it was.

Secretly, Lois was pleased to escape from the drabness of the living room and glad to see sunshine and a bit of colour. Dark rooms gave Lois depression and hurt her eyes.

There was a strange shape blocking out the light. Lois readjusted her G-string which had been making in-roads into her not-so-secret passage. She opened the door. She closed it instantly.

The person on the other side knocked on the glass.

'What do you want? Lois asked nervously.

'I'd like to talk to Mrs Grey, please,' came back the reply.

'Go away, Desmond... Haven't you done enough damage,' Lois whispered, trying not to arouse suspicion.

It went quiet. He then started to bang the door. 'Let me in....! Please let me in!'

Amanda appeared in the hallway. She had to refocus her eyes to readjust to the daylight.

'Who is it Lois?' she could sense that something was wrong.

'It's the.... It's the milkman. He wants to know if you would like some yogurt with next week's delivery'

'I don't have a milkman.'

Lois was thinking on her feet. 'On no... It's not the milkman... How silly of me.... It's the coalman.'

'Lois I've got gas.... What are you talking about? What's going on?'

The voice called through the letterbox. 'Let me in.... I need to talk.'

Lois shot a glance at her friend.

'Open it, Lois,' said Amanda as a stern look ran across her face.

'No!' Lois stood in the way, blocking out the light from the door.

'Open it'

'OK...' She pulled back the latch. The door moved inwards, Amanda stared at Desmond. He stood there in a black mac and matching head scarf, tied in a bow under his chin, flowers held in his hand.

'What do you want?' Amanda asked, without showing any emotion.

'I would like to see Daryl.'

'He's dead,' Lois interjected heartlessly.

'I know he's dead... She killed him.' He looked more insane than normal, which was frightening considering his appearance always scared the kids half to death as it was.

'Then you can... Fuck off then.... You weirdo!' Lois screamed at his face, trying to slam the door shut.

His foot stopped it from closing. He put all his weight into prising it open. His finger clutched at the door frame. Lois sank her teeth into them. He yelled out and pushed the door open in one movement.

'What do you want Desmond?' Amanda was too tired for all this. It was the last thing she needed right now.

'I want my Daryl back.... I need him.' the transvestite spoke softly.

'Desmond? Aren't you forgetting he was my husband, not yours?'

Lois piped in. 'Yeah! He was hers, not yours. She was married to him.' She pointed at the wedding ring on Amanda's finger.

Desmond held out his hand. It had a large engagement style ring on his finger. 'Well.... We both had rings off him.... He bought this for me last month.'

'Bought it.... By the looks of it he had it out of a Christmas cracker from the Poundshop,' spat Lois.

Amanda stared in disbelief, she was lost for words. Pressure built up in her temples. She finally spoke, 'Desmond, please tell me what you want.... Please?'

He looked her square in the eyes and muttered, 'I want to sit next to the coffin in the church and I would like to give a speech and read a poem like that bloke did in "Four Weddings and a Funeral".'

Amanda tried hard to rewind different scenes from the British movie in her mind. She had only seen it once and then she had fallen asleep. She wasn't a fan of those middle class kinds of comedies, especially staring Hugh Grant; the upper-class, chinless twat got on her nerves.

'Sorry Desmond…. I don't want you to…. This is hard enough as it is… I don't want to turn it into some freak show.'

'That would be the fuckin' understatement of the year,' interjected Lois, lighting up another cigarette. 'Especially with the elephant man in lipstick over here.'

Those words sparked a chain reaction of anger inside the normally quiet and placid man. He started to shake outwardly.

'Lois… Behave!' Amanda jumped in again. 'Look…Desmond… It's impossible…. Please can you accept that?' She pleaded with the man.

He thought for a few seconds. 'Well…. Perhaps I wouldn't do the poem, but I insist that I must carry the coffin.'

In Amanda's mind this was worse. She pictured the comical scenario of Desmond in black mini-skirt shuffling along, as the coffin procession waltzed into the church.

Lois piped up again. 'Carry the coffin…. Why don't we ask the rest of the characters out of "Wacky Races"…? Then we will have the full set of nutcases.'

Amanda held her head in her hands. 'Lois shut up…. No Desmond…. I don't want you carrying the coffin… In fact, I don't want you there at all… If it weren't for you we wouldn't be in this mess.' Her words were cutting. She turned and walked back towards the kitchen, despondently.

Lois smiled to herself; she was happy that Amanda wasn't blaming her after all. She began to close the door. Suddenly, the man launched himself into the hallway, a knitting needle clenched firmly in his right hand.

Lois was first to react, her foot connected with the advancing man; he tripped and fell into Amanda. His weight knocked her into the kitchen. She crashed onto the table, plates smashing on the tiled floor.

In one movement, Lois picked up the telephone and whacked it over Desmond's head. He fell down onto one knee. Blood zigzagged down his head, disappearing under his collar.

'Get out, before I call the police… Get out…! You fuckin' creep' Lois yelled at him. Amanda was too afraid to say a word; she shivered and shook next to the overturned kitchen table. She could see the hatred in his eyes.

He gathered his senses and slowly said, 'I've come for my Daryl…. And you ain't going to stop me…. He loved me….Daryl loved me…. Don't stand in my way.' Tears welled up in his eyes.

He turned his head quickly as he listened to Lois speaking to the police officer on the end of the line. 'Quick…! We have an intruder… And he's armed.'

Desmond realised he was in trouble. He had been warned at the clinic that they would only consider his application for a sex-change if he was a model citizen. He knew that standing in someone's hallway brandishing a weapon would probably spoil his chances. He growled at the both of them. 'I'll get you…. Mark my words.' He then fled up the street.

The desk sergeant on the phone at the local police station bolted upright in his swivel chair. 'What did you say, Madam…? The suspect is armed… is it a gun?' He couldn't believe it. Trust his luck to be working a double shift when some madman goes crazy bonkers, or some big gangland drug war breaks out on the estate. To be truthful, he was still recovering from shock after the incident with the pile cream at the department store. Three of his best officers had been wounded in the frenzied attack by that woman in the wheel chair. They had all put in sick notes for four months, suffering with work-stress (and all on bloody full pay, including benefits). The doctors in the area were always very accommodating in that respect. Always concerned about their prescribing budgets, but happy to cause local business all sorts of grief by giving out stress-related sick notes like they were Smarties.

'No...It's not a gun,' Lois replied, watching Desmond sprint around the bend. 'It's a knitting needle.... Quick.... Hurry.'

'A knitting needle... Is it sharp?' the officer commented.

'Yes.... It's a size 16..... Hurry he's getting away.'

'Oh shit... That sounds nasty,' the officer hesitated. 'We'll be over straight away.'

Within two minutes, five policemen had barged into the tiny office, already kitted out in bullet-proof vests. 'What are we talking about Sarge? Guns, knives, tubes of deadly pile cream?'

'No boys... This is bad..... It's a bloody ten inch knitting needle.... Size 16.'

One officer visually shook with fear, before slowly adding. 'Shall we take the stun gun with us, just in case?'

'I think so... And a big ball of wool as well.... That's what my gran used to use to make her needle safe.'

'Sarge... We haven't got any balls of wool.' one policeman replied as he searched in a box marked 'Miscellaneous'.

'No problem.... We'll stop at Geraldine's the wool shop on the way.'

They piled into the cop car and raced towards the incident, wondering how much a ball of wool would cost and could they pay for it out of petty cash?

Chapter 10

Mud

The church was full on the Thursday morning of Daryl's funeral. Outside, the rain lashed down as the long, black hearse pulled up to the entrance. The tyres of the large, elegant vehicle crunched over the gravel track of the driveway of the church.

Amanda sat in the front row, squeezing Lois's hand tightly. A black veil covered the widow's face. She could feel every set of eyes in the cold room boring into the back of her head, all except old Mister Murphy who had severe cataracts and was actually looking the wrong way. He stared blankly at the confessional boxes, waiting for some action to start.

Organ music sailed upwards; candle smoke danced above the altar and then disappeared into the cold atmosphere of the church. The pall bearers regimentally paraded towards the altar; they carefully put the coffin down. The six men were soaked through from the rain. They slowly backed away to the spaces in the pews that had been reserved for them, leaving small pools of water in their wake.

Amanda glanced at the wooden box, dripping water onto the cold, hard stone floor. It was hard to think that her husband of fifteen years lay inside, dead, cold and about to get buried. It seemed so surreal, like a dream, or one of those television shows where a hidden camera waited in the wings, filming the reaction on the face of the widow who was the butt of the joke. She imagined Daryl suddenly springing up out of the coffin, to the great amusement of the entire crowd who had been part of the great 'Funeral of a Husband' farce.

Nothing stirred from the box and Amanda knew it was for real; not even the Japanese would be that sick and invent a game show like that (well, not yet, anyway).

It was only now starting to sink in that Daryl wouldn't be part of her life, ever again. Of course, there would be memories and photographs to thumb through and she assumed that every time a man in drag came on television, she would think of him and Desmond. But, after today, she knew that that would be it, the final countdown, kaput, the last of the Mohicans.

She looked beyond the coffin at some of his so-called friends. They wouldn't make eye-contact with her. Sadly, since his death, no-one offered any encouragement or help, except Lois. The recent attack by Desmond hadn't helped her cause. Rumours had spread around about how Desmond had popped round to Amanda's house with an Aran jumper he had knitted for Daryl to get buried in, only for the two women friends to viciously beat him black and blue and kick him out into the street.

It was only then that she realised just how old his mates were beginning to look. They were the worse for wear. She wondered if she appeared as old to other people, as they did to her. She bloody hoped not. Their faces were full of deep lines; they all owned a matching set of unflattering bags under their eyes and a mass of grey, which had quickly replaced the black hair on their heads. They looked like her father. It was unnerving; she hoped she didn't look anything like their mothers. She shivered at the thought.

The priest stood on the pulpit fiddling with the pages in a red book. She turned to her left and caught the stare of her mother-in-law. The eyes of the old hag spelt out exactly what she thought of Amanda. The invisible hatred from the woman scratched at Amanda's insides, causing her to bleed from way down in her heart.

Suddenly a new arrival distracted her. A man stood at the back, shaking the raindrops out from an umbrella. He was dark and very handsome, Amanda thought she recognised him, but she couldn't think from where. He shook someone's hand and sat opposite her. He acknowledged her with a nod of his head; he then glanced at the altar and made a sign of the cross.

Just then the service started. The priest looked solemn as he spoke, but his words were filled with lots of richness, strength and meaning. Amanda closed her eyes, and tried to shut the world out. She drifted into her own inner space. She felt as though she was the one drifting out of her body like a soul about to go on its last trip. She imagined floating high above the ground in some kind of helicopter, staring down on the entire congregation.

A young workmate of Daryl's was given the responsibility of saying some words about him. The man was very sincere and told one or two amusing stories about Daryl's exploits in the foundry. It was both sad and happy at the same time.

But that was all to change with the sudden arrival of a loud banging noise and a high pitched cry from the entrance. Everyone's attention switched towards the back of the grand old church.

'Daryl.... Daryl,' a single voice shrieked out. 'It's me... your cuddly Desmond Bear.'

All heads turned to the back of the small building. Their jaws dropped in pure amazement at the sight of a distraught Desmond, dressed all in black with mascara running down his face. He was clutching a photograph of Daryl to his chest. He began to shuffle slowly towards the altar and more worryingly, the coffin.

Amanda had made it quite clear to Desmond that he wasn't welcome, or allowed at the service. Several undercover police officers (wearing knitting-needle proof vests) got up from the pews and attempted to usher him outside. He refused to go without a fight. He may have looked a nancy-boy, but he was as strong as an ox. In the end, six of them had to physically pick him up and march him to the door and throw him out. They were going to lock him in the van, but it was raining and they didn't fancy getting soaked.

The priest instructed someone to close the giant wooden doors behind them and bolt them shut. There was still a shocked silence, the priest glanced to the heavens and shook his head. He coughed to clear his throat and was about to start again, when the banging resumed.

Again it was Desmond. He hammered on the door with all his might for several minutes. The priest decided to continue regardless, trying to ignore the noise. Then it suddenly stopped. The masses inside sighed with relief. What they couldn't see from the comfort of the uncomfortable church, was Desmond preparing to run at the great wooden doors like a goat about to head butt a rival goat, because the she-goat he loved was two-timing him with a creature from the next field. There was an almighty crash, then it went silent again. Desmond recoiled and fell onto the gravel path. He saw stars and his head was bleeding. Father John tried to make a joke out of the situation. It fell on deaf ears. Slightly red in the face, he continued once more with the service, but at a brisker pace.

The funeral was back on track.

'Where was I?' the priest asked himself. 'Oh yes... Daryl was a hard working man, always willing to lend a helpful hand,' he droned on.

Amanda was thinking that nothing else could possibly go wrong when, out of the blue, there was the sound of a mobile phone going off to the tune of 'It's a kind of Magic'. It caused everyone to jump. Everyone quickly checked their own pockets or handbags first, before glancing suspiciously at the person next to them.

'Who the hell is that?' Lois whispered to Amanda, after checking her own purse.

The ringing caused Amanda to start crying. It continued for what seemed like an age. She thought she was on the verge of turning into a mental train-wreck.

Finally, Father John took the bull by the horns and piped up, demanding that the perpetrator of the mobile device knock it off immediately. But still it rang and rang.

Then an observant altar boy tugged on the priest's robe. 'Father... Father... I think it's coming from inside the coffin,' the fresh faced boy indicated, while pointing to the pine box.

'Don't be so stupid,' Father John hissed.

Several people crowded around it to investigate.

'It is,' someone shouted, 'it's coming from in there.' They all backed away as if the coffin was about to explode, several people crouched down amongst the seats with their hands over their heads.

Every single person in the church stared at Amanda again, and this time it included old Mister Murphy. They all waited for some sign from her.

'Don't look at me,' she cried 'I didn't know that he owned a bloody mobile phone.'

The priest made a sign of the cross, and asked the funeral director to open the box and retrieve the mobile at once.

It took several more painfully embarrassing moments to lever the lid back of the pine cask. In the meantime, Desmond had climbed up a drainpipe and was balancing on a ledge, mobile phone to his ear and peering through the dirty stained glass windows above the altar.

The man searched Daryl's jacket and found the offending device.

'What should I do?' he turned to ask the priest, while holding up the still ringing phone.

'What do you mean, "what should you do?"' the priest stuttered.

'Well, should I answer it or just switch it off? It could be important.'

Again the crowd turned to face Amanda.

'I think you'd better answer it... just in case,' Lois whispered to her mate.

'Just in case of what?' Amanda bit back hard. Now she was sure that she was being filmed on some TV show, but didn't know why.

Lois replied sheepishly, 'It was only a suggestion. It may be good news.'

'Good news? For whom....? Daryl's bloody dead!' Amanda yelled. 'What kind of good news? He's just won the lottery or something...? OK! Give it here.'

The man holding the phone passed it over to Amanda. She reluctantly pressed the receiver button and held it up to her ear. There was silence. The entire congregation edged closer to the phone, dying to hear what was going on. Several leant over so far that they tumbled over the wooden railings and crashed into the people in front of them.

Then a voice cried down the receiver. 'Daryl it's me.... Desmond.... Your little bear. I Love You... I love you.' Desmond, positioned high in the sky, banged on the window and waved to the crowds. 'Look! I'm up here.'

All and sundry looked up. Amanda yelled before chucking the phone at him. It smashed into the wall, breaking into a thousand pieces. Desmond tried to duck out of the way of the advancing device but in doing so he accidentally fell off the ledge and landed face down in a skip.

The church went noiseless again. The priest grabbed his bible and the silver ball containing the smelly stuff and told everyone he'd see them at the graveside in ten minutes. He stormed from the altar to get a drink.

The long black car floated across the gravel path and parked up next to the freshly-dug grave. The rain belted down so hard, it was almost horizontal. As usual, the graveyard was grey in colour, with just the odd splattering of red and yellow coloured carnations, still in their Asda wrappers, that decorated the many graves.

Everyone in the town knew full well that it always rained on funeral days. It was the law in these parts, like some unwritten golden rule. Even on the rare occasions when it didn't rain and the sun actually shone, the funeral would be postponed until it started to piss down again, or someone was made to fire a water hose over the gatherers while the priest said the last rights. The logic was spot on. Rain was for funerals and sunny days were for weddings. The only problem was it rained for 345 days of the calendar year and the days when it didn't, it snowed, so the balance was completely uneven.

'It's unlucky to put someone into the ground if it's not raining,' Amanda's grandmother always told her.

'Unlucky for whom?' Amanda wanted to ask but never did.

The priest stood at the top of the shallow pit, Amanda by his side. Lois held her hand. They were followed by six pall bearers, his supposed best mates; all dressed in cheap, black, Matalan, washable suits, with matching black, washable, polyester ties. Friends, family, undercover cops, and a few sad, twisted, thrill-seekers made up the rest of the fifty, or so, people who had braved the elements to lay Daryl to rest.

The priest coughed to indicate the start of the proceedings. In the background the piercing sound of an ice-cream van sailed and bobbed around on the wind.

'Who the fuck would want to buy a Mister Whippy on a day like this?' Lois whispered to Amanda. 'Sorry Father.'

The priest gave her a cold stare before adding under his breath 'It's not selling ice-cream... probably drugs.'

'Are you sure Father?' Lois asked.

'Positive.... Little Johnny Bond told me in confession last week. You can buy anything off them.... Speed, Crack, Charlie, uppers, downers and unbelievably they also sell 'Haunted House' ice creams.... I haven't seen one of them since the seventies.... Apparently they import them from Russia along with the drugs.'

The two women were both impressed and a little unnerved by the priest's knowledge of hard drugs and discontinued ice creams.

Amanda took the opportunity to scan the crowd to see if she could see the handsome dark-haired man who had caught her attention in the church earlier. She failed to spot him. It was probably for the best, she wondered if she should really be looking for a dark haired stranger in the middle of the ceremony to bury her husband.

Instead, she yet again caught the full-stare of her mother-in-law. Amanda smiled at her weakly. The old witch didn't respond, except to make a growling noise from deep down in her throat. Amanda could sense the hatred escaping from every pore of the old woman. For whatever reason, she had personally blamed Amanda for her son's death. She hadn't spoken to her since.

The priest waited for the jingle from the ice-cream (come drug-selling) van to subside before continuing.

'Family, friends, and poor Amanda..... I'll try to keep this brief, due to the weather conditions.... And other stuff... We are gathered here today...'

Unexpectedly, a strong gush of wind blew the wig off one of the pall bearers; it landed inside the hole in the ground. The priest stopped again. Firstly, all eyes stared at the artificial hair-piece floating in the pool of raindrops and mud. They all glanced at the man with the newly exposed bald head. The priest waited, very annoyed.

'Amanda, I'm so sorry,' the man said, as apologetically as he could. 'I need to get it... sorry... I'm so sorry..... I haven't finished paying for it yet.... my wife will kill me.... She hates baldy men.'

'I'll bloody kill you if you don't shut up and get the poxy thing... and quickly,' the priest hissed under his breath.

The rest of the pall bearers formed a daisy chain and lowered the wigless man into the pit. He stretched and stretched but was still inches away from grabbing the hair-piece. Amanda didn't know if she should laugh or cry, be happy or extremely sad. What she did know was that no one would ever forget this day in a very long time, perhaps they would make it into one of those classic comedy sketches. This was the saddest day of her life and it seemed to be overrun by the cast of the Keystone Cops. At that moment, to add insult to injury, one of the bearers lost his footing and the human chain broke. The wigless man crashed into the sludge at the bottom of the open grave.

'Quick, fill the bloody thing in,' the priest yelled. He was deadly serious.

Amanda and Lois giggled as if they were at the back of the classroom, and not in a place of sorrow and mourning.

The man finally scrambled onto safe ground, the wig held firmly in his dirty, mud-caked hand. The priest stared at him again. He was even more annoyed. Although he was a man of peace, at a time like this he wished he had a gun and a licence to use it, in the name of God. He wondered if the Ice-cream/drug-van sold guns as well and made a mental note to stop him and buy one.

'Well?' Father John asked him.

'Well what?' the man was confused. He stood there shivering with cold, soaking wet, covered in mud and embarrassment.

'Well, I think you'd better put that bloody wig on your bloody head, after you've ruined my bloody service.'

The man did what he was told. He placed the wig back on his head, small muck balls crept down his face.

'Please can I get this over with?' the priest sighed, placing one of his hands on his hip.

'Hey… doesn't Father John look a bit gay standing like that?' someone, near the back, mentioned to the person next to them.

"Schhhh….. Show a bit of respect for the dead… but that is a good point. We'll start that rumour tomorrow,' another person answered back, while jotting down the observation about the priest into his little green rumour-book.

At the same time, over by the crypt at the far end of the cemetery, behind the headstone embossed with gargoyles, which some brave teenagers from the estate would use for carrying out séances and sex parties during full moons, a person hid, his face streaked by dark mascara.

Back by the freshly-dug graveside, droplets of rainwater trickled into every dry space. The priest had now been given the all-clear to continue. He signalled for the pall bearers to start the operation of lowering the wooden cask into the very muddy ground.

Desmond peered over the top of one of the gargoyles. He looked like Alice Cooper on his 'Welcome to my Nightmare' tour, from the early seventies. He was sobbing, he was heart broken. He stood up, erect. His breath was short and sharp. He started to run towards the ceremony. After a couple of strides he stopped and took off his specially-made, size eight women's shoes. He placed them, and his matching handbag, on an unkempt grave stone. He continued on his mission, gathering speed with every stride.

The priest picked up a handful of earth and sprinkled it over the descending coffin.

'Ashes to Ashes…,' he muttered, raindrops running into his open mouth.

Amanda moved closer to the edge. In the background, like a bat out of hell, the transvestite in bare feet sprinted towards the crowd. The coffin inched towards its final resting place. The pall bearers were once again finding it awkward to keep their footing. They balanced precariously, their cheap plastic-soled shoes finding little purchase in the slippery mud.

All eyes were transfixed on the pine box. Desmond, panting and puffing, was only a few feet away from Amanda and directly behind the priest.

The madman sprung through the air. Everything appeared in slow motion. Desmond had Amanda in his sights. Just before contact, the handsome, dark-haired stranger pushed Amanda out of the path of the Kamikaze transvestite. She landed by the side of the grave, the body of the stranger enveloped around her.

Desmond sailed straight passed. He accidentally knocked the priest into the hole. Both Desmond and the holy-man landed on top of the coffin. The force and weight of the two men pulled the six pall bearers holding the ropes into the grave as well.

It took everyone several minutes to appreciate what had happened, and then no-one could actually believe what they were witnessing.

Pandemonium broke out, as legs, arms, wigs, mud and everything else wrestled around at the bottom of the pit. There were screams. There were yells; punches were thrown by the priest. They all scrambled around looking for a foothold in the mire in order to get out.

People screamed, cried and ran for cover; even the rain stopped for a while, giving the sun a chance to have a look at the comical scene being played out in the cemetery below.

All the men imprisoned in the hole were clambering about wildly to get up the side. The mud stopped all progress. Finally the altar boy dropped a wooden plank for them to use to get themselves out.

Desmond, on the other hand, wouldn't budge, he hugged the coffin refusing to let go. They couldn't get him to release his grip. The priest was thoroughly soaked and completely pissed off. He snatched a shovel off one of the council workers employed to fill in the hole after the ceremony, and he started to splatter the coffin and Desmond in earth.

'Ashes to Ashes…. Dust to fuckin' dust,' the priest cried and worked at marathon speed to fill it in. Eventually, someone persuaded the Catholic priest to cease burying the cross-dresser.

Someone tied a rope around Desmond's ankle and attached the other end to the hearse. After a count of three, the funeral director shifted the car into gear and slowly moved off. The transvestite was hauled up out of the grave, feet first, his dress around his waist and the coffin lid still gripped firmly in his hands. He jumped up and said, 'I'll get my revenge.' He pointed towards Amanda, who was still in the arms of the dark-haired stranger.

He then ran off between the graves, only stopping to retrieve his stilettos and handbag. He reached the perimeter wall and used the coffin lid to pole-vault over it. He disappeared into the forest. Some of the pall bearers and Daryl's mother (on imaginary broom-stick) had given chase; a pack of hounds in plastic-soled shoes after the hare in a skirt.

The handsome, dark-haired stranger held out his hand and helped Amanda up from out of the mud. The scene at the graveside was comical, with just a hint of sadness and a small pinch of regret. People were crying, some women had fainted and lay face down in the dirt.

Amanda wiped the dirt out of her eyes. 'Thank you,' she said turning to the man by her side, her face caked in mud.

'My pleasure… Are you OK?' His voice had a strong accent, which she struggled to place. He continued, 'I haven't been home for several years now, and I had forgotten how bizarre life was around here.' He looked at the posse of individuals scampering through the woods after Desmond.

'What do you mean... you haven't been back home?' Amanda enquired, studying his rugged features.

Before the man had a chance to reply, Lois appeared on Amanda's shoulder and piped up 'What a right fuckin' fruitcake? Oh sorry again, Father,' she apologised to the Catholic priest who was sitting on the edge of a gravestone, smoking a cigar.

'It's OK my girl.... He is a fuckin' head-case.... If I had my rifle, I would have shot the bastard.' He turned to the people dotted about the grave and asked if anyone was going to the pub.

Father John then picked up his tunic and bounded towards the local ale-house, where he apparently stayed by the bar, underneath the dart board, drinking whiskey and Red Bull for a week and two days.

Back by the grave, someone walked up to where Amanda and the stranger were standing. The man directed his question towards the stranger, 'Hey Jacob... you must miss this place.... fancy coming for a drink?'

Amanda was taken aback. 'Jacob,' she whispered softly and asked 'Are you Jacob? Jacob from the second year... the quiet and mysterious one?' she found herself blabbering hysterically.

He nodded coyly.

'Lois... Lois... its Jacob... you remember... Jacob... Oh,' she turned back to face him and said, 'And by the way... I knew that group were called the Clash and not the Crash.... I was only pulling your leg.'

He smiled. Inside he felt quite honoured that she had remembered the last words they had spoke together so many years ago.

Lois as usual was less complimentary. 'I thought you were in prison for killing your entire family with a garden pitch fork while high on drugs?' Lois always knew how to spoil a moment with a poorly thought-out sentence. She was the queen of dousing cold water onto a memorable situation.

'Neither,' he said confused, 'Well I must go... I'm running late as it is... and I've got someone to see before I go back.'

'Are you going for a drink?' Amanda asked in hope, turning her back on the grave.

'Sorry... I've got to get back to London. I have a flight back to South Africa in a few hours,' his reply disappointed Amanda. She felt as if a rug had been swept from under her feet yet again.

She couldn't believe that over the last twenty years she had only managed to speak less than three sentences to the man she had found extremely attractive (and still did).

He shook her hand, said his goodbyes and left. As he walked to a waiting car and got in, the rain started to fall from the heavens again.

Amanda believed that after the last few months of crying she'd be all out of tears, but as Jacob's car disappeared out of sight, wet droplets rolled down her cheeks again.

In the distance a gun could be heard ringing out from somewhere in the forest.

Boy, Girl, Fruitcake, Flower

Part 2

Heads or Tails

Chapter 1

Stone

He sat on the cold toilet seat, with his head resting in his hands, contemplating where it had all gone wrong? He couldn't for the life of him believe it could ever have turned out this way. He had never envisaged it ending up so messy and so damned complicated.

The funeral had been an utter nightmare. The final nails in the coffin, so to speak. Since that terrible day he had decided to keep a very low profile. He didn't want to pour more suspicion onto the already saturated situation. Rumours were already being thrown about like plates at a Greek wedding.

He knew it was time to act, and act fast. It had been over six months since the 'incidents'. He hadn't seen or heard of Amanda since the day she had finally laid Daryl to rest.

The widow hadn't been seen much since then. She had been given compassionate leave from her job until she got her life back on track (if her life could ever be put back on track after such a fiasco). His opportunities to contact her had now been greatly reduced. He needed to take stock and consider his options. He wasn't going to give in. he was now on a mission since Daryl's death.

He finished his mucky business, washed his hands thoroughly, and quietly tiptoed into the warm front room. He smiled at the sight of his mother lying there so peacefully, so child-like, and lifeless. He noticed she hadn't touched any of the food on her tray. Maybe she wasn't hungry. He scooped her up in his arms and carried her back to her room. He kissed her gently on the cheek.

He closed the door and walked back downstairs. He sat in the kitchen and scribbled feverishly on a piece of paper. He made a list of what he needed to do to make the situation right again. This time nothing would go wrong. No stone would be left unturned.

He considered that maybe it was time to go straight to plan D. Plan A had begun well, but had ended in disaster that had been the catalyst for all the unrest. And, to be honest, he didn't have any confidence in Plan B. The less said about plan C the better.

So, with this in mind, he went down into the basement to the secret room and rummaged through the stacks of boxes by the fireplace. He eventually found the things he had been searching for. He smiled as he swirled the chain around his wrist and clutched tightly onto the small chemical bottle. There was no time to lose. Firstly, there were a couple of individuals that he needed to be got out of the way; he needed to erase them from the picture; this time around nothing or no-one was going to get in his way.

Chapter 2

Daggers

The summer months' had come and gone without Amanda realising, or really caring that temperatures had reached an all-time high throughout the country. So outside, where tarmac on pavements bubbled and melted and ice creams sales rocketed, in the confines of her mind she felt as though she was left hanging by her feet in a large storage freezer, like some poor stool-pigeon in a gangster movie; helpless and all alone.

Understandably, the beautiful sunshine had left little impression on her. Locked behind the darkness of thick curtains there was no need for a sun tan, no thought of beach towels and the only reason she wore dark glasses was to hide the tears which constantly flowed from her eyes.

She established her mood was more aligned to the arrival of the autumn season. The sight of leaves dying and dropping from branches reminded her of the direction her life was heading: downwards and lifeless.

Over the last few months she still found herself carrying the millstone of guilt which hung heavily around her neck. She didn't really know why. She found herself rooted to the settee in her own form of purgatory, praying for the return of long lost souls whilst the world outside her window just carried on regardless, content to mill about placing temporary sticking plasters on the gaping holes of their battered and bruised lives. It left her isolated. She tried desperately to figure out how to patch up her shattered life. She didn't know where to start or if she really wanted to.

Since the funeral she rarely ventured out. Instead, she decided to lose herself in the comfort of the darkened room and the all-too-convenient bottom of a gin bottle. The room where she sat was gloomy; it mirrored her heart and her mood. She was soulless; she could happily stay in this state forever. Broken dinner plates and shattered glass from photo frames lay in a thousand pieces on the floor of the kitchen. Some days she felt angry, other days quite sad, but most of the time she felt nothing at all. She sat there motionless. As the Mickey Mouse second hand revolved slowly around on her internal body clock, she realised she had been dealt a poor fake of a life. She sulked and tried to figure out where it had all gone wrong.

And just to make matters worse, she was going to be forty years old in a month's time. As if that wasn't bad enough, now she was going to face that unwanted milestone in her life with no children, the distant memories of a dead husband who had just happened to kill himself after falling in love with a transvestite crane driver, and the regular daily sighting of that same transvestite crane driver standing motionless outside her window. By the look on Desmond's face he was still very mad with her and blamed her (wrongly) for everything that had happened.

The jilted lover hadn't physically come into contact with her during this time; instead he would lurk way back in the bushes outside her house. Every time she opened her bedroom curtains he would be staring up at her, never blinking, standing perfectly still.

It was reminiscent of the scene from the film, 'Halloween,' where the maniac killer, Michael, would stand in Jamie Lee Curtis' garden. The only difference was that in the movie the psychotic murderer had been wearing a pair of black overalls with an ice-hockey mask covering his face. Desmond, on the other hand, was a bit more flamboyant (and comical) in his disguise. The mad transvestite was trying to blend, unsuccessfully, into the foliage, dressed in a blond wig, a cerise PVC cat suit (two sizes too small) and his mother's floral headscarf. It was both frightening and highly amusing at the same time. It was similar to being stalked by a cross-fusion of Purdy from 'The Avengers' and Dot Cotton out of 'East Enders.'

The strange man never moved or attempted to communicate. He just stood there glaring intensely and menacingly at the widow. Amanda would shut the curtains tight, afraid to peer outside. So, as the days grew longer and the night crept in, she had decided to leave them permanently closed, even in the daytime. The mental torture it caused was simply eating her up from the inside out.

She sat alone wondering what was happening in the real world. She pictured everyone having a whale–of-a-time, partying until they dropped, while she was locked away. She frequently believed that maybe all wars had stopped and everyone was living together in harmony. Americans and Iraqis, Catholics arm-in-arm with Protestants, and, to top it all, even Liam and Noel

Gallagher, the turbulent brothers from Oasis, getting on like little thatched houses-on-fire. So, as the sun shone on everyone else's lives, in her world she was left to get soaked to the skin by the emotional raindrops in her front room.

She even began to think that perhaps she was the cause of all the evil. Maybe it was God's way of punishing her for committing hideous crimes in a past life. Maybe she had been an arsonist responsible for igniting a forest fire; or a bank robber whose stray bullet missed the chasing coppers and killed a child. Or perhaps it was divine retribution for that illicit first blow job behind Lipton's. She continued to beat herself up badly before beating herself up some more.

'I bet fucking Suzanne 'the longest legs in the school' Jackson, (her rival from high school), isn't living such a shambolic lifestyle,' Amanda taunted herself, as she buried her head in a pillow.

Suzanne was the prettiest girl in her form, and she bloody-well knew it. She was the girl that all the boys, and most of the teachers, wanted to make-out with. She was the girl that all the other girls despised. In Domestic Science lessons they made voodoo dolls in her image and stuck pins in them. It didn't appear to have any effect as she continued to look stunning and get the best and fittest looking boyfriends.

'I bet she's probably got the perfect life,' she hissed to herself. 'She's married the perfect husband, who's got some great job, and a bloody big car, and I bet she has seventy-six children, who all look like Donny and Marie Osmond. And I bet she still has a figure to die for.' Amanda stated crying again.

She peeked out of the curtains to see if the late autumn sunshine would brighten up her day. Sadly, the dark cloud known as Desmond was still standing in the long, uncut grass. For some reason he had changed the colour of his wig to bright ginger, had a Day-Glo pink patch on his left eye and was squeezed into a tutu.

'Desmond's in a tutu,' the irony made her for a split second smile. She soon became serious once again.

'Why me, God? I wasn't that bad in my life.... was I?' She eyeballed the heavens, waiting for a sign. 'OK... so I could have gone to church more often.' She rephrased it. 'Alright.... alright... maybe I could have gone to church once in a while.' Her words forced her to look down into the fires of hell.

She found tears rolling down her face for the zillionth time since she had got up this morning. It was only then did she realise how she had distanced herself from any part of religion since she'd grown into an adult. She guessed that, since she married, she had only visited church for the odd wedding or the time of her Aunty Lizzie's and, of course, Daryl's funeral.

'But God,' she looked up again towards the overcast grey sky, 'you must realise that there are lots of things to do. Washing, ironing, cooking... and the dishes don't do themselves you know.' She was trying hard to convince him of the reasons behind her actions; the rationale for her heathen ways was hard to come up with. She gave up, knowing he had probably heard the same excuses a million times from millions of people down the years.

A roar of thunder rose up from the heavens. She bolted upright. 'Perhaps... Daryl's suicide was a sign. Maybe it was God's way of showing me the light.' She topped up her glass to the brim, not even leaving room for a drop of fresh air to climb in and splash about.

'Maybe.... I should become a nun... like that Mother Theresa person.' She closed her eyes and pictured herself looking at least two outer-skins older, in a light blue wrap-around habit, or whatever that thing was called they wrapped around her head.

In her mind she stood next to a long queue of sick people, all lined up waiting for the small religious wonder-woman to cure them. There were several different queues for all sorts of ailments. One for old men with inflamed piles; another for various skin issues; a long line for teenagers with spots to the left, a shorter one for people suffering with genital warts on the right and a massive long line for grumpy people (her mother-in-law was at the front of it). She then refocused to the present.

'That's it... I'm going to become a nun.' She stood excitedly. This was her calling, her vocation, the perfect way to cleanse her soul; to wash the pain away.

At that moment, by the back entrance to Amanda's house, the handle of the kitchen door moved slowly downwards. It creaked inch by inch. The catch finally released from the lock and the door swung quietly open.

'Yes, that's what I'm destined to become,' Amanda's voice sailed out from the living room.

The intruder was silent, careful not to make a sound. The footsteps were measured and calculated. On entering the house the person quietly opened the cutlery drawer, rummaging around until they located the right instrument. When they felt the cold metal object in the palm of their hand, they turned in one movement towards the small hallway.

The figure paused momentarily outside the entrance to the living room, listening to the mad ramblings of the woman inside. The person waited for the right opportunity before attempting to rush in, waiting for the moment to cause the maximum surprise. Inside Amanda was oblivious to the danger looming only feet away. She was too concerned with speculating if nuns were allowed to have the odd cigarette now and again.

The door handle journeyed downwards. Amanda suddenly became aware of its movement. She immediately stopped what she was doing. Her heart pounded. She could hear it beating. The lounge door inched opened, Amanda had a scream balancing on the tip of her tongue. She picked up an ashtray, fag nips fell to the floor like soldiers parachuting out of a bomber behind enemy lines. The person stepped inside.

'Lois... for god's sake.... you frightened the life out of me.' Amanda sat down on the chair, shaking visibly.

Her mate sauntered in carrying a jumbo packet of crisps, a large bottle of wine and a bottle opener which she had retrieved from the kitchen drawer.

'Hey... who were you talking to?' Lois said looking about, 'and what are you going to become?'

'Hang on a second... where have you been? I haven't seen you for ages,' Amanda asked before answering. 'And if you must know I'm thinking of becoming a nun.'

Lois plonked the wine on the table. 'Girl, slow down and swallow a reality pill, I've only been away for three weeks and you've found God? Hey, don't worry. I'll sort you out... I'll put you back on the wrong side of the tracks... I've taken the devil for a lover, and I've got his bastard son to prove it.' She wasn't joking!

'Why not...what's wrong with being a nun?'

'Because.... because... you can't become a nun especially if you gave Mucky Murphy a blow-job in a doorway behind Lipton's.'

'I never did!' Amanda was shocked, 'I didn't... I....'

Lois' stare was cold and to the point. No further words were required.

'Ok, I did, but I was sixteen... that surely can't count against me becoming a nun....? And it wasn't a blow-job... it was a hand job... if you must know.'

'It doesn't matter. Listen girl, a fuckin' sixty year old Amsterdam hooker wouldn't give Mucky Murphy a blow-job or any type of job, so there. And I think it's written in tablets of stone, verse one, chapter six in the Bible, the part about the 12 apostles and the drunken donkey..... Blow-jobs behind Lipton's....no way a nun.'

Amanda's face was solemn. Lois laughed out loud; it was the sound that had been sadly missing from the room. She began to uncork the wine. They stared into the silence, as Lois poured the white sparkling liquid into her glass.

'Oh, Lois... what am I going to do? I liked being married. I will be forty years old next month... and I'm so alone for the first time in my life, I feel that I've just sunk to the bottom of the barrel. Where will I find someone like Daryl again?'

Lois opened the big bag of crisps while searching around for a plate or a container to put them in. She eventually poured the potato crisps onto the top of the glass coffee table. Amanda was glad to see that her mate hadn't lost any of her working class charm and high-rise sophistication. She knew she could always rely on her best mate to bring any situation down to street level.

She still giggled with horror and shame when she thought back to the time of her and Daryl's wedding day. It had all started well enough, cars on time, husband there with best man and flowers still blooming. It was a scene from a picture postcard. There was Amanda dressed in a long flowing white dress, standing on the altar next to Daryl. To be fair to him, he had also scrubbed up extremely well, but Amanda wished he could have lost the grey slip-on shoes and white socks from Asda.

The intense-looking priest carrying out the ceremony had just reached the part where he was about to ask the immortal questions that all girls were born and bred to hear, at least, once in their sad, predictable lives.

'Amanda…, Elizabeth…, Willis…, will you take…, Daryl…, Peter…, Grey…, to be your lawful…, wedded…, husband?' the priest's strong and purposeful voice boomed around the church. Amanda couldn't help noticing an egg stain on the holy-man's gown around his crotch. The bright yellow stain looked dry and old.

If she was truthful with herself, on that day, of all wedding days, those were not the exact words she had wished to hear. When Amanda thought about it again, she would probably preferred to have heard the priest, with the thick bushy eyebrows filled with dandruff, muttering the following well-rehearsed words that she had memorized in her mind ever since she could remember.

'Amanda…, Elizabeth…, Willis…, will you take John…, Nigel…, Taylor…, the handsome and talented bass player from Duran Duran, to be your lawful…, wedded…, husband…, to love and to hold…, to lie in bed with all day on Sunday's…, and explore each other's erogenous zones…, nooks and crannies…, until thy kingdom's come?'

As she quickly muttered her reply, 'of course I bloody will…, wouldn't you?' She pictured the rest of the world famous rock band suddenly bursting out with a chorus of 'Save a Prayer' from up in the balcony of the old eighteenth century church building.

'Now, that would be a perfect way to get hitched,' she thought, as the priest and the rest of the congregation waited with baited breath for her reply.

Sadly and regrettably, John Nigel Taylor was unavailable on that day. He was probably off in Rio, screwing some gorgeous, ugly model whore with long, stumpy, perfectly hairy legs. Amanda wasn't at all bitter and twisted. So, with that being the case, Daryl unknowingly had stepped in as the poor substitute for the rest of her life, in his crap shoes, white socks and thin red tie.

As the priest's words swam around in Amanda's head, she took one last look at the man she was about to sign her life away to. The 'I DO' words' stuck deep down in her throat. She was about to leave go of them when she was temporarily saved by a loud farting noise. It came from Lois' direction.

The noise was amazingly loud. On a scale of one to ten, it bordered on seven-and-a-half on the Richter scale.

Even some of the friends of the groom were shocked by the ferocity of her outburst. And these were Stone Age men who prided themselves on sitting in social clubs playing dominos, while competing in childish games of duelling bottom burps with each other.

Lois' enormous gaseous escape echoed around the perimeter of the cold church walls. A statue of the Sacred Heart wobbled precariously and nearly toppled onto Daryl's grandparents.

Everyone turned, shooting daggers of disapproval at the perpetrator. People sitting next to Lois held their noses and moved sharply away from the ever growing pong. Some clambered over the wooden pews, trampling each other in the rush to get away.

'Bloody hell, father!' Lois said angelically, 'must be something you put in that bread-stuff.' She nudged a deaf old man by her side, who had been confused by the sudden, swift movement of people.

Eventually, it took fifteen minutes to restart the ceremony as everybody waited in the car park while the altar boys sprayed the church with air freshener. The rest was history.

Looking back, Amanda couldn't help but think how different it may have been if the statue had actually fallen on Daryl's grandparents. It would have been shocking at the time, especially if the wedding had been cancelled, but think of all the heartache it would have saved later on. Her entire life could have ultimately been saved by Lois' uncontrollable bowel movements.

Back to the present time: Amanda turned to Lois and continued, 'Do you think I'll ever see him again?' She looked pitiful. 'Do you believe that people can come back from the dead…like in that film Ghost?'

Lois put a handful of crisps in her mouth and snapped, 'Hey… if Patrick Swayze had come back from the dead to see me…. I would have had him do more than help me make a bloody clay pot…. unless he would have allowed me to make a plaster-cast of his old boy.'

Amanda ignored her mate's stupid comments. 'Lois be serious…do you understand … I'm forty years old soon?'

'Of course I do, and that's why I've organised something for us to do to celebrate it…. and in bloody style.'

'Like what?' Suspicion crawled out of Amanda's mouth and escaped from her pores.

Lois pulled a piece of paper from out of her handbag. 'Here goes,' she said and started to read the writing on the scroll of paper. 'Number one… next Friday morning you are going for a full body transformation,' she replied, while gulping down some wine, in a very unladylike way.

'What the hell is a full body transformation…? You make me sound like a Frankenstein monster!'

Lois smiled. 'You are going in for a new woman MOT, probably get your oil checked and a bit of a clean up of your old engine.'

'Urrrrgggghhh.'

'It will transform you from an old wreck to a foxy chick…! By the way, look at these.' Lois pulled her boob-top down to reveal a brand new pair of shiny 'DD' cup breasts, complete with extra large, brown-coloured nipples.

'Good God Lois, where did they come from?'

'Well, not from bloody Argos… let me tell you. I thought I needed a new look, so I pawned-off a couple of things and got a pair of these. I feel wonderful, what a difference, eh?' Lois flashed them to her. 'They're still a bit tender… but well worth the pain.'

Amanda was tempted to poke them; she didn't know what to say. 'Well, I'm not going to get mine done!' she insisted.

'You don't need to; you've always had a smashing pair of tits, the best in the school, including bloody Suzanne 'I've got the mankiest legs in the world,' Jackson. She was all toilet-roll and padding.' Amanda smiled in satisfaction. She loved it when Lois stuck up for her.

'This is only the start,' Lois added, 'I'm having a Designer Vagina next.'

'A what?'

'A Designer vagina…. It's when the doctor tightens-up the walls of your thingy.'

Amanda joked that the operation would have to be a pretty long procedure to get Lois' bits back to normal size. Amanda instantly pictured a doctor lacing her mate up like a footballer lacing up a brand new pair of football boots. She wondered what they would do with the left overs. She muttered. 'Well, what am I having done then?'

'Just a little pruning... nothing to worry about.' Lois added, 'Then in the night there is a school reunion, and me and you are going, and what's more, we are going to flirt with every man worth flirting with and hopefully at the end of the night we'll have a slash on Mrs Price's piano.... I've always wanted to do that.'

'Do what, flirt with men in a school reunion or piss on Mrs Price's piano?' Amanda looked at her for the answer.

Lois smiled back. 'You figure it out.'

Amanda shook her head. 'No way... there's no way I'm going to a school reunion.... especially looking like this.... and definitely not after what I've been through... I'll be a laughing stock.'

'Exactly... and that's why you need a full-over body transformation first.... And don't worry about the Daryl thing... that was yesterday's news, no one cares about that anymore.' Lois lied a little for her friend's sake. 'And finally, on the 20th, we are off to Blackpool for the lights, and more importantly, we are going to pick up gorgeous young men who, hopefully, have tongues like anteaters.... and can breathe through their ears.'

'Lois, that's disgusting.'

Lois lit up two Bensons. 'So, what about that for starters then? There's no need to thank me... the hotel's booked, the bus is organised, and I have a suitcase full of luminous condoms. Now let's finish this wine before it goes cold.'

Amanda was speechless. She knew Lois wasn't joking about any of it, but she decided maybe it was about time she rejoined the real world. She knew it couldn't be any worse than her hermit like existence.... or could it?!!

Chapter 3

Yanked

It was body transformation day. Amanda was scared stiff. To make matters worse, it hadn't helped that she had watched a cosmetic programme on Sky about a pretty, normal and healthy 48 year old woman with a few wrinkles around her eyes, who went into hospital to get them ironed out. As the programme unfolded, the woman came out after the operation looking like a deformed pig in a wind-tunnel.

Amanda knew she wasn't having anything that drastic, but it had affected her badly. She hadn't slept. She had tried everything to get out of the visit to the beauty salon, but to no avail. Lois had threatened to blackmail her mate if she didn't turn up, by making up a story about her and telling everyone in the Butcher's shop.

It was 10.45am on a Friday morning and they were sitting on the uncomfortable, grey plastic chairs in the clinical, cold waiting-room of an establishment aptly named 'The Beauty Box.' Looking around at the clientele it could easily have been christened the 'Ugly Mug' and no-one would have blinked a false eyelash. Amanda couldn't help but stare at some of the odd-looking women who lined the perimeter of the room, all preparing to change from colourless caterpillars into beautiful butterflies.

She had spent some time slyly analysing the woman opposite her. The lady must have weighed around sixteen-stone in her bare feet. The features on her face were lost in a range of chins, with the added bonus of having large clumps of hair sprouting from unsightly brown moles on her face. She looked like Sasquatch's sister with a five o' clock shadow at lunchtime.

Amanda wondered what hellish treatments the fat, hairy yeti was about to put herself through in the name of beauty. She checked the long list of procedures on offer to see if she could possibly take a wild guess.

Lois nudged her and whispered, 'They will have to be miracle workers to make that look half decent.... I've seen better looking cows hanging on hooks in the slaughterhouse at the top of town.'

'Schhhh!' Amanda giggled, but secretly nodded in agreement. 'What do you think they'll give her?' she asked quietly.

Without batting an eyelid Lois said, 'A book on dieting, a Bic razor, advice to stay away from mirrors and small children and a fuckin' brown paper bag to put on her head.' She was brutal in her honest assessment.

'Lois... you are terrible.' Amanda shook her head. 'By the way, what have you ordered for me?'

'The same.' Lois picked up a magazine and opened the pages. 'Only joking.... Wait and see.'

Amanda copied her friend but was really too nervous to take in anything that she was reading. She just skimmed through the pictures.

Suddenly there was a loud 'Urrrrrrgggghh' sound from the small cubicle at the far end of the room. It caused Amanda to sit bolt upright in her seat. Her magazine on Japanese decorative gardening dropped to the floor.

Amanda glanced over towards Lois. 'What the hell was that? It sounded like that woman was having a baby... or a small elephant.'

Lois hadn't flinched; she just sat thumbing through some glossy magazine looking for the sexual problem pages. She loved reading about other people's issues, especially when the letters went into graphic details.

'Well?' Amanda spoke again.

'Well... what?'

'Well...? Why did that woman scream as though she was being butchered with a kitchen knife?'

Lois rolled her eyes to the ceiling and slowly replied. 'Well, I didn't hear anything.' Lois turned to the other woman and winked, 'Did you hear anything?'

'When?' the hairy woman replied, scratching her hairy armpits.

'Arrgggghhh.' A similar scream rose up again from the same place.

Amanda was losing her temper with Lois's patronising attitude. 'That noise.'

'Oh! That Aarrrrrggghh noise...! She probably saw a spider.' Lois continued to read the problem page of the magazine.

'A spider?' Amanda picked her feet up in case there were more running about.

'Or it could have been a snake.' Lois smiled. 'Anyway don't worry about her..... Listen to this.' She started to read an article from the pages.

'Dear Dr Zelda..., I am a 38 year old woman who's been married for over 16 years and in that time I have never had an orgasm during sexual intercourse with my husband. What should I do? Beryl, Leeds.'

'What did she tell her to do?' the hairy woman grunted.

'Read it for yourself....some right shitty advice... that's utter nonsense.' Lois passed the magazine over to the woman. The yeti-woman shook her head in agreement, passing it over to Amanda. Amanda could smell the woman's BO. They waited until she finished.

'Well I think it was quite sensible advice actually,' Amanda piped up after scrutinizing the response herself.

'Urrrrggghhh!' The scream pierced the silence again.

'The spider has probably come back.... And I bet you... it's big hairy one... sorry no offence,' Lois motioned to the woman opposite.

Luckily the woman appeared unaware and didn't understand what Lois meant. This pleased Amanda because by the look of the woman she could have squashed both their heads with her bare tattooed hands.

Lois snatched the magazine back from her friend and added, 'There's no way she should have told the girl to do that... that advice is crap. I would have told the girl to get down to Anne Summers and buy a Billy-goat vibrator.... It's got an attachment on it that could dig up tarmac... that will get her to Pleasure Island in no time.'

'I don't think they could actually print words like that in Cosmopolitan and even if they did what about the relationship with her husband?' Amanda whispered back.

'Amanda.... Bollocks to her husband. If my Ex is anything to go by, men can't satisfy women even if they have a manual in front of them. Most men couldn't find our king prawns if we painted them bright yellow and had a fuckin' neon sign pointing straight at it. They are all bastard useless. It's the vibrator every time.' She leant back on her chair.

The fat woman's mouth dropped wide open.

'I think I'll start my own in-agony aunt column.' She motioned her hands as though a star was shooting effortlessly across the darken skies on a bright winter's night. 'If you're looking for help with love, come to Dr Lois.'

Another yelp came from the mysterious woman behind the door.

Amanda piped up, 'Yeah, I can see it now… and in the small print it will say Doctor Lois…. recovering alcoholic, on probation for scalding the foreskin off her cheating husband, and the girl who's had more inches of willy than steel in the Eiffel Tower… that would look good on your résumé.'

'Hey… that's not a bad slogan,' Lois searched in her bag for a pen. 'It shows I've got experience and I've been scarred by love…. So don't mess about with me when it comes to matters of romance.'

Out of the blue, the door of the room, where all the screaming was escaping from, swung open and out strolled two young teenage girls, dressed in white overalls. Both of them had nose piercings and way too much foundation on their young faces. One had the appearance of a milk bottle. The other was only one shade away from being a human tangerine.

Amanda could sense they were both the type of girls who acted older than their years. They reminded Amanda of teenage grandmothers who knew everything about everything and who didn't have a good word to say about anyone. These were young ladies with chips the size of canoes on their shoulders and attitudes that could burn down a block of solid brick flats covered in a fire blanket, and with a solid concrete foundation.

The milk white girl yawned and studied the roster for the rest of the day.

Amanda watched in fascination as, eventually, they were followed out of the room by a lady who seemed to be in some discomfort. Amanda guessed that she must be in her late forties, but by the expression on her face she seemed to be ageing by the minute. She was not so much walking, as swaggering from side to side like a gorilla suffering from a serious bout of haemorrhoids. She appeared to be in shock; an ashen white face locked in a vacant stare with a painful grin visibly fixed around the corner of her mouth.

'Saw the big spider... did you love?' Lois joked, winking at one of the beauty assistants.

The lady didn't acknowledge the sarcasm in the question. She was more interested in heading for the safety of the door. She appeared to be in a trance, small steps accompanied by large tears rolling down her cheeks.

'See you next month Mrs Williams... and I hope that Mr Williams' loves his birthday treat.' The one girl folded her arms, making devious 'I couldn't care a fuck' eyes at the other assistant.

'What do you think she means by 'his birthday treat?'' Amanda's innocence was genuine as she looked for an answer from her friend.

'She's just had a Brazilian,' the more orange of the two assistants replied, folding her arms even tighter, before yet again rolling her eyeballs to the ceiling in an increasingly impatient manner.

'A what?' Amanda looked confused. The only Brazilian she had ever heard of was some bloke called Polo or Pelo, or something like that, who scored a touchdown in the FA cup final of some soccer game during the war, or something.

'You are out of touch.' Lois jumped in to save her friend from certain embarrassment. 'Sorry girls.... she's just come out of a nasty divorce and she's thinking of becoming a nun.' Lois turned back to Amanda, 'She's just had a waxing.'

'Waxing.... What her legs?'

'Amongst other things.' Lois lit a fag, she pointed down below. She could tell by her face that Amanda was still lost. She quickly added, 'She also had her 'See You Next Tuesday' done.'

'Her what?' even the assistants appeared stumped.

Lois tried again. 'You know... C….. U….. NEXT…. TUESDAY,' she motioned down below with her hand. 'Bloody hell…. She just had her beaver buffed, her minge manicured, her twat tweaked, her crack coiffured … her F. A. N. N. Y. waxed.' For some strange reason Lois felt it necessary to spell out the last word.

Amanda mouthed the word in silence. 'Why did she do that?'

'Because her priest told her to do it in confession… you plonker… why do you think?'

Amanda felt like heaving. 'If I knew why I wouldn't be asking you.'

'Cos… it's all the rage,' the fat, hairy woman bent towards her to add her two-penny's worth to the wacky conversation.

Amanda knew everyone was staring at her as if she was some kind of alien that had just landed from the planet Zog. She pondered a few more seconds before enquiring why they called it a Brazilian. She couldn't work out what the significance was.

'Because it was invented there.... on the beaches of Rio... where the sands are white and the bathing costumes don't leave anything to the imagination.... You know what the South Americans are like..., hairy thighs and dental floss g-strings. That's why I'm having one done today,' the yeti-woman replied. 'Men just love a smooth vagina.' Both beauty therapists glanced at each other and cursed under their breath.

Amanda thought she was going to be sick. Her eyes searched about for a bucket. Instead they were drawn to the woman's groin area. She couldn't imagine a worse job in the world than that.

'No wonder the assistants wore faces like slapped arses all day,' she thought.

She envisaged that working down a damp, rat-infested coalmine for twenty-three hours a day, without food or water, would be better than having to pluck the pubes from old fatties' nether regions.

Amanda closed her eyes to try and clear her head. The solitary-feeling the darkness gave her helped her to refocus her mind. It made her think what would have happened if a Brazilian waxing hadn't been invented in that warm, beautiful country which instantly conjured up images of sun drenched beaches and gorgeous women with pert bottoms. What if it had been conceived in a little rundown council estate on the outskirts of Scunthorpe? She pictured millions of would-be models throughout the world, pulling off their knickers, and asking for a 'Scunthorpe, without the smog from the Steelworks please.' She tittered to herself.

'I don't know what you're finding so funny... you're having one next!' Lois interrupted, while getting to her feet.

'Who... me?'

'Yes you... and don't who me...? And don't worry it's my treat for you. But watch out for that spider.' Lois turned to the young assistant. 'Look girls... I'll pick her up in two hours...and don't forget, give this lady the full works... no wrinkle to be left unturned or hair unplucked.' It was her turn to laugh out aloud as she exited the building in search of a dress to buy.

'But....but' Amanda struggled to find the right words to express the terror she was feeling. She felt like a dog that was about to get neutered, or a convertible automobile about to drive through a car wash with the top down. It was as though she was about to walk the green tiled mile into the room of pain to face a modern day execution. She took tiny steps.

Behind the closed door the assistants were very matter of fact and very ignorant. They talked about Amanda as if she wasn't there, dismissing any attempt the older woman made to make human contact.

'I can't believe fatty's back,' one of the girls spoke about the woman still slumped in the waiting room. 'I only did her three weeks ago.... I'm sure she must be on bloody strong hormone tablets... or bathing in Baby Bio... her hair grows faster than my granddad's nose hair. Last time I did her I filled two black bin bags right up to the top.'

'Do we have to do her...? Can't we refuse...? She smells as well.' The girl with the David Dickinson skin made a contorted face; her nose piercing nearly touched her forehead.

'But she tips well.'

The girl with the scrunched-up features spat her chewing gum into a swing bin and added, 'Well.... I'd like to give her a tip.... Stop eating bloody cream donuts so much and have a shower now and again.'

They smirked at each other for exactly ten seconds, and then their faces became serious again. From where Amanda was sitting they were two robots in white overalls, devoid of all feelings and emotion, two C3PO's with waxing pots and eyebrow tweezers.

The prettier, pale blonde one, who looked no older than 12, but assured Amanda that she was 18, scanned the treatment card before saying, 'OK... this one's booked in for a 13,17,74, followed by an 81 and a .....' she checked the list before continuing.

For the first time in her life, Amanda felt as though she had suddenly developed into a take-away Chinese meal overnight. She half expected them to pour soya sauce over her and put her in a foil container with a bag of greasy prawn crackers.

'She's also having an 84 as well as a 93 to finish,' the mouthier assistant whispered, a smirk appeared on her face that Lucifer would have been proud of wearing to a Sunday afternoon execution of a couple of goody angels.

'What's an 84...? does it hurt?' Amanda sounded nervous.

The other girl remarked, 'don't worry.... it doesn't hurt half as much as an 85. We normally call for an assistant to hold you down when we do that one.'

Amanda didn't want to ask what it entailed. She was asked frostily if she fancied a cup of tea before they started.

'Only if you put some pain-killers in it,' she joked nervously.

'How the hell did you know we did that?' the dark-skinned one said solemnly.

Amanda didn't know if the girl was joking or not. The expression on the girl's face never altered. They were like shop window dummies, but with half the intelligence and a third of the personality.

'What is it about youngsters today?' She looked around the treatment room. 'They all act and look the same.' She wondered if God had run out of funny-bones after 1985 and had used a dodgy supply of East German sarcasm bones instead. The younger generation were like no other generation before them. Techno-junkies with mobile phones permanently attached to their ears and frowns stretched across their faces.

'Why are they all so gloomy?'

'Why did they appear to carry the weight of the world on their ever-shrugging shoulders?'

She remembered when she was that age; she tried hard to be pleasant to everyone. At that time she wanted to talk to other people, basically to find out about other people's lives. But these modern-day girls seemed almost too afraid to smile. Maybe they were scared that if they showed any sign of happiness they would be disowned by some teenage demi-god. She wondered if their lack of manners was to do with watching too much TV, or maybe growing up on a diet of fast-food that had, no doubt, eaten away at their brain cells, or perhaps the decline in family values had robbed them of even being able to hold a normal conversation. She decided to see if she could lower their drawbridge, let their tongues run free for a while, so she could enter their world.

'Out tonight, girls?' she asked, smiling pleasantly.

The girls' stared over in shock. It was as if Amanda was speaking in a foreign language. The quieter one looked for help towards the cocky, brown-coloured one. Amanda could see her thinking. She was sure she could make out a thought travelling around the inside of her mind. The girl gazed at her for a while before saying,

'Maybe we'll see you at the bingo tonight, or are you staying in to do some knitting?'

Amanda's tongue was tied. Before she had a chance to counteract, the two girls carried on preparing the stuff they needed. So that was that. No more words were exchanged between the women from the different generations. The moment was lost forever. She was left dangling on the end of a sarcastic comment and the door to their secret world was closed forever.

She shut her eyes, leaving the assistants to carry out their duties.

The first two treatments were very pleasurable and very relaxing. The milky white assistant manicured her nails and the other carried out a pedicure. She was beginning to enjoy all the pampering and fuss. She could feel the years drop off her in chunks and fall to the floor like icebergs falling from a glacier. The build up of stress slipped out of her opened pores.

They may have looked just out of infant school, but Amanda had to admire their professional approach, if she disregarded their lack of interpersonal skills. They actually appeared to enjoy their job. Next on the agenda was a very relaxing face pack. As she waited for that treatment to finish she listened to the girl's explicit conversation about a recent night out in the town.

'Did you see what's-his-name snogging with that little slut in K's last night?' one girl asked the other.

'Yep... what a dirty slag.... she had her hands all over him.... I could hardly look.'

It took Amanda several moments to realise that the `K` was the town's nightclub called the Kirkhouse. She knew that abbreviating words was not a new thing to this vacant generation, now especially with the invention of texting, but Amanda wondered how long it would take until everyone spoke in single letters abbreviation or AB…. for short.

The orange girl slapped on some gloves and instructed Amanda to strip her knickers off, and place her feet in the stirrups. It was pain-time.

The girls were well organised; they worked as a pair, one on the top half doing her eyebrows, the other on the lower half of her anatomy. They were a synchronised body hair removal team.

'It's a dirty job…but someone's got to do it.' Amanda said, while thinking she'd try to break the ice while they carried out this obviously embarrassing procedure.

The girls didn't raise a smile at her comment. There was no movement of their facial muscles, except from the rolling of their eyes again, but this time in a more 'What a fucking moron' expression.

It was like being in a dentist chair but this was a dentist run by two ignorant teenage butchers, who'd completed their apprenticeship while working in a concentration camp, experimenting on chopping private parts off their victims.

They still chatted between themselves as though she wasn't there, or she was a dead body on a cold slab at the mortuary.

Amanda lay on her back wondering if they actually rotated their duties during the shift. Maybe they worked an hour on, an hour off. Or perhaps they did an hour between the legs, then an hour on the eyebrows. Or maybe one was an apprentice and her training meant she had to do the bottom half, until she got issued with her pube removal certification papers.

Amanda was amazed at how explicit and beyond shame these girls were during their discussions. But then again, when she considered that they yanked pubic hair from women's nether regions for a living, then perhaps it wasn't surprising that it hardened their outlook on life.

'You never let him do that... did you?' the ghostly-looking girl asked, as she tugged what seemed like a clump of hair from Amanda's groin. 'Did it hurt?'

Amanda screamed at the sudden sharp shooting pain. 'That bloody did.'

They ignored her and continued.

'At first it did,' the girl replied 'but look what he gave me.' She flashed a ring the size of a Jammie-Dodger at her colleague.

'Is that real?'

'Yep....pure nine carat gold, with a real cubic zirconium middle.' She looked so proud.

Another strip pulled away; another scream from their victim.

Amanda's mind closed down. She was in too much pain to even listen to their conversation. She wanted to tell them to hurry up, but she decided she had better not anger them. They were the ones with the waxing strips and didn't appear to be afraid to use them.

'Uruughhh,' Amanda yelled as another chunk of hair was dragged out. She hadn't realised how much pubic hair she had below. She looked at the waxing strips laid out on the table top. They looked like a herd of large, hairy caterpillars queuing at a barber for a long overdue trim. There was enough to make a small wig. Amanda thought about the bloke at Daryl's funeral whose hairpiece had blown off in the wind. She recalled meeting him in the Spar shop recently and she had noticed he had attached a string to it which fitted under his chin.

'Better be safe than sorry,' he motioned to her and shuffled off towards the video section.

'How much longer?' She thought she was going to faint. In fact she did and when she finally came around Lois was standing over her. 'Well what do you think?'

Amanda painfully got to her feet and looked into the full-length mirror. She resembled a plucked turkey getting ready for Christmas. She was hairless and covered in red patches. She didn't recognise herself. She got dressed and struggled out. She saw the two girls sitting at the back of the shop tucking into a McDonald's happy meal. They didn't pick their heads up, they just continued to stuff French-fries into their dirty mouths.

'Wait until you walk into the hall for the school reunion. You'll knock 'em dead.'

'Lois… I'm still not sure why the hell I needed a waxing to go to the school reunion…. what the hell will I be doing there…. Pole-dancing?'

'You wait!' Lois' words hung around and then followed them out of the shop and down the high street. The thought of pole dancing at the school reunion worried poor Amanda to death. Her cellulite was not ready for public exposure.

Chapter 4

Milkshake

The two women headed up the path to Amanda's house. While Lois bounded along, without a care in the world, in front, Amanda followed behind gingerly, wincing with every bent over step. She couldn't wait to soak her tender bits in a nice warm bath.

Amanda unlocked the front door and shuffled into the hallway. Lois, not far behind, mimicked her mate's walk. Suddenly, the widow stopped in her tracks. As she stepped inside she could sense immediately that something was wrong. The atmosphere didn't seem right. For some unknown reason there was a distinctive smell of toast floating around her house and a draft blowing through the hallway. She sniffed the air like a tracker dog before slowly moving inside.

'What's up?' Lois asked.

'That's strange…. I never made toast this morning.' Amanda rushed into the kitchen.

Once there, she noticed the back door was ajar. A small pane insert in the wooden frame had been smashed. Splinters of glass lay all over the tiled floor. Amanda was too confused to be afraid. There was a mug of half-drunk cold tea on the table, next to a butter-covered knife and a plate littered with bread crumbs.

Nervous, she felt like shouting out, 'And whose been fucking about in my kitchen?' but then the seriousness of the situation took hold.

She bounded upstairs, clearing two steps at a time, memories of her painful de-plucking almost forgotten.

'Lois…. Quick!' she screamed from her bedroom, 'I think I've been burgled!'

She scanned the room. Her bedroom was a mess, drawers had been opened, cupboard doors unlocked; some of her clothes were strewn around the carpet.

Lois strolled up the stairs, casually. 'Are you sure?'

'Of course I'm sure! I've been burgled…. Just look at the mess!' Amanda snapped her answer sharply back at her mate.

'To be honest, it looks better than the upstairs of my house does now.' Lois lit a fag and sat on the bed, before adding nonchalantly, 'What's been stolen then?'

Amanda was frantically picking stuff up, examining the items for damage, then throwing them back on the floor. 'That's weird.' She shook her head, her mind raced in several directions at once. 'Really strange…'

'What is?'

'Well…. The only items that seem to be missing… are all my…. all my… black stuff….. Shoes, blouses, all my jumpers are gone. Even the black dress I was going to wear to the school reunion tonight.' She slumped onto the bed, mentally drained.

'Perhaps it's a sign,' Lois smirked, while reaching into a bag, and pulling out a slinky red dress. 'Maybe…. just maybe… Morticia Adams… you will have to wear something other than black for a change.' She held up the vibrant dress next to her friend. 'What a bit of luck… just the right size.'

Amanda always knew she was a bit slow on the uptake when it came to working out subtle hints, but this situation was taking an age to sink in to her thick skull. She was still extremely confused. Suddenly the light bulb came on as she saw the smirk on her mate's face.

'Lois…. did you have anything to do with this?' She stared at her mate. 'You did….. Didn't you?'

'Don't be so stupid…. Why would you think that?' Lois' grin grew wider.

'You did… I knew it…. You probably had your son to break in didn't you? I can't believe it.' Amanda paced around the room. 'And….and the cheeky bastard's not only whipped my stuff but he made himself some bloody tea and toast in the bargain.'

Lois ignored her; she was busily searching through Amanda's wardrobe for a matching pair of red shoes.

'He's a bastard, and you're one as …,' but Amanda purposefully didn't finish the sentence. She realised that Lois wasn't a bastard at all. She looked at Lois and smiled tenderly. She appreciated her mate was a good and thoughtful friend. She may have been rougher than three day old stubble on a pirate's chin, but deep down she had a heart of gold. Again, maybe not really expensive gold like the stuff displayed in the shop window of Samuel's the jewellers, but at least a cheaper version bought off a bloke with a suitcase from a stall in the outdoor market on a Tuesday.

She knew Lois meant well. It wasn't her fault she had been born on the wrong side of the tracks. To be fair to her she had had a tough old life. When she was only two months old, she was found in a Co-op carrier-bag, sleeping soundly inside a shopping trolley. She hadn't been abandoned by her mother; it was just that the forgetful woman had forgotten about her baby while out shopping-lifting. The police eventually tracked her down playing telly-bingo in the Theatre. Her mother had been a likeable Valium-junkie, who was always doing stuff like that. On the other hand, her father was a different character all together. He had been an unrepentant alcoholic with a selfish streak and who had little or no time for the seeds of his loin. He had left them all high and dry when she was still in primary school. Looking back, Amanda sometimes wondered how Lois survived at all.

'I wonder what else your son's taken.' Amanda checked her jewellery case.

'Hey, he'd better not have taken anything else. I instructed him to only take your black gear.' Lois was cross at Amanda's accusation. 'He may be a useless junkie but he's got morals.... and I bloody well warned him that if he did half-inch anything else... I would throw away his needles.'

And to be fair to Lois' son, he had listened to his mother's gypsy warning and carried out her orders to the letter of her law. But this included lifting three pairs of black panties and a pair of black hold-up stockings. He may have been a drug addict but that didn't stop him having urges, and he knew Amanda was quite an attractive woman.

The two friends walked back down to the kitchen.

'Right,' Lois clapped her hands, 'your horse and carriage will pick you up at seven on the dot.... so be ready and look beautiful.' It was Amanda's turn to listen to orders.

'Have you booked a taxi?'

'Fuckin' taxi...? This is our school reunion...We ain't turning up in a smelly taxi... We are going in style... I've ordered us a fuckin' twenty-foot limo with a bar in the back. See you in two hours, Cinders.' Lois sauntered out of the house looking pleased as punch.

Amanda slowly climbed the stairwell. She began putting stuff back into the drawers. She stared at the red dress laid out on the bed. It looked wonderful, if a touch slutty, but she could work around that.

'Trust her to do that for me.' She began to cry. She loved Lois. She couldn't have asked for a better mate in the entire world, even if Amanda had been the first in the queue when God was handing out friendships. Lois was special, a one in a million.

Amanda bathed and began to get herself ready. It had been a long time since she had an excuse to really 'tart' herself up. Even when Daryl was alive, the furthest they went was the social club. She could have dressed as a dockside hooker and she wouldn't have looked out of place in that shit-hole. She was enjoying this new experience; it was exciting.

Once ready, she glanced in the full-length mirror positioned in the spare room. She wasn't looking that bad after all, she thought to herself. She moved in to examine herself a little closer. She noticed the crow's feet around the eyes, but considering the year she'd had, she had escaped quite lightly in the worry-line department.

For the first time in ages, she actually felt quite womanly. In fact, she visualised herself like Cinderella, Snow White and Lady Diana, all rolled up into one wonderful, fairy princess. She sparkled like a diamond in a coal mine which glistened brightly through the gloomy shadow of her past life.

A car horn honked and snapped her out of her trance. 'Your chariot awaits.' She smiled at her reflection and strolled out into the cold night air.

The limousine was magnificent. It was all white and must have been the length of a football field. Inside, it was all black leather with chrome accessories. It was warm and inviting. The heat wrapped itself around her as she stepped into another world. It took her a minute to take it all in.

As the vehicle cruised slowly away from her home, she could see the neighbours peeking out of their net curtains. She could sense their disapproval and jealousy engrained on their long, drawn-out faces. To rub it in even more, Lois gave them all the one finger salute. Amanda loved her mate.

After a few minutes, Lois piped up at the driver in the cap, while she finished off her bottle of lager. 'Hey drive... see this girl here?'

The driver fiddled with his rear view mirror until he caught a glimpse of the lady in question.

He nodded in acknowledgement while paying particular attention to the fleshy area where Amanda's skirt had risen up, exposing her thighs. He moaned to himself.

'Ain't she beautiful?' Lois asked.

The lust in the man's eyes agreed with Lois' observation. He didn't need a formal education with top grades and high scores to appreciate a good looking woman. He licked his lips before replying 'Sure.... very nice.'

His devious mind changed up a gear. Like most men in the world, deep down he knew she fancied him, it was so obvious. It was the uniform that did it every time. He straightened his tie and winked at her. As he smiled Amanda caught a glimpse of his lovely, yellow teeth.

There was always something about taxi drivers that unnerved Amanda. She had read somewhere that most of them had been in the clay class in school. This one looked like he couldn't spell clay class, never mind play around in one.

The desire in his eyes had now quickly travelled down to his underpants and something stirred down below his belt line. He readjusted his position, perspiration dripping from his forehead, falling off and onto the steering wheel.

'Did you know?' Lois continued, catching his stare in the rear view mirror, 'she's had her beaver shaved this afternoon.' Lois pretended to lift up her mate's skirt.

Amanda spat neat Bacardi onto the car floor. She just knew that Lois would say something to spoil the mood. While Amanda was feeling like Dorothy, in red sparkling slippers travelling back to Kansas, as usual, up pops Lois, the wicked Witch of the West, to end her fairytale journey with some choice words. She was a master at it. Amanda hated Lois at times.

Amanda turned a bright shade of crimson red to match her dress and pushed Lois' hand away. She was upset; she hadn't been prepared for that. The driver, on the other hand, started drooling and was lucky not to drive into an oncoming bus. The limousine swerved. The girls fell about in the back, two traffic cones went flying across the road, narrowly missing a cyclist in tight lycra shorts and crash helmet, causing him to smash into a sign, which warned drivers to take care. After fifty yards and a squashed cat the limo driver finally regained control of the wallowing vehicle.

'Lois... now see what you did...?. You nearly got us killed.'

'Hey…. it was your snatch he was bloody looking at… not mine.' Lois glared at the driver.

'I wasn't…. I wasn't,' the driver pleaded his innocence, while trying hard to regain his composure and correct the tent that had appeared in his trousers.

Lois shot his feeble excuse down in flames with her famous look. It made him slump down childlike in his seat and he pulled his cap down to the bridge of his nose.

The rest of the journey through the decaying urban wasteland leading up to their old comprehensive school was shrouded in mortified silence. The car eventually stopped opposite a bus stop. Amanda clambered out, ensuring the driver couldn't see up her skirt, while Lois did the opposite.

They walked through the old rusty gates of their school. Butterflies flapped around in the pit of their stomachs. Amanda had warned Lois that if she dared let slip to another person about her lower anatomy again she would hit her over the head with something heavy.

'I won't do it again… promise.'

'You just told the fucking caretaker,' Amanda hissed, 'and his bloody wife.'

'Sorry…. I must be nervous,' Lois said 'Don't know what I'm saying… but did you see the face on her…. She looked like a bulldog licking stale piss off a nettle.'

The two girls fell into some kind of silent trance as they strolled down the corridor, past the battered school lockers and towards the main assembly hall, where the event was being staged. They were drawn towards the entrance similar to bees towards a blossoming flower. There was no turning back.

Amanda had always believed in the principle of having school reunions. She thought they were a great idea. But what she couldn't for the life of her make out was why they didn't hold them in some proper club, instead of the old school assembly hall. She deemed that there was no need to actually go back to the place where she spent five miserable years, with a few days of happiness sandwiched in-between, to meet up with old school friends. She imagined it was the last sick joke thought up by a sadistic headmaster who was bored silly with bullying spotty kids in torn blazers.

She pictured a headmaster shouting out to his overworked secretary. 'I know! Let's have a school reunion.'

'That's a good idea headmaster.... Shall I try and book a restaurant or a nightclub; maybe Stringfellows; or a nice restaurant in downtown New York for the event?'

'No...! No such thing...! Lets hold it here... here in the freezing-cold, smelly school assembly hall, where all the furniture's been made to fit the seven dwarves... and I tell you what else we'll do... we'll have the school bell to ring and we'll get the school canteen staff to work overtime and give them all sausage, beans and cold chips and strawberry milkshake....it will be great.... Just like their old days.'

Amanda dismissed the thought as she pulled up a chair. For the second time that night she'd felt like Judy Garland in the Land of Oz. She double checked under the piano, just in case there was a set of witch's legs with ruby slippers sticking out from beneath it.

A fifty-something man, who had the demeanour of a headmaster came across to greet them. He was small, bald, and dressed very formally in extremely shabby clothes, covered in chalk dust, his shoulders bearing the snow drift of bad dandruff. The leather elbow pads were shiny.

'Fuck me... it's the mayor of Munchkin land...and here comes the rest of the lollipop boys,' Lois hissed, smoke drifting into her eyes.

Amanda looked over to see three teachers following behind the man. They were all dressed in a frighteningly similar fashion and appeared to be all joined at the hip. Amanda burst out laughing. The effect of the Bacardi was starting to swallow her nervousness up in some alcoholic haze.

'Hello Ladies... nice to see you.... My name is Headmaster Phillips.' He held out his hand in a welcoming gesture.

'Where's Headmaster Black gone?' Amanda asked, slightly shocked by this impostor posing as a headmaster.

'Ho...ho,' Headmaster Phillips chuckled, holding his stomach. His three stooges joined in. 'Headmaster Black retired years ago. He lives in a shelter now... sad really. Anyway, we've had several heads since then.'

'It's about time he ordered a new one, then,' Lois whispered in Amanda's ear. 'His head looks like its way past its sell by date.' Amanda nudged Lois with her elbow.

The man continued, 'There was Headmaster Grey, then Headmaster Peters.' He paused, and whispered. 'We even had a Headmistress,' he closed in and added, 'she didn't last long... it's not a job for women you see... too much responsibility and stress. There's more thinking than you could possibly understand in this role.'

Amanda looked at him in disgust. She hadn't liked Margaret Thatcher at the best of times, but she wished the old iron lady could have been walking past at that moment, as the stupid man uttered those words. She would have put him in his place.

'Anyway ladies,' he grinned. 'Enough of me... what are your names?' a smile fixed across his chubby face.

Amanda introduced herself first.

'Nice to meet you... and who's your charming friend?' He stared across at Lois.

'I'm Lois.'

The gang of school teachers glared at each other then glanced nervously towards the headmaster.

'No, seriously.... Who are you?' he asked again, laughing weakly and edging back ever so slightly.

'I've told you... I'm Lois... they used to call me Lois Bug, because my mother looked like a centipede.... You must have heard of me.... I once burnt down the science lab?' She bared her teeth to the circle of teachers.

'You can't be Lois... I heard that she was still locked-up in prison,' one of the other teachers spoke up. 'Something to do with drugs in Thailand.... Smuggling I was told.'

'Smuggling... fuckin' Thailand,' Lois laughed out aloud. 'The furthest I've ever been to is fuckin' Chickenland.' She proceeded to walk away towards the bar shaking her head. She was in need of a stiff drink, and it was going to be a treble.

The four men stood like statues, unable to speak. Amanda could sense their unease. She eventually made her excuses and left them to go to the bar as well.

On the stage the DJ tried his best to create the atmosphere of yesteryear by playing songs from that era.

'God,' she thought, 'she hadn't heard the song 'Is Vic there', by whatever the band was called, since her teens.' She loosely recalled spending a night at a house party necking with a boy called Steve, when the song was in the charts. Sadly he got killed years later trying to dodge a bullet in Belfast.

Her eyes hopped around the room, trying to see if she could recognise anyone. Whichever way she looked she could identify people who she hadn't seen for decades. As if she was possessed by some evil creature, spiteful words popped inside her head when she analysed her former classmates in greater detail.

'She looked a lot prettier when she was younger!' she thought, spying someone walking by.

'She's had a face lift or bloody six.'

'He colours his hair.... He was going grey in third year.'

'Good god... how many chins can she get on one face?'

'Oh... bloody hell... that twat can't still be teaching... can he? I thought he was dead.'

The more she stared around the room, the more cutting her inner-thoughts became. She was sounding more like Lois than Lois. She wondered if her ex-classmates were thinking the same type of things of her. She bloody hoped not.

Out of boredom, she glanced towards the main door. It opened inwards. A dark figure strolled into the noisy room. The new headmaster and his teacher posse approached the man and shook his hand in turn. Amanda sat bolt upright, her breathing became shallow, and her heart beat wildly. She put her hand over her chest in case someone heard it banging over the whining of Adam Ant's old favourite, *'Stand and Deliver'*.

'Oh my God... it's Jacob.' She wanted to shout his name out, as he glanced around the room.

From where she was positioned his hair looked a little greyer around the edges than she remembered, but he was still as gorgeous as ever. He glanced straight at her, but before she had time to wave at him, someone else shook his hand violently and pulled him toward the bar.

'Did he see me?' she asked herself, as she straightened herself up. 'He must have.... but why didn't he acknowledge me then?' Her brain hurt with all the questions she asked herself. 'But it's dark. Maybe he's short sighted? Should she go over and say hello?'

She wanted to talk to him. She would have loved to stare into his hazel green eyes. She resisted the urge to walk straight up to him and demand to find out more about his life, and, more importantly, when was he going to ask her out for a meal and get to know her.

She watched from afar as people went out of their way to say something to him. She hadn't realised how popular Jacob had been. Old school mates buzzed around him as though he was either dripping with money, or coated in honey.

She was determined not to screw it up. There would be no shy, tongue-tied school-girl approach this time around. She had waited since the third year of school to get to know him and this was her big chance; here he was, presented to her on a silver platter.

During her unashamed lusting for him she hadn't noticed the beautiful brunette hovering by his shoulder. Amanda was too busy wondering what would be her excuse to go and chat with him to have seen her.

It was then that the bullet with the words 'Reality Check' etched on the side of its casing hit her square between the eyes. The sudden realisation that the stunner in the long black evening gown, standing by Jacob's side, was actually with him caused a sharp pain to pierce her heart. She became visibly deflated in her chair.

'Perhaps she's just trying to get past?' she hoped. It soon became obvious that the woman was going nowhere,

Amanda's heart weighed as heavy as a house-brick in her chest. It dropped to the pit of her stomach, making her feel sick. Her legs turned to jelly; all her senses mingled into the music.

'Stand and deliver.... Your money or your life.'

The words from the song belted out of the speakers.

'Fuck right off.... Adam fuckin' Ant, and get a real bloody job,' she muttered. 'You useless pirate... or whatever you were suppose to be.' She was upset. She needed someone to take it out on, and poor Adam Ant took it with both barrels between the war paint on his flat, boyish chest.

Jacob shook some other man's hand. They then turned and Amanda could see him introduce the man to the girl. The three of them laughed, sharing some joke between them.

Throughout her life Amanda had never been a violent person. She had always tried to treat individuals as she expected them to treat her. But at that moment in her old school assembly hall, if she could have got her hands on a gun she would have blasted the beautiful bitch, then cut out her heart and eaten it in front of everyone in the room.

'Wonder what Mrs Price, the piano teacher, would have made of that?' she hissed though her dry lips.

She couldn't believe that, yet again, her world was suddenly collapsing around her. Her new found confidence sunk down in a pit of faltering quicksand. She knew it was stupid, but she somehow thought that Daryl's death was just the end of one chapter in her life, and maybe, just maybe, Jacob would be the person to take her to the end of her book of life.

For various reasons the romantic side of her, which had been dormant for so many years, had somehow always envisaged a truly happy ending with this man. Many future unwritten chapters full of passion, laughter and hot, sweaty sex were waiting on each future page to greet her. She had been so deep into her fantasy that she hadn't even stopped to listen to the logical half of her brain which had been continually yelling out that Jacob probably had lines of beautiful women begging for his services; scores of would-be wives, with size eight figures, dripping in diamonds and pearls and Brazilian waxed beavers.

'How stupid of me!' she cursed to herself. 'Why did I think that? Did I honestly imagine that someone as handsome and successful as Jacob would be waiting just for me?' Tears welled up her eyes; her posture slumped into defeat.

She felt as if someone had drenched her entire body with freezing cold water as she lay sleeping on a sunlounger by the edge of a swimming pool on a warm, Mediterranean day.

She must have been completely barmy to think that she, Amanda Grey (or soon to be Willis, once again), could have the style and the panache to tempt this man into her low, shallow existence.

She necked the half-glass of Bacardi and coke in one go and topped it up from the bottle that she had smuggled into the event in her handbag.

'Is there no justice in the world?' she said, watching Jacob whispering something into his girlfriend, or, worse still, his bloody wife's ear.

The girl said something back to him and they both headed towards the far end of the bar. Amanda felt sick to her boots; she was in shock, denial and the other one.

'My kingdom for a magnum 45 and a magazine of bullets,' she wished upon a star. Then, as if by magic, Lois appeared, full of smiles and bursting with energy.

'Amanda... Amanda,' she shouted above the music 'Quick, come and take a fuckin' look at what I've found.' She grabbed her hand and dragged her towards the other side of the hall.

'Look, Lois... whatever it is you want to show me .... I'm not in the mood... I wanna go home.'

'Not until you see this.' Lois stopped in front of a table and positioned Amanda at a right angle to the stage. 'Right....who do you think that is?' Lois pointed to an overweight woman sitting all alone in a horrible, cheap, green dress.

'I don't know... Porky Pig's mistress?' Amanda was not really interested who she was. She was more concerned in losing the love of her life, so easily, and without putting up a fight.

'No, smart arse.... that is the one and only.... Suzanne 'I'm the prettiest girl in the world' Jackson.' Lois smirked, knowing full well that she had uncovered the best discovery since Julius Caesar caught Cleopatra doing lewd things with an asp. This was miles better than the man who had unearthed the remains of that mummy in Egypt, or the other guy who came across the face of God on that tee-shirt, shroud-thing in Turin.

Amanda squinted her eyes 'No way... that's not Suzanne 'all sugar and spice and everything is nice' Jackson?'

'Honest to fuck.... cross my heart. I've just been talking to her. It was hilarious ..... She told me she's been married and divorced three times, has five kids and works as a cleaning woman on the weekends... and, wait for it... in the town hall.'

'So there is a God;' Amanda commented, as the two smug women made a bee-line to go and say hello, and, of course, to gloat some more.

After taking the piss out of the poor woman for a while and then having to suffer non-stop eighties disco music belting out from the speakers, Amanda found herself sitting alone. Lois was again nowhere to be seen. Amanda was starting to feel sorry for herself. She contemplated leaving; assuming Jacob was still in the bar-area with some old school mates and that beautiful, but ugly troll-model.

She searched under the table for her handbag. A gentle tap on her shoulder caused her to jump. She lifted her head up very annoyed.

'That was a bloody stupid thing to do?' She was ready to give the person who had tapped her on the shoulder a verbal bashing for causing her to hit her head on the edge of the table. She stopped in full flight on seeing the handsome features of Jacob occupying the chair next to her.

Her immediate reaction was to kiss him. This took both of them by surprise.

'I'm so sorry...I don't know what came over me,' she whimpered with embarrassment, looking around to make sure no-one else saw what she had done.

He smiled; she had to concentrate hard to stop herself doing it again. The disc jockey announced he was going to slow the pace down a notch or two, and give long-lost lovers a chance to find their long-lost love. Amanda grinned at the romantic gesture, but let out a groan when he spoilt it all by putting on the song 'True,' by that group with the stupid trousers and hair.

'I didn't expect a greeting like that.' Jacob tasted her lipstick on his lips and asked, 'May I have a dance with the most beautiful girl in the room?' His words made her knees buckle slightly. She inched closer towards him; her body ached for his touch. But then the hand of reality slapped her full-force across her cheek again.

'But what about your girlfriend, or is it your wife?' He could make out from her tone that she was fishing for some kind of answer or reassurance. He followed her line of sight; her eyes were firmly fixed on the stunning lady milking up the admiration of every man by the bar. 'Her... how old is she...? 32...? 33...?. 12?' The venom in her voice was obvious.

He laughed and shook his head. Amanda took offence; she didn't appreciate being made to look a fool by anyone, and she didn't care if he was the man of her dreams.

'What's so funny?' she asked; her words were bitter.

'You!' He rocked back in his chair, grinning

She searched again for her handbag. 'Well...I'm leaving.'

'No....wait.... you don't understand. That's not my girlfriend or my bloody wife. Me and my wife parted company a long time ago... thank God.' Amanda must have looked more confused. Jacob continued. 'That's my baby sister... Natalie... You must remember her... and by the way, she's 34... but she does act like a twelve year old from time to time.'

'Yes?' Amanda didn't mean the joy to be so evident in her voice. She stared up to the heavens and whispered 'Thank you God... I'll promise to come to church on Sunday.' She turned to Jacob and added 'Oh, young Natalie.... Well I'll be.... She's turned into the most beautiful lady.' Amanda could feel her heart come to life again. It floated up and found its rightful place back where it belonged; it was as if a large sun had appeared to spread sunshine over her gloom.

'I wouldn't say she's a lady,' he replied, 'but I've been told by many that she is quite pleasant to the eye.' He stood up and offered her his hand. 'Fancy a dance?'

'Of course I'll dance with the most handsome man in the world.' She rose immediately to her feet, cursing herself for saying that.

The first thing she noticed when they held each other tight on the dance floor was how nice he smelled. She couldn't identify the brand of cologne, but it oozed class and smelt so manly.

'Makes a difference from 'Hi Karate,'' she informed him after he told her what it was. She then told the story of how some shifty character that drove a lorry to France for a living had smuggled back a truck-load last year and sold it cheap around the clubs. Ever since that day, every male, of all ages, had smothered themselves in it. Even after Daryl had died, it took at least three months to get the pungent aroma out of her bathroom. She hated 'Hi Karate' more than football.

He laughed and held her tight. Amanda thought she had died and gone to heaven, especially when she witnessed her rival Suzanne 'You ain't no model now, fatty' Jackson, picking her bag up and leaving the disco, all alone. But she immediately suffered a pang of guilt.

'What a pity' Amanda felt sorry for the poor woman as she trundled out, obviously upset. She knew she shouldn't have cared less about her, but she wasn't made like that. She promised herself that she would phone Suzanne 'I'm looking for a friend' Jackson in the future and take her out for a meal or something.

Meanwhile, Jacob pulled her in closer. His strong hands moulded to her body. She tingled underneath her skin, a thousand nerve endings exploded, reminiscent of fireworks on a cold, November night. She cursed herself for wanting him so much. She didn't know if this was a normal reaction to all the mad things that had rebounded around her life over the past few months. She tried hard to stop her lower-regions from grinding themselves into his groin area. Her sex organs had suddenly found a reason for living; they were coming back to life.

It was then that she became conscious of the fact that she hadn't had sex, or love, or even an orgasm, in any way, shape or form since Daryl had jumped to his death. In fact, it was longer than that; she couldn't recall the last time her and Daryl had actually put in the effort for a serious bout of rumpy-pumpy. She thought his lack of sexual drive was due to the long hours he was spending in the foundry. More fool her! So, with everything that had gone on over the last few months, sex hadn't been high up on her list of things to do.

Jacob stroked the valley of her back. She bubbled inside like a bottle of pop, shaken, and, hopefully, soon to explode. Her feet floated on jets of invisible air on the wooden tiled floor of the assembly hall. Her heart melted as his breath left a warm trail on the hairs at the back of her neck.

'And now, everyone's favourite,' the DJ interrupted. 'It's Hot Chocolate with *'So you win again.'* He lowered the lights; his work for the night was nearly done.

Their bodies smooched for several more slow tunes, until the disc jockey got restless and decided to release upon the group his extensive collection of party songs which included the stupid song where everyone in white trousers, or whiter skirts, clambered onto the dirty floor and pretended to row like slaves in a galley.

'Who the hell came up with this routine?' she unwittingly spoke aloud.

'Beats me… but do you fancy having a go or getting a drink?' he whispered into her ear.

'A drink please… I'll have a strawberry milkshake,' she wistfully replied.

He stepped back, confused.

'Only joking,' she laughed. 'School always reminds me of strawberry milkshakes. I only have to see someone in a school tie and my taste buds start to drool.' She regretted saying that as soon as it escaped from her mouth.

'Yeah… I know what you mean…. I think!'

They headed in search of a drink. Jacob introduced Amanda to his sister. Amanda was so glad the girl was his flesh and blood, because she was unbelievably gorgeous, and also very pleasant; all the things she never wanted a beautiful woman to be. It was bad enough that these types of women were so stunningly stunning without having the bloody cheek to be nice to talk too as well. That was just so unfair.

She and Lois had often discussed the issue of the virtues of beautiful women until they were blue in the face. Lois always claimed that really pretty girls had the looks, but no personality; none at all. It was a proven fact. While, at the other end of the spectrum, fat, lumpy girls had no sex appeal, but came top in the personality stakes.

Amanda had thought long and hard over this, and one day phoned her mate and asked. 'Ok, clever clogs… what happens if the fat girl with the great personality suddenly goes on a mega diet and becomes thin and gorgeous?'

There was silence on the other end of the receiver. Amanda was chuffed. She had finally beaten her best mate in one of life's conundrums. But Lois wasn't giving up that simply. She replied 'That's easy. If they do get slim, the only way to ensure they don't pile back on the pounds is if they trade in their brain for a slim body… It's like doing a deal with the devil… same goes for men with big C.O.C.K.S. they always got small brains. Oh, and they will also be left with hideous stretch marks so they can never wear anything skimpy.'

At the time, Amanda had thought that Lois had made her point quite well, but now there appeared to be a big glitch in Lois' observation in the shape of Jacob's lovely sister. Amanda couldn't wait to show how nice this beautiful girl was to her pal, but, on second thoughts, she decided that the further Lois was away from him or his family the better.

Over the loud blast of the music Jacob suggested to Amanda it would be a laugh to wander around the old corridors exploring their past, stirring up ghosts of the 'class of 81,' and all that stuff. She mischievously agreed. They set off, drinks in hand; two naughty grown up school kids, bunking off lessons.

After a short while, they found themselves in the large sports hall. The light from the street lamps outside illuminated the musty smelling room. The contrast between black and white gave the hall an eerie feel, as shadows bounced off the wooden climbing frame equipment and crawled up the walls. The apparatus had been set up ready for the first session on Monday morning. The smell of sweaty boy's armpits hung heavy.

They strolled around. An awkward lull crept into their conversation. Finally Jacob spoke, 'How are you feeling now?'

'To be truthful, I'm feeling a little drunk,' she admitted, giggling unashamedly to herself, eyes wide open.

'No.' He stared deep into her eyes. 'Not at this moment… with your life in general… you know after

Daryl's…hum…passing away.' His original accent sliced through parts of his South African dialect.

For once in her life she was careful to choose her words. She thought about what she was about to say before spouting the words out in one mass lump. She didn't want to appear the hard-nosed, widow-type who had already forgotten about her poor husband, as though he was a wilting flower placed in the bin; but on the other hand, she didn't wish to give off a signal that she was going to spend the rest of her days grieving. She looked to get the balance right in her reply.

'I'm taking each day as it comes; I'm getting over it slowly.' She lowered her eyes to the floor.

'Hope I don't appear to be forward,' he said, 'but you look beautiful tonight… simply wonderful. Have you done something different with your hair?'

It was now Amanda's turn to back away. She instantly thought that Lois had purposely gone out of her way to mentioned to Jacob about her all over body transformation.

'I'll kill her if she has,' she told herself inwardly. Outwardly, she stuttered 'No… not really… have you spoken to Lois tonight?'

He shook his head, reassuring her that he hadn't quite had the pleasure yet and he wasn't sure if he was looking forward to it. She breathed a sigh of relief. He took the half-empty glass out of her hand, and balanced it on a set of climbing bars. She didn't know what to do with her hands, but she knew exactly what she wanted him to do with his. Nine months of pent-up frustration, stress, and every emotion under the sun, was waiting to explode through the pores of her skin.

He stepped a little closer. Her face was less than six-inches from his rugged features. Her breathing became more pronounced, her lips puckered up by themselves; her eyelids became heavier.

She felt peculiar all over. She was sure she was on the verge of having a stroke, or a seizure of some kind. 'That's all I need right now is to go into a spasm.' She had to concentrate hard as she pictured herself having a fit on the floor, spit rolling down her chin, her body convulsing violently.

She decided to make a move. Her hand touched his face, moving over his cheek to his lips. He kissed the tips of her fingers, his tongue gently flicked out on her skin. Electrical impulses raced randomly through every inch of her aching body as he placed his hands on either side of her face, his mouth moved closer to hers. Then suddenly, from out of the back store room, where all the sports equipment was kept, there came a low moaning noise. They immediately stopped what they were doing. Amanda held her breath.

The moaning turned into a deep growl and got louder and louder. Amanda knew straight away it was the sound made by a man. It appeared that whoever was making the noise wasn't in serious trouble. For all intents and purposes it was the sound of someone on the verge of climaxing, or maybe, in the intensity of a bad nightmare.

'Oh…oh….oh,' the words became faster, 'oh…yes…oh…yes yessssss.'

Amanda and Jacob were too stunned to utter a word. They held each other tightly, without actually realising what they were doing. They were cheek-to-cheek, staring at the room where the noise was coming from. It was as if they were cat burglars who had been disturbed whilst stealing the world's biggest diamond by some guard doing his hourly rounds in an art museum.

Then out of the store room appeared Headmaster Phillips, heading for the exit whilst hurriedly pulling up his trousers, re-buckling his belt and doing up his fly. He yelped as he caught the tip of his foreskin in the zip. He didn't notice the couple standing there as he rushed out, his cheeks flushed, sweat glistening on his forehead as the droplets caught the light from the street lamps. He proudly sniffed his fingers as he exited the room.

Amanda and Jacob started giggling. 'Well I never, what a dirty......' Amanda didn't actually finish her sentence. She stared in horror as Lois was next to emerge, rearranging her skirt, a wicked smile balancing menacingly on her face.

She also appeared not to see the pair, frozen like statues by the vaulting horse. She sauntered towards the door, but before she opened it to leave, she stopped to light a cigarette.

Without looking back she muttered cockily. 'Hey Amanda... I hope you and Jacob are not up to no good in there.... And, by the way, Jacob, did she tell you about her new hair style? Ask her about it. See you by the bar,' she cackled and closed the door behind her. They could still hear her sniggering all the way down the corridor.

Jacob was flustered; Amanda was deep scarlet with embarrassment. 'Fancy another drink?' he asked hesitantly, taking one step backwards.

They walked silently back to the assembly hall, both knowing the moment they nearly shared was now lost, but they both hoped that it wouldn't be forever.

For the rest of the night, Amanda and Jacob chatted about this, that and the other. She was relieved to finally find out that he was happily divorced after a tortuous eight-year marriage to a lady from Cape Town. He also explained that he intended to sell up his business and move back to his country of birth as soon as he could.

Sadly, he had to leave around midnight. She gave him her phone number. He promised to give her a ring as soon as possible.

The hall emptied. People exited into the wind and the rain, leaving behind a few more memories of the class of '81 or, in Lois's case, the headmaster of '69.

Amanda sat in the limo, waiting for Lois to come into sight, while trying to ignore the lusty glare from the driver. Amanda noticed he had put on a new shirt and had covered himself in 'Hi Karate.' She lowered the back windows.

'Where have you been to now?' she shouted at Lois as the girl dragged herself into the back of the car, straightening her dress.

'Just been paying my last respects to Mrs Price's piano,' Lois replied, before turning in one movement and telling the driver that she would give him a blow-job if he drove around the centre of town with the sun-roof open for a bit.

Chapter 5

Rock

As Amanda looked out over the promenade, she had forgotten just how tacky Blackpool Pleasure Beach actually was. It had been about twenty-five years since her and her family had travelled to the land of the Big Dipper. On that occasion, like most times when they had ventured this far North, it rained as if it was going out of fashion and her parents argued from the start of the vacation until it, thankfully, all came to an end, a week later. All-in-all, it had just been a typical British holiday, with a typical British family, in a typical British resort.

To be honest, as she glanced around at all the rows of bed and breakfast houses, she really struggled with the fundamental fact that someone had the damned cheek to name it a Pleasure Beach in the first place.

'Unpleasant stretch of waste-land with a few fairy lights,' she had reflected, would have been a much better description to sum the place up.

Across the main high street, bright-coloured light bulbs dangled on every man-made surface, waiting for the night to draw in so they could twinkle into life. It all added to the place's urban sick-appeal. The biggest thing, that instantly struck her, were the miles and miles of greasy fish and chip shops which conveniently catered for families of obese, blob-shaped people. The men waddling across the oil-stained sands in yellow and purple shell suits, the woman wearing t-shirts two sizes too small, were showing off their bloated, pierced stomachs at the front and their tattooed arse antlers at the back.

Whatever way she turned, there were overweight people fighting to shovel large amounts of food (which weighed nearly as much as them) into their mouths while trying desperately to keep their cheap 'Kiss me quick' hats from blowing away on the gale-force winds.

She knew that the United States of America was renowned for being the place full to the rafters with its fair share of fatties; the land of the lard-arse, the country built firmly on the greasy cholesterol burger. But, on reflection, it appeared that Britain and its public weren't far behind; in fact, it was definitely in silver-medal position, with most of the other western nations still a long, long, way behind in third. Her place of birth was now a country full of hungry hippos in acrylic nylon and cheap Hi-tech trainers.

Lois, Amanda and some of Lois's mates sat in the Tower Ballroom on a grey, damp Saturday afternoon, in the Las Vegas of the North. To anyone on the outside looking in, the gang looked like inmates from Alcatraz on a day's outing to Strangeways. They were all kitted-out in bright pink tee-shirts, with the words 'We are the Pussy Posse' printed on the back, with each girl's name across the front. Of course, Lois had designed them. She had come up with the slogan in less than a blink of an eyelash.

Lois had explicitly warned Amanda that she was on a personal mission to get the widow laid, and maybe drawn and quartered before the end of the weekend. She had given Amanda strict orders to start to relax and enjoy the great sights that Blackpool had to offer.

'Well, what great sights?' Amanda snapped back, looking out of the window at the windy street. A deck chair tumbled towards her, crashing into the window before continuing on its journey.

'Don't look out there. Look in here, there are lots of great sights,' Lois answered back, as she pointed to a young twenty-something boy who was walking past carrying a tray of drinks for his mates. 'I wouldn't mind sucking on his Blackpool rock for a bit.'

'Lois... you're disgusting.... But I like it!' Helen, one of her mates, indicated before chanting, 'OK then girls... lets have a game of 'Truth or Dare'.'

This worried Amanda. Helen was just as crazy as Lois. Earlier that day, while they sat in the bar of the hotel waiting for the rest to arrive, the girl had shared her famous tattoo with Amanda.

The example of skin-art, which was positioned on her shoulder blade, was a near life-size print of her late, husband's head. Unlike Amanda's dead husband, Helen's hubby had systematically drunk himself to death in between regular bouts of beating her black and blue and pissing the bed.

'Serves the bastard right,' Helen told her while sipping on a double helping of Rum and coke

'Good God! That must have hurt!' Amanda said, wincing at the thought of the needles piercing her skin.

'Not really.'

Amanda stared dumbfounded at the ink portrait that lined the woman's back. She was befuddled, not least because the face looked the spitting image of a cross between Eddie Munster and Ziggy Stardust after a bad night on the tiles, but also she just couldn't understand why, if her husband was that much of a bastard, go to all that bother and have him imprinted on her back, forever? It just didn't make sense.

'Let me explain,' Helen tried to comfort her with her logic. 'Since he died.... I've made sure that I've gone out of my way to hump all of his mates from the social club.... Doggy style.... Then I tell them all to cum over his fat ugly face... serves the prick right.... It makes me feel great.' Helen ordered another drink.

A poor family on the next table had accidentally heard her sick explanation, and were so repulsed that they immediately left the hotel in a rage, never to return.

Back in the tower lounge, Lois cried 'Yesssssss.... I love truth or dare. Bags me spinning the bottle first.' She emptied the remains of the Holston Pils bottle onto the floor and cleared up the beer-stained table in preparation for the game.

As the bottle revolved around with a mind of its own, Helen explained the rules of the game. 'Right... if the neck-thing of the bottle stops opposite a person, that person can choose anyone on the table to either ask them a saucy question or do a saucier dare.... Understand?'

'What's the forfeit if you don't do it?' Amanda asked nervously, knowing fully well that Lois' mind was already thinking up crazy things to get her victims to perform.

'Wait and see,' Helen smirked.

Amanda was feeling nervous. She held her breath as the bottle spun menacingly around. It eventually stopped and pointed directly at Helen.

'Great....' Helen smiled. 'I would like to ask you all one major question.'

'You can't ask us all one question... that's not in the rules'' a girl in a sparkling boob-tube and large, saggy breasts piped up.

'It's in my rules... so there. Right, starting from my left... I would like to know if you have ever swallowed a man's cum and more importantly, what did it taste like?'

Of course, as if by magic, Lois was first in the firing line. Without the slightest hint of hesitation, shame or regret, she spat out her reply to the rather personal information request. 'I've done it once, or twice,' she smirked. Everyone else tittered to themselves.

'Once or fucking twice... in the last two hours... you dirty bitch,' someone screamed out. It was followed by a blast of laughter from the rest of the girls.

'Well, Lois, have you or haven't you?' Helen demanded.

'Hey.... does a bear shit in the woods?' Lois asked sarcastically.

'Not if it's a polar bear' Amanda quietly whispered to herself rather than the rest of the group.

They all looked at her with pure disdain and not a hint of humour on their council estate faces.

'Be quiet, Amanda,' Lois said, annoyed. 'Your turn will come soon.' She continued to try to answer the question by adding, 'By the way, I think men taste magnificent... nectar from the Gods.... Honey from the bees. I wish they sold it in Asda in big jam-jars with a child-proof lid, next to the Nutella. They could call it Spunkella.'

Amanda thought she was going to be sick. Two thoughts sprang regretfully into her mind. Firstly, she pictured Lois spreading the gooey substance onto a slice of toast or a warm crumpet on a Sunday morning, while scanning the gossip columns of the News of the World.

But the second image was too disturbing to mull over, as she contemplated how a clever child would react if it had some how worked out how to prise open the jar and had gulp down the contents. The image in Amanda's mind near made her sick, but luckily she switched it over quickly and envisaged something else.

Sian, the woman next in line and who also had a formidable reputation as a man-eater, enlightened the gaggle of semi-drunk, horny females that she believed the taste of man's seed varied from bloke-to-bloke.

All of the women around the table stopped drinking and stared at the woman.

'And I should know'' she added, 'I've been doing it since I was fifteen. I swear. You can divide it into three categories. There's the 'no taste at all'…nuffin'… completely tasteless. Then there's the 'thick stuff with a strong hint of ready salted crisp flavour'.'

Some of the women started to nod their heads in approval. One or two even put their fingers on their chins resembling educated professors debating one of life's important topics.

'And the final one…' Sian made a face reminiscent of someone sucking on a sharp lemon 'The last one… tastes kinda sour…a bit like how detergent tastes. It brings water to your eyes and a burning sensation to the back of your throat.'

Lois offered her support. 'Exactly…I've always said so…. Haven't I?' She nudged Amanda's arm.

Amanda was lost for words. She wanted to ask Sian how the bloody hell she knew what detergent tasted like in the first place, never mind bloody semen. But she was too afraid of what her reply would be. She was looking for an excuse to get up and leave,

Lois shouted out to a waiter walking past. 'Hey gorgeous... two thick spurts of ready-salted please, and a bag of nuts.' The hilarity from the table caused other people to stare.

Amanda couldn't help but join in the merriment. Maybe it was the constant flow of weak beer, or the gang of mad, deranged misfits she was sitting with, but whatever it was, it was working. Tears of laughter started to roll down her cheeks, as she finally relaxed enough to enjoy the humour.

'So! What about you then, Amanda?' Helen asked. 'What tickles your taste buds?'

All the attention focused on her. She felt uneasy again. 'Well, to be truthful... I've only ever done it once, and that was by accident.'

'What do you mean by accident?' Helen asked, intrigued.

Lois jumped in before she had chance to answer. 'Never mind that... what do you mean you've only done it fuckin' once? And you call yourself a Catholic? I'm so disappointed,' Lois commented. Again, more girly hysterics filled their space. Someone spat beer over the top of the table, someone else followed suit.

Amanda gave her friend a cold stare, and then continued to fill in the gaps. 'Well, Daryl was drunk. I think we had been to a wedding or something... or was it my Aunt's sixtieth birthday party?'

'Amanda, I don't care if it was the Corpus fuckin' Christy parade lead by bloody Nelson Mandela... what the hell happened?' Helen had rejoined the interrogation with some purpose.

'Well he was enjoying it so much, and I must have been tipsy myself, because I didn't detect the warning signs. One minute I'm bobbing up and down thinking about making a couple of cheese and onion rolls, the next BANG.... I'm choking on the stuff... some of it even went up my nose.'

The rest of the girls were now rolling about like the aliens from the 'Smash' instant potato advert, arms swaying, legs wildly kicking up in the air.

Lois waited until the noise quietened down before shouting out, 'Can you make an insurance claim for that type of accident...? Maybe third party fire and accidental ejaculation. Or were you fully 'cum'prehensive.' Lois was on form. She may have been dragged up on a rough housing estate but she had a great sense of timing and humour. She loved to be the centre of attention when the subject was dirty and she had the invisible microphone. This was her stage and all the material was original.

'But what did it taste like then, when you had your little accident?' Helen interjected, trying to keep a straight face.

'I know this will sound stupid.' All the girls crowded in. 'It reminded me of chicken soup.'

'Chicken fuckin' soup.... Are you real?' Lois's voice was first out of the blocks. 'Most of my men's love-froth tasted like Dettol, and the only time you have done it....by accident.... and it tastes like chicken fuckin' soup.'

'Well he had some soup the night before. I read once in a magazine that a man can taste exactly like the food he's been eating.' Amanda looked smug with herself.

'What type of chicken soup?' a shy woman asked, before ducking back behind her glass of cider and black.

'What do you mean, Trisha?' Amanda batted the question back. All the girls' eyes focused on the poor girl, who now wished she hadn't said anything.

'Well...,' the girl was slow and deliberate in choosing her words, 'was it rich and creamy like Heinz soup, or watery and lifeless like that Tesco's own brand variety... there's a massive difference.'

The stares shifted back towards Amanda's side of the table. It was like some game of Suck & Tell felatio; table tennis of the dirty minds.

'Neither, really.' Amanda thought about it. 'It was more like those packets of weight-watchers cup-a-soup thingies.'

This was a cue that Lois needed to switch the spot light back to her. 'Cup-a-soup...? you are telling me that your dead husband's semen tasted like a weight watchers chicken flavoured cup-a-soup?'

'Yes.... guess so.' Amanda's face reddened. She wanted to sulk under the table.

Lois shook her head violently. 'And now you're bloody telling me. I love cup-a-soups, me... I would have been milking him like a cow in farmer Morgan's field if he was my husband... That reminds me... I'm starving.' She scanned the room licking her lips searching for a man to provide her with some fast food.

Helen waited for the din to die down and she took control of the game once again. 'Right,' she announced positively. 'Last roll of the bottle, then it's all back to the hotel to get our pulling gear on... and don't forget tonight's the night for an all out shag-attack... I don't want to see any gorgeous hunky men left standing.... I want them all limp by lights out.'

'We won't let you down, Sarge,' Lois jokingly replied, making a saluting-motion with her left hand.

The spinning bottle landed opposite Amanda. She took a few minutes before notifying Lois that she wanted her to go to the next table, which was occupied by a gang of boys, and flash her knickers at them.

'No problem.' The girl rose up immediately, pulled her pink G-string as far up her crack as was humanly possible without slicing herself in half, and she sauntered over towards the table.

'Hey... you lot... how about some of this?' she yelled, as she bent over to expose her derriere to the world.

One brave, ginger boy stood up and cried back 'Hey... not bad... but I need to get a fuckin' brown paper bag out of my car to put over your head first.' He led the chorus of laughter as his mates joined in. He sat back down to lap-up the adulation from the rest of the gang. He prided himself on his quick wittedness and slight of tongue. Other boys patted him on the back.

Lois waited for the wails of laughter to die down before launching into her own witty reply. 'Oy... you ginger minger... I've French-kissed better looking pigs than you.'

'Yeah... it was probably your fuckin' brother.... Or maybe your uncle with the one tooth!' He was, once again, fast on the draw. 'Who's plucking the banjo here?' He pretended to play an invisible instrument.

Amanda was impressed with the boys return serve. He may have looked like a nerd, but he was hitting Lois's returns back faster than Andre Agassi on Centre court. He grinned at Lois.

Sadly, his wide smile and choice words were all but defenceless, as a full pint of cider, thrown by the enraged woman, followed the end of his sentence.

At first the boy was too shocked to react or retaliate. Before he had a chance to gain his senses, Lois had stormed out of the pub. The bouncers marched over looking for an excuse to throw someone head-first out of the bar. This they duly did. Amanda and the rest of the Pussy Posse decided it was time to drink up and escape out of the emergency exit.

Time had moved on a couple of hours. It had been a quick shower back at the boarding house, and several attempts at dolling themselves up for the night ahead. The upper floor of the cramped guest house smelt like a hair lacquer factory that had had a nuclear explosion in one of its most potent chemicals tanks. It was so strong it discoloured the ceilings and killed the landlady's rare Norwegian Blue parrot. She wasn't pleased and had issued a last warning to the girls.

Two hours later the girls found themselves packed, 'sardines-in-a-can' style, in one of the seaside town's premier, and sweatiest, nightspots.

The club was full of amphetamine-fuelled males; all seeking out their one-and-only beautiful princess, for a night of incredible, mind-blowing sex, or at least, a quick blow-job behind the hot dog stand down by the pier.

On the other side of the coin were housewives who were slightly past their sell-by-date, desperately searching for some hunky Latin lovers, with looks like Ricky Martin, and, hopefully, were hung like Champion the Wonder-horse.

On the surface it should have been a match made in heaven. Except that, all the heavenly princesses on parade just happened to be hard-nosed assembly workers from a light bulb factory in Redcar, while most of the greasy Latin lovers were small time gangsters from Glasgow, kitted out in cheap Chino jeans, loafers with white socks and carrying flick-knives.

The music was so loud it hurt the ear drums with its constant, moronic rhythms. The drinks were watered-down and unlawfully expensive and the dance floor was the size of a glass coffee table in a dentist's waiting room with blinding strobe lights which should have carried a health warning.

Amanda and the girls sat at the back near the toilets. Unbelievably, they had been joined by the gang of lads from the pub earlier that day. To make matters more unreal, Lois was playing duelling-tongues at five paces with the ginger boy who she had soaked with the cider.

'Hope you've got that brown paper bag ready?' she had told him, while squeezing between his legs to check out his tackle. She probed his ear with her tongue. Lois never held grudges especially when there was the hope of some male action at the end of it.

Sadly, by a process of elimination and seating positions, Amanda found herself being chatted up by a twenty-three year old car mechanic named Matt, with oily skin, black finger nails and an extensive knowledge of the workings of combustion engines. He was as exciting as watching paint dry on a water tower.

The long night dragged itself about, until it was completely out-of-shape. It was purgatory for Amanda. She couldn't for the life of her understand how the hell she had let Lois talk her into taking the two boys back to their digs. So, whilst Amanda lay on the bed in her room, fully clothed, desperately trying to fend off Matt's advances, next door Lois had already passed third base and was on the verge of getting a home run. The ginger boy couldn't believe his luck, as he lay back watching Lois, the master, go to work on his pale, freckly body.

Meanwhile, Matt seemed to be on his own special mission to conquer the mountain called Amanda (and in extra fast time). He had changed from an ordinary Dr

Jekyll, who bored her to death about cars, to a sex-deprived Mr Hyde, octopus-type creature, with eight flailing hands that squeezed, pinched and tweaked her in all the wrong places.

'Come on,' he whispered in her ear. 'I've just popped a Viagra tablet... I'll be hard all night.'

Amanda really didn't want to be there, and she definitely didn't want to feel his hardness boring into her leg all night. There was no way in a million months of Sundays that she was going to succumb to the advances of a boy nearly half her age, who used expensive aftershave to disguise his cheap and meaningless conversation.

She was both angry and upset by her stupidity. She was annoyed at coming to Blackpool in the first place. She should have known it would end up in disaster. She had been friends with Lois long enough to realise that her mate would definitely pull some bloke while she would get dragged along for the bumpy ride.

She didn't want her first time since Daryl's death to be in a flea-ridden bed-sit with some car mechanic, who needed a bloody Viagra tablet to get aroused... and at the tender age of twenty-three.

'What the hell is the world coming to when a twenty-three year old stud needed a tablet to pass a sex test?' she asked herself. It wasn't like that in her day, but, to be truthful, Viagra wasn't around to tempt individuals. She had been out of the mating game for so long, perhaps the rules had changed; maybe the little blue pill was an essential accessory for a night of passion. The concept popped into her mind of a gang of Viagra-addicts meeting in some church hall to share sad tales of their experiences like some A.A. meeting. She imagined, one-by-one, nervous men standing up in the circle to spill the beans while sporting tented trousers of all shape and sizes.

She conceded that if she was going to make love with someone it was going to be on her terms, and with someone special. If she was to do it, she wanted it to be with someone other than the creep in her bedroom. If she was going to take the plunge she wanted it to be with Jacob. She didn't know why, but deep down she really wanted it to be him. She longed for the man of her schoolgirl dreams to take her in his strong arms and make love to her all night. There had been a vote of strict no confidence in her self esteem, after the 'husband knocking off the transvestite' episode had surfaced and she needed someone to give her that old loving feeling back. She needed to feel exclusive and wanted.

Back in the heat of the bedroom, she managed to release herself from Matt's sucker-like lips and came up for air. She made an excuse to go and use the bathroom. It had been quick thinking on her part, because the cheap guest house only had one toilet facility per floor, which was situated down the hallway. She escaped from his grasp, closed the bedroom door and stood shaking in the dark passageway.

She quivered as she tip-toed quietly towards the safety of the bathroom. She activated the switch for the hallway light. It didn't work. She suddenly became aware of how dark the corridor was. It scared her. Goosebumps crept up her arms. She felt uneasy, as though she was being watched. She glanced behind her, jerking her head around. The shadows were playing trick-or-treat with her mind. She hurried in to the tiny room, locking the door in one swift movement.

She hitched up her skirt, pulled down her panties and sat down exhausted on the plastic seat. She listened. She could make out the rhythmic sounds of what seemed like a hundred bed-springs being activated from behind the line of closed doors in the tiny boarding house.

'Everyone must have taken Helen's warning seriously,' she told herself. 'We'll shag them on the beaches.... We'll fuck them in the air.' She did her best Winston Churchill impression. 'Your country needs you, girls.'

It had all the ambience of the old Western days, where dusty, unwashed cowboys, in fake Calvin Klein boxers, rode into town to spend their hard-earned cash on whisky and the pleasures of the flesh in the form of tattooed women. She wished she could go home.

All of a sudden, her mind snapped back to the present, as the handle of the toilet door moved. Her heart missed several beats, her blood raced through her body at a hundred miles per hour. Someone was trying to get in.

'I'll be out in a minute,' she shouted to the faceless person on the other side of the door. She cursed as she thought that it was probably her young chaperone for the night, high on Viagra and with an animal glint in his eye.

'Look Matt... if that's you... I'm not interested... I'm not feeling well.'

There was silence. Then the door shook harder. Someone put their shoulder into it. She started to panic. She looked around for a window to escape out of. There wasn't one, only a sink, a tiny shower, and a noisy extraction-fan.

'Money grabbing bastards....what if there was a fire?' she grunted, looking about for something heavy to use as a weapon, if needed. She picked up the toilet brush but replaced it immediately when she saw the state of it. She nearly puked.

The door creaked and groaned under the pressure. Her mind started to do cartwheels in her skull. Perhaps it wasn't Matt; maybe it was someone with evil intentions, or even someone suffering from the runs.

She screamed out. But unfortunately for her, a second later, another girl in the throws of her third orgasm screamed out from one of the bedrooms. Amanda's plea for assistance was drowned out by the shrieks of passion.

So, no one came running; they all thought it was just someone getting their rocks off, reaching the point of no return. Lois heard it and was actually jealous. She sharply told her pathetic, ginger lover to pull his finger out, or put his finger in, or just bloody do something to get her going.

Then the handle sprang back to the horizontal position. The pushing ceased. It went quiet. She eavesdropped again, hearing a set of footsteps tottering away.

Amanda waited several minutes before building up enough courage to open the door and make a dash for it. The noise of bed-springs bouncing faster and faster engulfed the long corridor. She scanned the hallway, before bolting to her bedroom. Once inside, she quickly locked the door, her heart pounding in her chest.

She turned towards the bed to update Matt about the strange goings-on. For the second time she found herself letting go a scream, as she saw the young man laying unconscious on the bedroom floor; blood dripped from a deep wound on the top of his head.

She fled without thinking of the consequences which could be waiting for her in the shadows outside the room.

'Lois... Lois.' Amanda burst into her mate's bedroom. 'Quick... I think something is going on... I think someone's after me.' She stopped dead in her tracks.

Lois was lying on her back on the double bed; her hands were tied to the headboard with a pair of her stockings. She opened her eyes and grunted, 'You could have bloody well knocked before barging in... this useless bastard had almost worked out what he needed to do with his tongue, but I had to draw him a sketch of where it was first.' Lois nodded to a rough lipstick drawing of a woman's vagina, with an arrow pointing at the clitoris with the words 'lick here, you tosser,' scrawled on the mirror.

It was then that Amanda noticed the shape of a person way down at the other end of the bed, positioned between Lois's thighs. She could see his white socks sticking out of the edge of the bed clothes.

The boy clambered to the top of the bed, popping his head out of the sheets. He appeared like a hungry rat scurrying out of a drainpipe (but this was a five feet, eight inch rodent, with a mop of ginger hair and matching freckles.)

'Aarrrrrggghh,' shrieked Amanda on seeing his face.

'Hey... he's not that frightening,' Lois snapped at her mate, but then cried out herself on seeing the boys face.

'What's the matter? What the hells wrong?' The ginger boy sprang to his feet, looking around for a mirror. The boy knew he was no oil painting, but he felt that their reaction on seeing him was way over the top; even if they had both sobered up.

Amanda stared in disbelief at the boy, who was toddling around the bedroom in the nude, with a luminous condom still dangling off the end of his old boy.

'No... it's your face... it's, it's ...it's ... what's on it?' Amanda couldn't bring herself to say the words.

'It's what's on my face.... What do you mean...? So I've got a couple of spots.... everyone's got some... I'm only nineteen.' Now he was annoyed.

Lois piped up. 'You told me you were twenty-three.'
'Does it matter?'
'No... not really.' Lois winked at him.

He picked up a compact mirror. It took a full thirty seconds before he let out the mother of all earth shattering screams.

Again, copulating couples in other rooms didn't take any notice, and just continued to bang away.

The boy shouted at Lois, 'Where's all this fuckin' blood come from?' He was too confused and scared to move. He stood there as if cast in stone. His entire face was covered in a red substance; thick splodges matted his ginger hair and stringy-pieces dangled precariously from his nose and ears.

'Oh shit,' Lois said casually, while pulling her hands from her bindings and lighting up a fag. 'I must have had my period when you were messing around in the river... never mind... it could have been worse.'

'How could it have been any worse?' he shrieked frantically.

'Normally I've got more chunks in it than that.... You're lucky it's my first day.... Sometimes it's like a tin of tomatoes.'

'LOIS... there's no need for all the graphic details,' Amanda protested, her stomach churning up at the image painted for her.

The ginger boy changed colour from a milk-bottle white, to an Ash Wednesday grey, before he threw up all over the floor.

'Hey... fuck face, those are my new shoes... now, get out you ginger bastard.... and take your skiddy pants and size seven hush puppies with you.' Lois pushed him out of the room.

'Aarrrrrggghh,' an innocent girl in the hallway screamed on seeing the boy run past.

Amanda slumped on the bed next to her mate. Suddenly there was a banging and thumping on Lois' door.

'Who the fuck is that now?' Lois was stressed from the bad sex. She knew she had to have an orgasm soon, otherwise she would crack up.

'Don't answer it... it's the person who's after me.' Amanda spread her body against the door.

Lois shrugged her shoulders. 'What person?'

'Schhhh.... I'll tell you later,' whispered Amanda, placing her finger to her lips.

The knock grew louder and more impatient. Then the landlady yelled from the other side. 'Hey... you in there.... Do you know anything about an unconscious boy in room 17 and a stupid looking ginger fucker covered in blood, smelling of spew and wearing a bright lime-green dunky, who's just caused two old aged pensioners to have heart attacks?'

The two girls burst out laughing and hugged each other.

'Let's go home,' Amanda said.

Chapter 6

Ladder

It was exactly a week to the day since the fateful Blackpool experience. Amanda was still trying to get the bizarre event out of her mind. It had been nothing short of a nightmare in the end. Firstly, the landlady had called the police, after Lois had given her a few choice words. The cops had arrived all gung ho, sirens wailing, lights flashing and looking for answers without really understanding the questions. Their interrogation techniques were sharp and to the point. They wanted to know who had knocked out the young lad. Amanda later found out he had a criminal record as long as an express train for dealing in drugs. They found forty three Viagra tablets and a bottle of date-rape mixture in his jacket pocket. She considered herself lucky to have escaped the experience unscathed.

When the police confronted the boy, he couldn't remember a thing about the incident, except that someone had returned into the room as he lay on the bed, naked and with a chemical-induced erection. After that he informed the police he blanked out and had woken up covered in blood. He was interviewed for several hours then charged with possession of illegal substances, with intent to cause an erection.

The police also informed the girls that the ginger boy, with the blood stained face and luminous condom, had last been seen racing through the streets towards the motorway. He was still reported missing presumed hiding somewhere near Bolton.

Amanda wasn't sure if the strange goings on were connected to her, or if it was just a coincidence that someone was wandering around boarding houses in the seaside resort, randomly scaring the life out of people for kicks and knocking-out Viagra dealers. Maybe the mystery person was a superman hero figure protecting possible date rape victims? She moved the entire notion to a quieter part of her brain. It was already overloaded with other important stuff to worry about.

Since coming home, she and Lois hadn't been speaking. It had started the day after their return, when Lois had been pestering Amanda about going to a singles bar. She'd said no. She was still annoyed with being paired up with Matt. The girls had a massive slanging match about it, which saw Lois losing her cool and storming out, but not until she had screamed, 'Amanda if you ain't careful girl…. Your M.I.N.G.E. will heal, shrivel-up and then die.' She then marched down the street, her white shoes on fire.

Amanda was not taking her comments lying down; she opened the front door and shouted after her, 'Well, you have as much chance of yours shrivelling up as hell has of freezing over….. Devil woman!'

What had also upset Amanda was that when she had confided in her mate that she thought she was in love with Jacob, Lois had told her to grow up and act her age.

'Love? Just because you had a snog in the sports hall... you think you love him?' Lois gloated.

'What do you know about love...?. You only ever do sex.' Amanda shook her head.

'Same horse.... different jockey.' Lois' annoying quip infuriated Amanda. 'Anyway... I don't trust him.... Remember he slaughtered all his family.'

'He bloody didn't,' Amanda screamed at her. It was immediately after they had the disagreement.

Now it was Amanda who found herself all alone in bed wrapped up in a thick blanket to protect her from the cold. She was miserable. She was staring intently at her alarm clock which ticked on the bed-side cabinet. She wished, and not for the first time, that she had the power to slow down the hands of time, or even just rewind it a few years.

The minute-hand on the clock appeared to be on some kind of mechanical anabolic steroid. It did not so much as race towards the midnight hour; it galloped on all fours with its springs and cogs hanging out. The twelve-o-clock finishing line was not far off in the distance. In fact, it was less than a few minutes away. Normally the time didn't bother Amanda, but tonight hearing the bells striking twelve was very much different, because in less than three minutes Amanda's relative comfort and safety of a thirty-something lifestyle would suddenly find itself in the undesired and murky swamp known as her '40's.

'Life begins at forty,' her friends (who had just past that square on the Monopoly board of life without collecting £200) would tell her. Or another favourite was 'Forty is the new Thirty.' She knew that that was complete and utter bollocks, and her forty year old mates knew it too. Everyone knows that life really starts at about eighteen and climbs to its peak at about 33, or at best 35.

After that, it just slides very quickly down a steep mountain-side covered in stinging nettles, sharp rocks and brambles while gorgeous, young twenty-one year old model types, with fat-free waist-lines, no cellulite and cheekbones to die for, smirk slyly on the sidelines.

'So, if forty is the new thirty,' she wanted to scream back at the darkness, 'what happens when you reach fifty? Is that then the new forty, or even maybe thirty?' At this rate, she pictured eighty year-old grandmothers wearing boob-tubes and fish-net stockings, as they were wheeled into cubicles to empty their colostomy bags, while injecting large fixes of collagen into their lips before being taken by ambulance to all night discos. She wondered where it would all end.

With each tick of the clock she could sense she was about to change; a Doctor Jekyll turning into a twisted Miss Hideous, without the need for a make-up department. She could see thousands of invisible age-lines queuing up on top of the dressing table mirror, waiting to select a part of her face to burrow into without mercy. To her right, millions of grey hairs dressed as Zulus hung on top of her bed-post for the order to advance and kill all of what was left of her natural coloured hair. She knew her locks didn't stand a chance, her hair was weak and badly out of shape; as she examined the split ends, she wished she had used conditioner more often. It would be a massacre and her remaining natural hair didn't stand a chance. She assumed that the way it was going, by teatime she would have the appearance of her grandmother or worse, Jimmy Saville.

The physical pounding that her body was about to take from joining the over forties club would be nothing compared with the mental scaring that age carried with it.

She once recalled her mother saying to her, while she was getting ready to go to youth club, 'Hey, just remember young woman.... You will be old and forty some day.'

'Mam... I'm sixteen and have more important things to worry about.... I'm covered in acne, and Suzanne 'bloody long legs,' Jackson is so nice looking its sickening.' She answered her mother back, while pounding her face with cheap foundation to cover up her spots.

Looking back now, she wondered how the time could have flown by so quickly. Where had it all gone to? One day she was squeezing blackheads in the bathroom mirror, getting ready to go to the big school dance, then, within the blink of a false eyelash, she was staring down the barrel of a double chinned gun called 'Old Age.' It was terrifying.

In her head, she knew forty was way too grown-up and responsible age for her. She didn't want to be knocking on that door; she would always be eighteen; perhaps not in body, but definitely in her mind and spirit. She realised that this was an ambitious desire. She had come to accept that, as the years progressed, the pounds rolled on and her body had a habit of moving in mysterious ways. Bits that had once been firm and pert were dropping to the floor, while other bits sagged like a set of deformed bagpipes.

She had become powerless to resist. She was now unable to simply pop to the gym and tighten up the parts that needed tightening by doing a brisk thirty minutes on the tread mill, or follow a strict non-food week diet that would have normally firmed-up the bits that needed firming-up. Now the rules had changed. This was different. She was now fighting an unwinnable war against the most cruel and evil of enemies.

But at least people said she looked younger than her years. Well, everyone except Daryl's mother who would always shoot her modesty plane down in flames whenever she called. It made her think that maybe her friends were just being nice to her, patronising her, making her feel wanted, and it was her mother-in-law who was being honest.

The hour-hand stood perfectly erect on the face of the clock, and Amanda knew that was that.

Ok, so she was forty; it was no good trying to hide it or fight it. Even super-rich movie stars living in Beverley Hills with all the money to fend-off the Age Monster didn't stand a chance. Ok, the big Hollywood hotshots may slow it down a little with their nip and tuck operations or their lift, suck and silicone procedures, but, in the end, age always came out on top, usually winning by two submissions to nil. The only difference was that, due to plastic surgery, film stars often went from looking ridiculously young sixty-year-olds, to frighteningly monstrous eighty-year-olds in the time it takes to brew a pot of tea and make a banana sandwich. No one can wrestle with Old Father Time; he's just too slippery; too crafty; too streetwise.

She knew she was getting older when policemen patrolling the streets in unsightly tight trousers looked like college students, and college students looked like primary school kids. She didn't understand a word of what the so-called modern day Rap artists were singing about. Unforgivably, on more than one occasion she had found herself actually saying they were just big 'Thugs' wearing too much jewellery.

She had heard herself saying 'In my day, the pop stars played proper music and you could understand every word they sang.'

She conveniently forgot to remember all the crap groups from her generation that were terrible and couldn't play or sing a note. The last time she had said that line to her little cousin, Amanda had rushed to the bathroom to check that, as well as sounding like her own mother, she hadn't physically turned into the miserable old cow. It was a sobering moment.

What saddened her most on this night was that she had no-one to share with this new, and maybe exciting, phase of her life. Her biological clock was tick-tocking away and she was on a treadmill, going backwards into space. She felt as though she was always running away from the future. And today was a true measure of how much her life was a failure. Forty was a land-mark in people's lives. A land-mark that they hoped would see them living comfortably with their best years to come. As she had advanced towards it, she had made a list of which rung of the social ladder she would be on by that date. On that list she hadn't dreamed of scribbling off 'Still married.' This thought hadn't crossed her mind; even after the first couple of years, when the sex started to get boring and the highlight of the week was staying in on a Friday night, sharing a tin of Fray Bentos pie and new potatoes together. She'd always believed her marriage was indestructible.

What was on her 'Reaching Forty' list were more materialistic things, like living in a big house with a reasonable sized garden for her children. Also she would be financially secure; nothing too flash, but a big car on the drive, two holidays in the sun every year. Of course, she still wanted to appear half decent, and still have her own set of teeth. She couldn't recall the rest.

The reality was that she had found herself to be halfway through her life's journey to death and other than still having her own set of gnashers; the rest of her dreams and wishes had been buried along with Daryl. She had not only failed to climb the ladder, she had skidded down the largest, meanest, most colourful snake on the board of hard-knocks, and every time she had the opportunity to throw the dice again, she landed on the same reptile.

So today she had come to a turning-point on life's road. She could surrender and live in the shadows of her past for the rest of her life, or she could fight back. She could drive forward, or forever glance over her shoulder at what could have been. She always hated people who talked about the past.

'I could have been someone,' or 'I was an inch away from being famous,' people would explain to her. She refused to listen to them; they didn't deserve air-time.

She had always wanted to scream at those people and remind them that if they looked at themselves a little closer they would see that they were an inch away from being complete alcoholics and arseholes, or both. But she didn't. She was too polite. Sometimes she wished she was more like Lois; more open and honest but maybe a little less brutal around the edges.

She concluded that it was probably fight-back time. It would start in the morning; a healthy breakfast, a walk around the block and no alcohol all day. Well, maybe that was just too much of a drastic approach in one step. She reconsidered. She would definitely do the walking thing, she would have the healthy breakfast after she finished the pack of bacon she had just opened, and she would still have the odd drink. She needed one bloody vice in her now boring life.

She assumed she wasn't alone in this journey; there must have been hundreds of individuals entering the gate of middle-age at that precise moment; all shuffling towards the edge of their mortal coil cliff.

Her mood-swing somehow made her think of Jacob. She longed for him to be lying there, kissing and touching her. To be truthful, her thoughts were a little less romantic than she was letting on; she wished he was lying on top of her pumping away like a seesaw in the park. During second-helpings of her fantasy, she imagined lying on top of him, in complete control, working his engine to maximum revs, changing his gear stick, oiling her parts. She thought she had better stop bothering with Lois so much; she was even beginning to think dirty thoughts like her.

She was determined to change, determined to make a go of it, to do whatever it took to take life by the scruff of the neck and swing it around. It was time to swim against the tide of depression. The next time Jacob phoned she would tell him how she felt about him.

He had contacted her a few times since he had returned to South Africa. He informed her he was having trouble selling up, but promised he would be back to see her soon. She didn't know what to think. She wanted more of him, a lot more.

That very night Amanda drunk herself to the edge of reason and then cried herself to sleep. She awoke next morning with an almighty hangover and swimming in a river of sadness.

She eventually got up and slowly pottered around the house for most of the morning, continually checking that her body hadn't all-of-a-sudden started to deteriorate due to the ageing process.

At around ten her parents phoned to wish her well. Her mother had kindly reminded her that it was time she grew up and acted more sensibly, and at her age she shouldn't be going to places like Blackpool, especially with some trollops, and with her husband hardly cold in the ground. Amanda couldn't even be bothered to argue.

An hour later, the postman delivered three birthday cards. One was from her mad Aunty June, who never forgot anyone in the family's birthday or anniversary but always forgot the person's age and often name. Amanda read the message on her card, 'Hi Anne…. I can't believe you are 50…. Only yesterday I was changing your nappies…. Hope the rest of the family is fine…. bye…Aunty June'

The second card was from some of the girls from her office. They wished her all-the-best on her special day. They had all signed it, wishing her well and a speedy return. Amanda felt sadder by the minute.

The last card was large and padded; it was unsigned except for a large 'X' on the bottom. She convinced herself it was from Jacob. She checked the postmark, which was blurred. She kissed it and placed it lovingly on the table by the side of her bed. She couldn't wait to show it to Lois when she finally turned up.

'What a bitch…. I thought she would have been here by now.' She cried out. She became increasingly upset as the day moved on.

Nevertheless, Lois never showed up. Amanda waited and waited for her mate to arrive. She even phoned her, but there was no answer. She was annoyed and a little angry. They had often had tiffs before, but within an hour or two all was forgotten, especially if it was someone's birthday or a special occasion. It was a golden unwritten rule between the two friends. Amanda cursed her again.

'Well, that's it… I'll never speak to that slut again,' she told herself, as she glanced up and down the street from her window.

Below the surface, one half of Amanda believed that it was all part of a big set-up. At any moment she was half expecting to hear a loud knock on the door and loads of friends lined up waiting to enter with bottles of bubbly and cake to celebrate with her. And, of course, Lois would be at the front, smiling and cracking dirty jokes. It was Lois's master plan, even though Amanda pretended she wasn't interested in having a party for her birthday.

'I just want a quiet night by myself,' she had told her friend when she had asked her.

But, deep down, Amanda wanted the big party, the big cream cake (with a couple of candles), even jelly and ice cream. She desperately wanted the attention; she needed lots of hugs and kisses. She wanted something to help plug the void, to fill the emptiness which was missing in her life; someone to care. She was secretly reaching out for it, crying for it, especially on this of all days.

But all she'd received were three poxy cards and a lecture off her parents. She felt depressed again. She walked to the cemetery to say hello to Daryl. She missed him more than ever today. He may have had his faults, but he was good at making a fuss on birthdays, Valentine's days and all those times designed by large card manufacturing companies to squeeze every last drop of hard earned cash out of romantic, working class idiots.

She cried in the rain; she longed for a drink. She arrived home and decided to put off her exercise programme until tomorrow, or the day after that. Her mood clouded over like the weather; black and overcast, with little sign of changing. She cracked open a bottle of gin, and phoned for a take-away pizza.

'Bollocks to everyone,' she yelled, while cuddling up to her birthday cards.

Chapter 7

Bucket

Locked somewhere in a rather vivid dream, Lois was about to fall off the edge of a large cliff. Her persistent attempts to let out a scream had thankfully shaken her awake before her body hit the jagged rocks below.

Back in the land of the living, she found herself facing a plain, white, blank wall. Groggily she lifted herself onto her elbows and began to scan the small room where she'd surprisingly discovered herself. A single light bulb hung from the ceiling. A grubby, piss stained mattress lay on the bare floor in the corner. A red plastic bucket with no handle stood to attention in the middle of some kind of small cellar basement room. It smelled of damp.

Once fully alert, she staggered to her feet, shaking the cob-webs of drowsiness from her mind. At first she wasn't too concerned to be faced with these odd surroundings. Down the years, she had woken up in all manner of strange beds and weird rooms. From her vast experience it wasn't the places which were the thing to worry about. The apprehensive bit was finding out what bizarre creature was lying next to her.

She peeped about. At least this time she was alone. That was encouraging. Unlike a few weeks before, when she woke up to find her naked body clinging on to a man covered from head to foot in tattoos of animals and mermaids, and who had his deaf sheepdog sleeping at the edge of the bed. After that episode she swore she would quit drinking cider through a straw when going out in search of one night stands. Although the situation she now found herself in seemed a little better, there was something that just didn't feel quite right. For starters, she was fully clothed, which was odd to say the least.

The strange thing was she didn't have any recollection of how she had got there. In the gloom she spied a door. She walked to it. It was locked. The whole thing made no sense at all.

Had she got drunk again and picked someone up? She couldn't honestly remember.

Had she been date raped? She checked herself down below with her finger. There seemed to be no sign of tampering. If fact, she was still on her monthly cycle and the string of the Lillette was still dangling where safe.

'What the fuck is going on?' She paced the room.

She closed her eyes to see if this would help to throw some light onto her predicament. Finally, she started to have flashbacks. She remembered feeling a little guilty about rowing with Amanda, so she had decided to try and surprise her and organise a little bash for her with some of her mates. Her car had broken down, so she had stupidly walked across the estate to start to let people know and to plan the night out in the local pub. There would be no men and no strings attached; just some old friends getting rat-arsed and talking about old times.

'What had happened to her?' Lois bit her tongue lightly while she concentrated.

She was also going to try and find out a little more about Jacob by seeing if any old school pal had any information about him. There was something about him that didn't ring true. He was too perfect; too flawless. After that, she recalled going to the chippy up on the estate to get supper for her and her son. She had a sausage in batter, chips and curry sauce, and a chicken and mushroom pie and ten embassy regal king-size for the lazy sod. She then realised that maybe she was dropping down into a little too much detail as she tried to piece the jigsaw together. At this rate she'd be here until a year next Wednesday and still no closer to the solving the mystery.

The next step in her journey saw her waiting at the bus stop. It was drizzling and windy, as per bloody usual. She stepped into the unlit shelter to light up a fag. The breezeblock structure smelt of fifty-seven different varieties of urine, including cat, dog and human (and probably some other strange creatures that lurked about the tenement blocks after dark).

She remembered thinking that she wished she'd brought her car, even though the exhaust was hanging off. But she had decided against it because it would have been noisy and may have attracted the unwanted attention of the police, and she didn't need another court appearance at this time.

Back in the bus stop, she pictured herself pacing about trying to keep warm. At the same time in the cellar room she bounced around deep in thought. Suddenly her body stiffened as an image flashed back across her mind. She had a recollection of someone slithering into the bus stop and standing beside her. It was a man. He had the collar up on his trench coat and was wearing a hat. She had thought at the time that it was odd. He was dressed a bit like Humphrey Bogart in one of those black and white movies that she couldn't stand. He also had a funny smell about him, unusual; it tickled her nostrils even over the stench of piss.

After a few minutes he mumbled something about the weather and asked her the time of the next bus. She felt rather uneasy, which was unusual for her. She nervously puffed away on her cancer-stick, watching out for the vehicle's arrival in the distance.

She jumped momentarily as he dropped his carrier bag of groceries onto the pavement. Apples and cans of beans spilled out onto the dirty floor. The objects seemed to be trying to escape, making a mad dash for freedom. He began to pick them up. She felt sorry for thinking the worst of him; he was just an average run-of-the-mill creep who lived on the estate. It was a rough old, tough old town, so she was used to peculiar people wandering about. She smiled before bending down to help retrieve some of the lost items.

It was as she stretched to reach for the last granny smith apple, which had rolled into the storm drain, that her memory went blank. The next thing she recalled, she was waking up in this cellar room.

What was going on? In her mind she searched for the right key to unlock her question.

She banged on the door and shouted out. There was no response only stillness from the other side. She wondered what the hell was going on. Did she owe anyone any money? Did she owe the Pozzoni Brothers, the estates equivalent to the Kray twins (only nastier), any rent?

She didn't think so, and even if she did, they were more into knee-capping than kidnapping. Was it something to do with her drug-addict son? She'd kill the scruffy little bastard if it was. She was sick to death of bailing him out of sticky situations. Now this was the last straw; not only was she locked up, because of all this nonsense, she was also missing Coronation Street.

All of a sudden, a small light shone in from an aperture that had appeared in the door. It was the size of a letterbox, but was positioned up at eye level. Someone was staring at her through the flap.

'Hey you... where the hell am I, and why is the door locked?' she demanded to know as she stuck her face up tightly to the flap so she could eyeball whoever was on the other side.

The person shut the flap and shouted. 'You don't need to know that just yet.' He disguised his voice by wrapping it up in a fake Scottish accent. He didn't know why he did this; she didn't really know him anyway.

'Let me out of here right now... or I'll call the police.' She searched around for her mobile phone which was in her handbag. She couldn't locate either of the items.

'Is this what you are looking for?' He was starting to enjoy his new Scottish identify. He imagined he was Billy Connelly on stage at the London Palladium. He threaded the remains of the smashed up phone through the flap; the remnants of the electronic device rained onto the floor.

'Hey, wanker,' she hissed at him. 'What the hell is going on?' For a split second an image flashed into her minds eye. She had a hunch who was on the other side of the big heavy door. She decided to go straight for the jugular.

'Desmond... is that you?' She wasn't fooled by the bloke's pitiful foreign accent. 'It's you...isn't it?'

There was no reply. She could hear him breathing on the other side. Then her mind flashed a more disturbing thought. It was a scene from the film 'The Silence of the Lambs,' where the mad killer had imprisoned his victim in a hole in the ground.

'Hey, freak... you'd better not try to skin me,' she growled after finishing her sentence.

There was a brief pause before the person replied, 'Why would I want to skin you?' He wasn't a big film buff and rarely watched television. He made a face as though someone had farted in a lift and got out on the next floor, leaving him to take the blame.

'Don't tell me you are not out there at this moment skinning dead women to make a girl suit for you to wear down the shops or when you go to bingo. You're a freak.'

The person didn't know what she was talking about. 'Shut, shut up... or I WILL skin you,' he commented frustratedly, his fake accent had been replaced with that of local anxiety.

She immediately stopped talking. She assumed that what with Daryl's death and all the stress of the funeral, Desmond had turned completely bonkers. She wondered how to turn the situation around. She wished she had gone to 'Dealing with disturbed people' classes now, instead of 'A Beginners Guide to Body Language' lessons.

She needed to be patient but, unfortunately, patience wasn't a virtue within Lois's make-up. She went straight to plan F without thinking about any danger.

'Ok... Ok,' she pleaded. 'I need to go to the toilet... please can you let me out to do that?'

'Bucket... use bucket.' He slammed the letter box shut and bolted it.

She was left in semi-darkness once again. 'But I need to have a S. H. I. T.' she spelt out the words to save them both embarrassment.

Several minutes later the flap opened again. The person threw some toilet paper and an air freshener into the room, then added 'You may need this!'

Darkness engulfed the room for the second time.

Chapter 8

Box

Amanda was woken up from her afternoon knap by someone knocking violently on her front door. She immediately thought of Lois as she clambered off the settee and rushed to let her in. Alas, when she opened it, she was wrong. Instead of Lois, it was her son, Ramone. He looked agitated and shuffled from leg to leg whilst chewing on a stick of gum. She let him in.

'Oh, your mother?' Amanda went to answer his question regarding her possible whereabouts. 'That slag is probably camped out in some crummy hotel room, performing 28 different kinky sex positions with the cast of Wacky Racers,' She really wanted to tell him, as he sat looking vacant on the chair in her living room. But she resisted giving her true opinion of his mother's possible movements; so as a substitute she went for the more 'concerned friend' approach. Amanda actually found herself saying 'She'll turn up soon… don't worry… you know what she's like!'

In a rather 'spaced out junkie' sort of way, he was quite upset and a little concerned about the disappearance of his mother.

'But she's never been gone for this long.' He was nervous. He hadn't had his morning fix and was trying to cope with life in the straight world for the first time in a while. 'I don't know… it's not like her to leave her fags behind and her favourite white shoes.'

'She left without her stilettos?' Now it was Amanda's turn to worry. Lois never went anywhere, especially on a date, without her 'lucky' shoes. Something didn't feel right; butterflies flapped around in the pit of her stomach.

'I think it's got something to do with that bloke who was shafting your old man.' Ramone didn't mince his words; they tumbled out of his mouth like meat spewing out of a sausage machine.

'Who? Desmond? Why would you think Desmond's got anything to do with it?'

'I heard he's been following you about…. And I've been told he's made threats to you,' the boy spoke more confidently and concisely this time.

Amanda passed the boy a mug of tea. 'Don't be so silly.'

'Well, I'm going around to the freak's house to find out what he knows… face-to-lipstick-face.' The youth rose out of his chair.

Amanda noticed how frail the boy's frame was. He wouldn't have looked out of place in a concentration camp. He was all skin and bones, held together by miles of scabs.

They were interrupted by a loud knock on the front door. They both turned towards the direction of the sound. Amanda spoke first, 'See…. that's probably her now,' she reassured him.

She rushed to the door, swinging it open in one movement, fully expecting to see Lois standing there, looking completely shagged-out and puffing on an Embassy Regal. Once more she was proved wrong. Actually, there was no one at the door at all. Amanda looked up and down the street several times. The pavements were empty; a taxi cab, looking for a fare, slowed down before sailing past.

It wasn't her day for predicting visitors. She shook her head, and then she saw the parcel resting on the doorstep, resembling a sorrowful puppy-dog trying to come in from the cold.

'Is it my Ma?' Ramone shouted out from the other room, while expertly pocketing a tenner from Amanda's purse. Now that his regular source of drug money had disappeared, he had to fend for himself. It wasn't that he was bad; it was just that his body was in need of repair and he convinced himself that he would pay her back later.

'No... it's a package.' She bent down to retrieve it. It was the size of a shoe box, covered in Christmas wrapping paper, with her name written in biro on the top. It wasn't heavy. She shook it, something rattled inside. She noticed it didn't have a post mark.

'That's strange...someone must have hand-delivered it and run off,' she talked to herself as she entered the kitchen, wondering if it was a belated birthday present.

Ramone wandered in to find out what was happening.

'Who was it then?' he asked, casing up the room for small objects he could possibly whip. He was starting to feel desperate. His entire body ached as if it was a giant rotten tooth that needed extracting. His veins required a hit of evil, and quickly.

'It was no one.... But someone left this.' Amanda realised her sentence didn't really make sense, but that was the way it was.

'What is it?' It was starting to feel like question time with Ramone the Junkie in the chair.

'It's a parcel,' Amanda was quick to point out.

'I know it's a bloody parcel... but what's inside?' he snapped, his body shook.

'Should I open it?' she asked. He nodded his head impatiently.

She took the scissors from the drawer and cut the Sellotape which bound it tight. Once undone, the wrapping paper fell away quite effortlessly. She slowly lifted the lid. She reached inside, and picked up an object. It was only when the image of the article in front of her had time to register with her brain, did she let go of it, and gave out a discordant whine followed closely by a louder scream. .

'Oh my God...' Ramone was the first to speak. 'Is that what I think it is?'

Amanda was too stunned to respond. She dropped the item onto the table and ran to the tap to wash her hands. She was transfixed by the thing lying on the kitchen work surface. Ramone reached down and slowly picked it up.

'It is you know.... Bloooooody hell.... I can't believe it. Someone's sent you a cock in the post.' The boy offered it up to the woman.

'Get it away... Get it away,' Amanda shrieked. 'Is it real?'

'Yep.... Think so. But don't worry.... It doesn't appear to work anymore.' He slapped it on the table top. It made a heavy thudding noise.

'Throw it away. Put it in the bin.' Amanda was covered from head to toe in goose-bumps.

The boy did what he was told to do. They then simultaneously stared back at the shoe box sitting there on the wooden table next to the mug.

'Was there any thing else in there?' the boy asked, moving closer.

'I... I... I think so.' Amanda backed away, leaning on the fridge for support.

'It wasn't his balls was it?' Ramone was actually being serious.

Amanda stared at the boy. 'Please have a look'' she requested.

The boy placed his hands on the box and rotated it over in one sharp movement. After what seemed like a lifetime of waiting, out fell a set of Chinese love-eggs. They clattered on the table top and automatically switched themselves on. They danced around like a bare-footed man on a hotplate.

'Arrgggghhh.... It is someone's ball,' he joked, while picking them up. Then his face changed...... 'Hang on... those are my mothers,' Ramone cried out, puzzlement spread across his thin, drawn face.

'What do you mean, they're your mothers?' Amanda was more shocked by his intimate knowledge of his mother's copious collection of sex toys than his observation.

'Those are my Mother's love eggs.... I'm telling you.'

'How can you tell they are hers?' Amanda was very curious to understand how he was so adamant about it. 'Love eggs are love eggs...ain't they?'

'Because she tipexed her name on the left one... in case she ever lost them.' He pointed it out to Amanda.

'Oh.... I see,' the woman replied. She didn't want to even think about where Lois would use them to actually lose them.

Ramone then developed a slightly more aggressive tone. 'Hey…. So what the hell are my mother's favourite love eggs and a dead cock doing in a fuckin' shoe box in your kitchen?' He may have been a drug addict, but his question was a good one, even though the subject matter was extremely bizarre and shouldn't ever have had the opportunity to be said.

Amanda really didn't know the answer to it and muttered, 'I don't fuckin' know…maybe someone's playing a practical joke on us.' Amanda turned to make sure someone wasn't peeking at them through the window holding a portable video camera. 'Ok maybe someone's delivered it to the wrong address.' That logic sounded worse than the first.

'Yeah, and maybe my names Tonto and I live in a fuckin' banana tree with my Uncle Sidney who is really my Aunt Basil,' his words spat out viciously from his mouth. He gawked at her, his eyes sunken in his gaunt face.

The conversation was getting too wacky for Amanda. She went for safe ground. 'Shall I call the police?'

'And tell them what?' He began to shake, partially due to the strange events and partly the need for drugs to feed his veins.

'Ok, let's go and see Desmond,' she said, reaching for her coat and stuffing a kitchen knife into her pocket.

The darkness was just arriving as Amanda and Lois's stressed-out son entered the red iron gate that led to the transvestite's house. Ramone was angry. He mumbled to himself constantly throughout the short journey across the estate. When they arrived he bounded straight up to the door and rapped hard with his knuckles. The sound echoed around the house. It was met by nothing but silence.

'Let's go,' Amanda whispered, realising that whatever happened someone would probably end up in tears, and the way her life was going that someone would probably be her. 'Let's just phone the cops and leave them deal with it.'

'No way... and any road I can't... I broke my probation last week and they have a warrant out for my arrest. I'm not supposed to be out after dark, especially after the incident with the chemist shop.'

Amanda didn't really want to know. She spoke up, 'Ok, but let's take a quick look around the back and if we see anything.... we'll go back home and decide what to do.' Amanda was feeling nervous. She held on firmly to the junkies hand as they tip-toed towards the side of the house.

Amanda stared through a window. The house was eerie in its inactivity. Ramone tried the kitchen door but it was locked.

'What shall we do now?'

'Well, I'll just have to unlock it.' And without hesitation the youth elbowed the small pane of glass positioned in the frame. It smashed into a hundred pieces. He reached in and unlocked the door. Amanda knew from his actions that it wasn't the first time he had done something like that. She remembered the 'Black Dress' robbery.

Once inside, the entire house smelled stale. Although the basic design of the house was the same as the rest of the structures in the estate, including Amanda's, it had the appearance of belonging to a completely different era. It reminded Amanda of how her late grandmother's house smelled and looked. It was lined with dark oak wooden panelling, and little animal ornaments filled up every nook and cranny.

She stepped lightly. Her heart pounded in her chest, her knees knocked, her legs struggled to carry her. She knew she was making a big mistake, but she needed to find out what the hell was going on. Things over the last couple of months were going from bad to worse without taking a spell out for a breather. It was time to face up to it and hopefully get some normality back in her life.

Ramone opened a drawer and rummaged inside before slipping a small silver ashtray into his denim jacket pocket.

'Hey Ramone! What are you up to?' she hissed quietly, bread knife clutched in the palm of her sweaty hand.

The boy stuttered before adding 'It may be evidence.' She knew he was lying, but she had reached the point where she didn't really care anymore.

She made her way to the hallway and inched herself towards the living room door. Every sound seemed to be magnified a thousand times. The large grandfather clock by the front door ticked without tocking. Suddenly it stopped all together. This was getting too spooky for words.

Of course, the door leading to the living room creaked as if it had been deliberately designed and engineered by Alfred Hitchcock himself. Amanda looked carefully around the door before stepping inside. Once inside the room, she noticed a large pink nightdress draped over a chair by the empty fireplace. More cheap porcelain figures decorated the shelves. On the wall a large portrait of Liberace rested above the mantelpiece. It was so unreal it made her laugh uncontrollably, until, on closer inspection, she saw a photograph of Desmond and Daryl next to it. It made her feel sick.

'Amanda.... Amanda,' Ramone muttered from upstairs. 'You'd better come and have a look at this.'

For some reason his words made her skin crawl. She began to slowly climb the stairs. 'What is it?' she murmured.

'You'd better take a look for yourself.' He was backing away from the door that led into the spare room.

The smell from the back room was unbearable. It hurt Amanda's nose. She ambled inside. The sight that greeted her didn't register for several moments, but once it did it hit her like someone had smashed her around the head with a baseball bat spiked with nine-inch nails.

Her mouth dropped. There, lying on top of the bed clothes in jeans and an Abba tee-shirt were the remains of a skeleton. On the wall behind the dead body hundreds of Polaroid photographs were sellotaped in neat rows across the wallpaper.

She knew she should have run, but her legs had seized up. She thought about screaming, but her throat was dry. Instead, she walked nearer to stare at the images in the photographs. They showed Desmond dressed up and snuggling up to the remains of the person. It took Amanda several snap-shots until she finally realised that the decomposed stiff in the photographs was, in fact, her late husband Daryl. All within the space of three feet, the picture before them painted a sickening tale of obsession gone mad. One of the last snaps even showed Desmond and the skeleton having Sunday tea out on the lawn, a highchair with a doll was positioned by their side. Under the photo was written the words 'Happy family.'

She was too upset to cry, too numb to move. She looked at Ramone; he shrugged his shoulders.

'This is fuckin' madness.... Is that your... your husband?' he muttered slowly, his eyes transfixed to the body. This was freakier than any acid trip he had ever been on in his life.

She stiffened again as a noise rose up from one of the bedrooms behind them. It was all too much for Ramone to take in. He fainted, landing on the floor with a crash.

'You can never trust a bloody man,' Amanda said to no one in particular.

She cautiously stepped down the long hallway. Her mind was still confused about what she had just seen. She could not begin to consider what else she would witness before the day was through. She gripped the knife tightly. Again another door creaked open. She peeked inside the master bedroom.

She automatically dropped the blade and backed away, bumping into the wall. There, lying on the carpeted floor, dressed in a nightgown covered in urine, was Desmond's mother. She appeared to be half starved and covered in her own mess.

'Hello love,' the woman's voice was strangely subdued. 'You couldn't pass me the bloody pile cream from out of the top drawer, could you? My haemorrhoids are the size of blood oranges.'

Amanda found herself joining Ramone in the land of the fainthearted.

Chapter 9

Print

The latest, unbelievable, episode in Amanda's life had, not surprisingly, made national news. It was the main headline across the entire country, even outstripping the government's latest sex scandal, for air time and coverage.

'Well, it's not everyday someone finds the body of their dead husband in the spare bedroom of his transvestite lover,' the young detective at the police station had passed the flippant comment, while handing Amanda a blanket and a strong mug of Bolivia. 'Especially in a….. Marc Bolan tee-shirt.'

'He was wearing an Abba tee-shirt actually… not a Marc Bolan one,' Amanda's voice was quiet but clear.

The man started to check his notes. 'Are you sure?'

'Positive…. It had 'Dancing Queen' written on the bottom of it.' She was surprisingly calm, considering the environment in which she found herself.

'It says here it was definitely Marc Bolan.' He made a note on the page and stared at the two-way mirror, where a gang of other detectives were positioned, analysing the woman's every move. They were checking her in case she knew more than she was letting on. They all checked their handouts.

Since the gruesome discovery on the estate there had been no sign of Desmond. The police concluded he must have fled and was hiding-out somewhere. Desmond was a wanted man (or a wanted woman.) To be truthful, no-one in the press could decide how they should report the incident. It was the day of political correctness spiralling out of control. His (or hers) posters were plastered on every television news channel. The images showed him (and her) in two very contrasting guises. The first shot showed him as a male and was the only photograph of Desmond when he had first started in the steel mill. He looked quite manly in his dark blue overalls, hard hat and safety glasses.

The second picture had been taken last summer when Desmond had been the winner of the 'Best Cup Cakes' competition at the local fete and gala. In this photo, he, (or she), wore a long blonde wig and glasses. The newscaster warned the general public not to approach the man (or woman) if they saw him (or her) because he (or she) was armed and extremely dangerous.

Back in the cold interviewing room at the police station, the unfeeling copper continued, 'Did you realise that Desmond was planning to take your husband on a two week holiday to Disneyland, Paris? We found two plane tickets and park passes in the lunatic's kitchen drawer.'

Amanda was too distressed to ask the stupid copper two basic questions. One was; 'How the hell was Desmond going to smuggle a corpse through customs in the first place?' and the second was, more importantly, 'How was he going to get them both onto the rides in the amusement park?' Instead, her scrambled mind instantaneously pictured Desmond and the skeleton happily riding on Space Mountain. She grimaced as she pictured Desmond buying the Disney photograph showing them both merrily going down the waterslides, waving their hands in the air.

'Am I going mad?' she posed herself the question.

It was then that Amanda realised she was on the verge of a nervous breakdown. Since she had discovered the gruesome findings, she had been interviewed, and then re-interviewed by dozens of different police officials, of various ranks and grades. They had all asked the same questions, made the same faces, written some stuff down in a big red file marked 'Secret,' and then left. Exactly ninety seconds after each session a smiling policewoman would enter carrying a mug of hot tea and a packet of Jaffa Cakes. Unluckily for her, Ramone hadn't been seen since to confirm her story.

The detective informed her that there hadn't been a positive ID concerning the rogue penis which had been sent to her in the mail. The copper had added, 'Well, it is definitely not your husbands. The item under examination was only two or three days old.'

He made it sound as if it was a stale loaf of bread, not someone's detached organ.

'But whose is it?' Amanda finally asked, emptying her mind.

'We are not sure,' he replied, 'but we have sent for assistance from MI5. Apparently they have designed a device that may help.' Amanda shrugged her shoulders, wanting some more details about it. He added, 'It works in a similar way to finger printing.'

'What do you mean? Are they going to finger print the....,' she lowered her voice, '....finger print it?'

'What?'

'The C.O.C.K... .' She sounded more like Lois spelling out the rude word.

'Well, technically… yes,' he hesitated, 'but it's not actually called finger printing…. That would sound stupid.'

Amanda thought for a minute then said, 'Don't tell me it's named Penis Printing, is it?' She felt like screaming. This was not lost on the policemen behind the screen. They scribbled on pieces of paper and nodded towards each other. They thought this maybe a clue.

The young detective was becoming agitated. 'No… we don't actually dip someone's penis in ink and roll it across a piece of paper…. That would be silly.'

In fact, that was exactly what happened.

'Well, how does it work?'

'I'm not sure.' He started to sweat; perspiration soaked the armpits of his shirt. 'I only got this job last week. I came from traffic control and to be honest this is my first real murder mystery…. case…. sorry… My first murder and dead-body snatching kidnap case.'

Amanda stiffened in her seat. She hadn't even thought about murder. 'How do you know it's a murder?' Her words stuttered from her open mouth.

'It's bound to be murder…. A cock in the post…. Dead bodies…. Well it ain't suicide, is it?'

The coppers behind the glass giggled amongst themselves. They couldn't help but be thoroughly impressed by PC Edwards professional reply.

Amanda asked again, 'But why?'

'It adds up…. Sounds like a religious thing to me…. A sign.'

'A sign? A sign of what for Christ's sake?' she was unintentionally playing along.

He changed the subject back to their original discussion. 'Anyway…. the finger-printing device is used to catch serial rapists; the bastards who cunningly wear gloves. Rapists are very smart these days, you know!'

Amanda stared at him straight in the eyes and slowly asked, 'What if the rapist cunningly uses…… a condom?'

The copper was confused. He hadn't thought of that. He wrote it down in the big file. He stood up and before he left he muttered, 'Well, if your husband hadn't started playing away from home in the first place…. all this mess wouldn't have happened.' He swung open the door and slammed it as he stormed out. The observing policemen behind the screen scratched their heads all at the same time. Within a minute, a smiling policewoman entered with a tray, a mug of tea and a Jaffa Cake.

After the police had completed all their tests on Daryl's decomposed body, Amanda was faced with the rigmarole of burying her husband for the second time in less than a year. Of course, the second funeral had been a quieter and more secret affair. She didn't want the world's press turning it into a media circus.

At the graveside service were herself, the priest, a few bearers, three policemen and a carpenter, whose job it was to ensure the coffin was securely locked. To be on the safe side, the craftsman had added extra locks and several bolts around the perimeter of the coffin lid, just in case.

'Fuckin' Houdini wouldn't get out of that,' the tradesman muttered out loud to himself on finishing. 'Oh, sorry father…. I didn't see you there.' He apologised to the priest who he hadn't seen leaning on a headstone smoking a nip.

'Well, it's not him getting out that is the problem… its odd perverts trying to get in,' the priest joked. 'Oh, sorry

Amanda... I didn't see you there.' Amanda nodded solemnly. She didn't have any tears left to cry.

'It's just that we wouldn't want to have to bury him for a third time, now, would we? That would really be bad luck,' the priest whispered to Amanda, as the last nail was hammered into the casket, on a surprisingly bright afternoon.

'More like weather for a wedding, than a funeral,' someone piped up, as the council workers hurriedly filled in the hole.

Amanda said her last goodbyes and headed home.

Out of storm clouds sometimes appears a silver cloud across the horizon. After hearing of the tragic news, Jacob turned up immediately, to offer his support to Amanda. He told her he had instructed his lawyer to settle up his business interests.

She was so pleased to see him. It had been bad enough having people talk about her the first time the Desmond and Daryl affair had surfaced; now people in the small town didn't even wait for her to pass before commenting. Teenagers wore Abba tee-shirts around the streets. The police put twenty-four hour surveillance around her house and the grave. Old ladies stood nattering away in the butchers shop, expressing their opinions on the whole sordid affair.

It was becoming unbearable. Jacob suggested maybe she should get way for a while until things sorted themselves out. He proposed they should go to somewhere in the country for a weekend. He knew of a lovely place where she could relax and forget about life. It would be peaceful and a million miles away from the current madness that surrounded her.

She had instantly said yes and rushed home to see what she had to take

Chapter 10

Tongue

In the cold light of day, Amanda did consider cancelling the weekend away with Jacob, and instead spend the time searching for Lois. She still hadn't been found. But the police assured her that they were doing all they could to locate her mate and it was no use phoning them constantly.

The police had even issued a missing-person profile of Lois to other towns in the area. To be honest, Amanda thought that the description they had circulated wasn't very flattering, to say the least.

So, in the end, Amanda had agreed to go. Deep down she was very glad to be getting away from it all. Being the main talking point, not once but twice, in a short period of time, in the small-minded town had taken its toll on her. She still wasn't sure where it would all end up.

She had been all of a fluster as to what to take with her on the excursion. It had been such a difficult decision. In the end she got the biggest suitcase she could find and filled it to the brim.

Jacob picked her up at exactly nine 'o' clock on a bright, but frosty, Saturday morning. The journey to the hotel was stimulating. Amanda wound the window down; she loved to feel the fresh air dancing through her hair. The further from the town they travelled, the further her troubles seem to escape her mind.

As they drove, she couldn't help but notice just how handsome her companion was. His casual dress and dark sunglasses gave him the appearance of a movie star, full of confidence, charm and mountains of sex appeal.

During the journey, Jacob did most of the talking. She was just pleased to sit there, taking in the sights, and listen to him. He told her all about his failed marriage, his reasonably successful business; the things he missed about the town, the things he definitely didn't. He mentioned his enthusiasm for fly fishing and his love of red wine. The drive made her feel so alive; made her feel like a teenager again, out on a first date. She felt warm and safe. It was as if he had somehow helped to move aside a large storm-cloud that hovered over her darkening sky. She knew it was too early to count her chickens, but at least there was a glimmer of hope shining through at last.

As the car pulled up the long gravel path to the beautiful country house hotel, the sight of the elegant building took her breath away. Her eyes found it hard to take in all of its splendour in one glance. She was awash with awe. A man in a top hat rushed up to open the car door for her.

The entrance to the hallway was even grander than the outside of the old building. A fresh-faced woman greeted them with a smile, which was both sincere and welcoming. Once again Jacob did all of the talking as the woman searched on the computer for details of their reservation.

A thought had crossed Amanda's mind. She wondered what arrangements he had made concerning sleeping accommodation. Would it be two single rooms? Or had he been more adventurous, chanced his arm and gone for one room with a double bed?

When the receptionist handed them two separate keys, Amanda didn't know if she was disappointed or relieved. She was silent, as a porter showed them to their separate rooms. On the landing they made arrangements to meet in the bar in an hour and Amanda let herself into her room.

The bedroom itself was magnificent, with its massive king-sized bed centring the room. It was the size of an aircraft hanger. Everything seemed too perfect to spoil. Unwittingly, she removed her shoes not to mess up the carpet. She tip-toed into the bathroom; it also took her breath away. She couldn't wait to climb into the gigantic tub. She discharged the water from the taps, before returning to the bedroom to unpack. As she slumped on the bed she came to the conclusion she was in heaven and she didn't want to come back down to earth.

'You wouldn't get this in bloody Butlins in Barry Island.' She laughed out loud and stretched herself out on the mattress.

As she lay there, for some strange reason, her surroundings made her recall the night she lost her virginity. She wasn't sure why. It wasn't because that night was perfect; far from it; it was just a disaster from start to finish.

It had been with a boy called Jean Paul Spaghetti-breath (or some Italian sounding name like that). He was quite conceited, always combing his greasy hair and looking at his reflection in windows and mirrors, but to his credit, he was nice looking. He had jet black hair, searching deep brown eyes, which he used to great effect that night to finally, break down Amanda's resistance as they lay in his parent's bedroom; they were off down the social club playing Christmas Chicken bingo.

The whole forgettable experience had been a bit of a blur to Amanda, mainly due to the four glasses of cider and black, and a shot of straight vodka that she had drunk to calm her nerves and to give her Dutch courage. It was supposed to be one of the greatest moments in a girl's life, up there with walking down the aisle in a flowing white dress, or giving birth to a child. According to the countless girls' magazines that Amanda read, the first time should be the perfect love scene, the night when all the stars explode in the sky. In reality, it was more like a scene from an A&E unit than any Hollywood movie set. It hurt; it was painful, dreadfully messy and Amanda couldn't wait for it to end. So, looking back, if she had to sum it up, she had given away her most precious gift for nothing, while trying desperately to stop the room from spinning.

It was a shame because it had started well. A few enjoyable rounds of heavy petting and fumbling had given him enough nerve to clamber on top of her. But then her head swirled, the room rotated, as the alcohol began to have an impact. The little sick button behind her ears became activated. Her jaw went slack; she had to concentrate hard to stop herself throwing up.

After several poor attempts by the Italian Stallion to actually penetrate her, (and missing the target by a long way), he finally got lucky and entered her in one painful thrust. There was nothing gentle in his action as the inexperienced youth impaled her.

'Ouchhhhhh,' she tensed up, her nails dug into his back.

''Ouchhhhhh,' he cried, 'that hurts.' He arched his spine.

'I bet it doesn't hurt as much as this.' She was angry at him. She forcefully dug her nails in deeper.

To try to blank out the pain she tried to kiss him, as he jerked inside her. She noticed that he was pulling an unusual and very off-putting face. It made her stop. It was her first, but not the last, time she witnessed a man pulling 'I'm cumming face' during sex. She believed, even to this day, it was the most off-putting thing that men do in the whole world, even worse than farting in bed or falling asleep downstairs with the telly blaring.

'Stop pulling that face...it's putting me off. It looks as though you've swallowed a pencil,' she said. 'And by the way, make sure you pull it out before.' Being a decent Catholic girl she knew that if she used any form of contraception she would be automatically sent to burn in the fires of Hell, so she didn't want to get pregnant on her first visits to the shops.

'Of course I will.... Now stop talking,' he panted in her ear.

A few jolts later and she could feel him tense up, as he started moaning loudly. She didn't feel well. She attempted to push him off, but she couldn't budge his suffocating weight. He jerked faster; she sensed he was close to lift-off and he wasn't going to stop. She started to panic. She used all her might and launched him off her in one movement. She did it with such force that he tumbled off the edge of the bed. Before he had time to get back on to his feet to complain, she was sick all over him.

He lay on the floor, helpless, covered in black liquid. He looked like a human Ribena that had been squashed by the wheels of a big truck. Not the first and probably not the last, teenage road-kill victim.

'My mother's bed… she'll kill me…. Oh no look at all the blood…where did that come from?' He was hysterical, stomping about, similar to a spoilt brat.

'Where do you think it came from…? My bloody nose?' His words incensed her even more.

She was still feeling dizzy from the alcohol. She staggered to her feet and got dressed.

'Come back and help me clean this up, my parents will be back soon,' he demanded, just as the front door opened.

'Jean Paul…Jean Paul…come and see what we won at the bingo,' his mother yelled out from the hallway.

Amanda gingerly toddled down the stairs. Jean Paul's father was struggling by the front door with a 22lb turkey which they had won on the last house. Amanda smiled at them both as she left, never to return.

A short while later, she found out he had boasted that he had deflowered her in an eight-hour sex orgy, and had even made her orgasm ten times. She told Lois the truth, Lois went out of her way to inform the school what really happened. Jean Paul was made to look a clown; they never talked after that and Amanda never drank cider and black again.

Back in the grand surroundings of the bedroom, she snapped out of the bad memory of the time she'd lost her cherry. She wasn't sure why it had popped into her mind in the first place. She waltzed back into the bathroom, a fresh, soft, white bathrobe wrapped close to her skin. On entering the tiled room she became aware that the entire bathroom floor was immersed in water. She looked at the taps belting liquid out from their nozzles. She panicked, rushing to turn them off before she got down on all fours to start to mop the water up with a bath towel. She cursed herself for being so stupid.

She couldn't believe that on her first time in a real posh hotel she managed to celebrate it by flooding the place.

'You can take the girl out of the estate, but you can't take the estate out of the girl.' Lois's famous statement came home to haunt her. It was only now, as she desperately mopped up the water, that she realised how accurate her mate's words were.

She wrung out the soaking towel in the toilet as she pictured the hotel management frog-marching her out of the elegant building and dumping her, and all of her cheap clothes, onto the lawn. She began to work faster, arms pumping, wrists aching.

She stepped out of her lovely white dressing gown, which had been laid out on the bed for her, and used it to help dry up the floor as well.

Meanwhile, down in the reception area, droplets of water were seeping through the floorboards; this alerted the bright-eyed receptionist, who, in turn, immediately buzzed for the maintenance department. All the staff at the hotel were well aware of the last time something like this had happened. The escaping water had fused all the electrics and the Georgian manor house had been plunged into darkness for three hours.

The old maintenance man and his younger side-kick headed up to the first floor to try and find the source of the leak. They were annoyed; it was only ten minutes into their fourth coffee break of the day.

They knocked on the door of room 206 and waited. After two minutes they let themselves in. The room appeared deserted, but they then heard some splashing and weeping coming from the bathroom attached to the suite.

The older man pushed open the door. Amanda was still bent over on all fours with her exposed rear-end pointing invitingly up towards the men. She was cursing to herself, completely unaware that she was being observed. The older guy gently coughed. Amanda screamed, spun round and saw them standing at the door, wide smiles across their faces, one holding a monkey wrench, the other a plunger (both instruments pointing to the ceiling).

'Sorry Love…. we did knock…. honest,' the older one took the lead. 'Anything we can do to help?' His words weren't meant to have sexual connotations, but the way it came out, they did, and in abundance.

Amanda shot up vertically, placing her hands over her delicate parts. She pushed passed them and hid in the cupboard, shaking from the cold and embarrassment. She sat there listening, afraid to come back out. She could hear them busily working away. The younger man had started cracking jokes and was sniggering.

Ten minutes later there was a gentle tap on the cupboard door.

'Miss!'

'What?' she replied, sheepishly.

'It's all done…. just finished,' the man's voice penetrated the sanctuary of her hiding place.

Amanda tucked her legs up under her arms. 'Thanks…. how much do I owe you?'

The both of them chuckled. 'Nothing Miss…. There was no damage done. But if it happens again… just give us a call on extension 76…. but try and put some clothes on first… I've just had a pace-maker fitted and sights like that could kill me.'

She could hear them leaving, the younger one whispering something dirty to his colleague about holes and plungers. She just wanted to curl up and die.

'How the hell could I have been so stupid?' she asked herself.

She sat in the safety of the darkness of the cupboard for another twenty minutes before ultimately stepping out to face the world.

A while later Amanda was still feeling extremely nervous, as Jacob led her by the hand towards the crowded restaurant. She hadn't mentioned the incident to him, just hoping that it would blow over. But as they walked she had the distinct impression that everyone knew about the episode in the bathroom. Then, just when she thought she was home and dry, they passed the old maintenance man, carrying his toolbox.

'Hey,' he said. 'I didn't recognise you with your clothes on.' He beamed and winked at her.

Jacob shot a glance at her, then him, then back at her.

'It's a long story….. I'll tell you later.' She swore under her breath, as the old man skipped away, memories of her backside still clear in his head, whistling a tune.

As they walked through the restaurant she felt intimidated by the surroundings. An elegant diamond-cut chandelier hung from the ceiling. The place oozed class, a burning candle sat on each table-top accompanied by a bouquet of red roses. For some reason, she perceived that she had fraud written all over her and her cheap dress. She was sure she saw the waiters staring at her, whispering that she lacked style; poking fun at her working-class upbringing. She was fully expecting the head honcho, the bloke in the dickey-bow and monkey-suit, to come marching over to expose her for what she was, while grabbing her under her arm and forcefully evicting her from the premises (yet again). She felt like Julia Roberts in Pretty Woman, a cheap tart waiting to be exposed.

She knew she didn't belong in a place so up market. She didn't even know what cutlery to use with her meal. Her self-consciousness was working overtime. She was sure people were watching her, nudging each other, lifting their noses in disgust.

'Oh my God... Sidney... what's that terrible smell. If I'm not mistaken she reeks of housing estates, cheap cigarettes, wheelie bins and pot noodles.... It's HER...the one in the fifteen pound dress from Matalan,' she visualised the posh women loudly whispering to their male partners while sipping sherry.

But when she took a second glance around, no one had blinked an eyelid in her direction except a couple of randy old men who were in fact sizing her up. Even the big head honcho had smiled at her as he pulled the chair out for her to sit down. This show of respect from her obvious betters had confused her.

She stared at the menu. It was written in some foreign language. She didn't understand any of it. Inwardly she panicked again, praying that the floor would open and swallow her whole.

'What would you like?' Jacob asked, his handsome face glistening in the flickering candle light. 'I'll tell you what.... I'll choose for us.... It will be a test to see if I can select something you like... OK?' He could sense her relief as her tension dropped from her shoulders onto the floor.

After he gave her a crash course in what knife to use, the rest of the dinner went off without any hitches. In fact, as Jacob stared at her, he didn't care that she couldn't read the menu, or that she had lapped her soup up with the desert spoon. He was just admiring her beauty. He wished he could kiss her at that moment, reach across the table to place his lips on hers. He wanted to pick her up in his arms and carry her off to his hotel room and make love to her for the rest of the night. They stared into each other's eyes as they sipped their coffees, barely saying a word. It was one of those rare moments when words were not needed. The silence said it all.

It took exactly twenty long minutes and twenty-three anguishing seconds from finishing the remains of their hot drink to eventually ending up locked in each others arms in Jacob's bedroom. His lips felt tender as they married themselves next to hers. She could taste his breath, as she tried to climb right inside of him, tongue first. His kiss was wonderful. It teased her and tempted her at the same time.

Most of the men she had the misfortune of kissing down the years, thought it was the least important act in the intimacy stakes. To be fair, Daryl had been quite good at it, until several years of marriage had prevented them from expressing affection with a simple kiss. But she had heard that forgetting the 'art of kissing' was just a typical married thing to do.

Most of the other men she had kissed thought it was just the means to get them to second base as quickly as possible. It always appeared to be a race, a two minute stop-gap in search of the bigger prize.

In fact, one of her past boyfriends, she couldn't remember which one, had shown her a five easy steps guide as to how to satisfy a woman (it had been developed by some guy called Big Mick).

She tried hard to remember how the guidelines went, and she thought it went something like:

Step 1 – Kiss them hard and make sure you roll your tongue around their mouth.

Step 2 – As soon as you see them shutting their eyes, go for the bra, if she stops, you kiss her a bit longer and put your tongue in further. This technique is guaranteed to get results. A nine-out-of-ten chance of success.

Step 3 – Once inside the bra, rub the breast firmly anti-clockwise for about five minutes. If possible try and lick her eardrum at the same time. Try and make it as wet as possible. This will drive them wild with passion. If it's your first time, don't attempt to do both things at the same time, this could end up in disaster.

Step 4 – If everything is going to plan go straight for the honey-pot. If you happen to find it dry, lick the palm of your hand and juice her up a bit. She'll appreciate it.

Step 5 – Climb on top and ride away. Don't forget to thank them when you finish; posh girls love that.

At first she thought it was a joke, a piss-take. She didn't think that even boys could be that dense. She was wrong. The boyfriend had informed her it was deadly serious and was the second most photocopied document after the new season's rugby fixtures.

Back in Jacob's arms it was obvious that he hadn't seen the pathetic rules, thankfully. His whole approach was very, very different. Sparks exploded inside her, blood raced around her veins; her breathing was short and to the point.

She could taste him. He tasted of manly desire, which again was a step up from tasting of cheap aftershave or cigarettes. His hands touched her cheeks, embracing the side of her face. Her knees knocked. She felt as if she was on a different planet. She felt weightless. There was no gravity in the air.

She couldn't hold back any longer. The woman that had been lost inside of her suddenly resurfaced. Gone was the shy, self-conscious girl, who had earlier hid in the cupboard; now she was replaced by the female of the species, with plenty of love to burn.

She couldn't believe how good it felt as his lean, naked body finally pressed against her bare breasts. A deep moan drifted from her throat. She was savouring the tingling sensation that engulfed her body. She closed her eyes and let her other senses take over.

He was incredible. He took control without being overpowering. He kissed her so passionately, that she thought she would melt or turn to jelly between the bed sheets. He was aggressive, yet sensual and she grew more receptive with every nibble of his mouth, every caress of his hand.

She felt ecstasy as he gently held her arms above her head and thrust deeper and deeper within her. She wanted the night to last forever. She could feel all the months of bitterness and pain escaping from her body. The sex was intense, and so much fun. He was full of surprises. They tried positions that she had only ever read about in magazines and dreamed about. Yet everything they did seemed so natural; so passionate; so true, there was nothing fake in the heat of the room.

Afterwards, as she lay exhausted in his arms, she hoped he would stay with her forever. Her mind told her not to let go of him again. It begged her to wrap her legs around him and to stick to him like glue.

She knew she would never forget room 206 or this beautiful man who had came back into her torrid life and had unknowingly turned her world upside down. She had forgotten the troubles still waiting for her back home.

She hoped he was sincere when he said he would love to see her again, because there was so much more she needed to learn about him. What were his dreams? How did he get that luscious derriere and the rest of his gorgeous body? Where did he get his sultry bedroom eyes, which made her go weak at the knees? Was it from his mother's or father's side of the family? And finally, where did his deviously, sexy smile and his great sense of humour come from?

He seemed too good to be true. He didn't even pull 'The man cumming face'. She was fully expected to be woken from the dream by the alarm clock or the postman, but she wasn't. This was real; the best thing that had happened to her in a long, long time. She cuddled back into him and fell into a delicious slumber.

Chapter 11

Waiting

He couldn't stand the delay any longer. It was definitely approaching the point where he needed to re-enact his idea and quickly. Time had somehow crept up behind him and threatened to pass him by if he wasn't careful.

It was becoming more critical for him to make himself known to her before the opportunities dried up, or were actually lost forever. He knew that would be no good at all, especially after all the planning, all the detailed preparation he had put into it. And what's more, he'd even put down a sizeable, non-refundable deposit on a cake.

So he sat motionless in the hiding place he had chosen. Looking around, it reminded him of the dark closet his mother used to lock him in when he was a naughty child. Hours, and often days, he was forced to stay in there, afraid to cry out, scared to make even the smallest of whimpering noises, in case she came back swinging the belt. He still had the scars on parts of his body where the leather strap and buckle had torn away at his tender skin.

But his imprisonment had given him one advantage in life over other individuals. He now had a skill for waiting; waiting perfectly still, akin to a hungry spider crouched at the top corner of a web, in anticipation of its next victim; mouth drooling, eyes focused, lips smacking.

So, as the world outside revolved around, he sat in the dark, curtains closed, a small bottle and a white handkerchief positioned firmly in his sweaty hands. He waited for her to arrive home from where ever she had been. He waited patiently to see his master plan come to life; he waited to, hopefully, celebrate the best day of his life.

Chapter 12

Sp-ce

Amanda had never felt so dejected in all her life. Jacob's car pulled off the motorway and headed to the entrance to her estate. She had to concentrate extremely hard from stopping herself bursting into tears and grabbing the steering wheel to turn the vehicle around. She had rarely, if ever, experienced such a high, then crashed to an all-time low, in such a short space of time. Of course, Daryl's death had been horrendous, but this was a different kind of sadness.

The entire weekend at the hotel had been a wonderful success; be that physically, spiritually, or emotionally, in fact, any other 'ally' that anyone wanted to add to the end of her sentence.

As they drove past the boarded-up police station, her body was still tingling at the thought of his touch. It had been a long time since she had felt so comfortable during love making. She had forgotten how powerful and leg-sapping an orgasm could be. Well not just one, actually, she had lost count. At one stage during the fabulous afternoon, she thought she was going to flake-out from the sheer pleasure engulfing her body.

'God what that man could do with his tongue and his middle finger beggars belief,' she smiled as the memory flashed back into her mind.

As she lay in his arms on that Sunday afternoon, he jokingly told her he used to practice his oral technique when he was in his teens by fixing a tangerine on a piece of string and flicking it with his tongue for hours on end. She wasn't quite sure if he was messing or not, but whatever he did, it did the trick beautifully. She couldn't wait to accidentally-on-purpose mention it to Lois. She'd be so jealous.

But now, sadly, it was home-time. It was like getting kicked out of a warm, friendly pub, because the grumpy landlord decided to ring the last order bell. Life was so unfair; why couldn't they have just stayed there in the bedroom? Why couldn't she stay there all safe and warm under the white sheets, cuddling up to his lovely, trim body?

She loved his smell, the way his body tasted, the way he took control between the covers. He was loving, experienced and experimental at the same time.

Back in the car, she glanced out of the window. The streets which embraced her town hadn't changed one bit.

Well what did she expect? A full urban make-over in the two and a half days that she had been away? As they drove on, dirty, faceless buildings stared directly at her. 'Welcome home,' she could imagine the houses mocking her, while sticking two chimneys up in her direction.

He pulled up outside her house. At first, she was going to ask him to drop her off at the end of the street so the nosey neighbours couldn't see. But she decided against that. After all, she had no reason to hide anything.

He leapt out and opened the passenger door for her, offering up his hand for support. She knew they would all be spying from behind net curtains, or over garden hedges; tongues at the ready and telephone fingers poised to spread the word of wrong doing.

But for probably the first time in her life she didn't care, 'They can watch until they're blue in the face,' she told herself.

She stared at every window in turn, just to let them know, that she knew they were there. This was the new Amanda, the rejuvenated model with extra confidence.

Jacob promised he'd return as soon as he could. He had some old, family business to sort out first. The sadness that crossed her face persuaded him to kiss her passionately right there and then, outside her house. She gasped with pleasure and automatically cocked her leg up momentarily. She was putty in his arms.

She waved him goodbye, then floated effortlessly down her garden path as if she was wearing a pair of anti-gravity space boots.

'One kiss for man…. One brand new step for womankind,' she giggled to herself, as she opened the door.

Once inside, she instantly thought about Lois. She wondered if her mate had surfaced yet. She checked her phone messages for any news. There was nothing. It was worryingly strange.

Back in the house, she was too excited to eat. Her animal instincts were already counting down to the moment when Jacob would return. She couldn't wait; she was horny just thinking about him. She contemplated using Lois' love eggs but she decided she was not that desperate.

She switched on the kettle; opened all the curtains and some windows. It was about time the room was given the opportunity to breathe fresh air again. She could sense the doom and gloom, which had been firmly locked in, finally disintegrating into small pieces and escaping into the daylight.

She dragged the suitcase upstairs. She unpacked slowly, smiling wickedly as she laid out some of the mementos of the weekend by the side of her bed. She had kept everything; soap, shampoo bottles, even the menu from the restaurant. She wanted to be near them forever, just to remind her that she hadn't been dreaming.

She burst into song, which was very unlike her. It was a mish-mash of all kinds of words and tunes that popped into her head. There was some soul, some R&B and a little Lionel Ritchie in there somewhere. She just made it all up as she merrily went along.

'What the hell!' she muttered out loud, 'I deserve to be happy for a change. There's no law against it'.

Unfortunately for Amanda, her singing drowned-out the quiet footsteps tip-toeing up her staircase. She had her back to the bedroom door, so she didn't see the person entering with the handkerchief in his hand.

The struggle was all over in a split second. The element of surprise was met with little resistance. The chloroform did its job well. Suddenly, Amanda's brave, new, shiny-world, blacked out abruptly.

Chapter 12 and a half

Timber

For whatever strange reason, Amanda felt as if she had been in a similar situation before. It was as if she was re-enacting a sexual déja vue moment. Just like an earlier dream, she discovered herself tied to a bed-post, unable to move her arms. Again, she was blindfolded and a piece of tape straddled around her mouth, stretched across from ear lobe to ear lobe.

She bit her lip and smiled to herself.

'I bloody hope no one wakes me up this time,' she told herself. 'I'm definitely going to have my way with Mister Clooney if it's the last thing I do.'

She knew it was a bit early to two-time Jacob, but this was a dream regarding a Hollywood legend, so it really didn't count. She stretched out the best she could to try and make herself more comfortable.

She waited for her new fantasy to start. Her heart pounded in slow motion. She heard someone enter the room. But there was something different about this dream to the last one. In the previous one she was more or less naked, except for her underwear, and a dangly set of earrings. This time she was wearing some kind of white, silky dress. It felt smooth against her skin. She dismissed it.

In her own, silent world, she muttered to herself, 'OK George…there's no need for all the foreplay this time round… just climb up on top and let's get right to it before bloody Lois turns up to spoil my fun, as usual.'

She could hear the person moving closer towards the edge of the bed. She was excited. It was then that she smelt a distinctive, but familiar aroma. She rummaged about in her mind, racking her brain, to try to recall where she had come across it previously. Then, without warning, the tape was ripped off her mouth in one sharp movement. The pain made her jump.

Before she had time to say something, the man stuck his tongue deep into the crack of her mouth. She found it hard to breath. There was definitely something not right. The person's breath was rancid. She thought she was going to be sick. She couldn't for the life of her imagine George Clooney having such disgusting breath. After thirty seconds of constant sword fencing with the intruding tongue, it abruptly stopped. She heard a rustle of paper.

'Step two,' she heard the person whisper to himself. 'Grab her breast.' He proceeded to rub it anti-clockwise.

'Hey… not so fast,' she protested, trying to move her arms.

This was followed by more rustling of paper then she felt a tongue embedded into her eardrum. He licked her as a child would devour an ice cream, covered in all the toppings, including strawberry sauce, on a warm summer's day.

'George…. or whoever you are…. Stop please.'

There was stillness. She exhaled as she felt the full weight of him lifting off her body. She wasn't enjoying this dream at all. In fact, she tried hard to wake herself up. Suddenly, the room illuminated as the blindfold was torn from her eyes. It took her many blinks before she began to focus properly. It was only after taking in the scene in front of her that she screamed loudly, and then passed out.

When she came to, time had moved on a few minutes, but the picture in front of her hadn't changed. Pitifully for her, there was no sign of the famous actor. That image had been crudely replaced by the freaky vision of the weird bloke from her office standing next to her in a pair of stained Y fronts.

'Arrgggghhh,' she cried out, feeling nauseous. 'This is not a bloody dream... it's a fuckin' nightmare.' She was definitely going to stop eating cheese before bedtime if this was the outcome.

Then the weird bloke spoke. 'Sssssssorry to have disappointed you,' his hiss resembled the snake, with the colourful rotating eyes, from the Jungle Book film. 'But this is not a nightmare either... this is real... or, what's more... this is going to be the happiest day of your life.' He smiled at her. His teeth had all the hallmarks of a New York City taxi cab; yellow, grubby and with bits of food stuck in every nook and cranny. Orange plaque lined every tooth.

Now she really was confused. She closed her eyes and again tried to shake herself into the real world; but once more it didn't work. When she opened her eyes again, he was still standing there, but she noticed that this time he had an erection in his soiled underpants. She tore her glance away from him at a right angle. Curiously, she saw what she assumed was a morning suit hanging on the back of the door. She couldn't imagine what he would be doing with a morning suit, unless he had stolen it.

It then hit her that she was not floating about in some dream-come nightmare; this was really happening; the weird bloke from her office had actually kidnapped her.

'Hey...,' she couldn't remember his name to make her questions more personal. 'Why I am here? What the hell is going on?'

He looked at her long and hard. 'You don't even know my name... do you?' His voice was filled with sadness; the lump in his underpants plummeted downwards.

She was quickly coming to the conclusion he wasn't just weird, he was completely bonkers and worst of all she was tied to his bed.

'Well... what's my name then?' he spoke again, this time with more anxiety in his voice.

She was too perplexed to think straight. He asked her again, but this time the volume of his tone increased a notch or three.

'Is it.... Ron?'

'NO,' he shouted, his left eye twitched

'Err... I know it's Ernie... yes it's Ernie.'

'It's not Ernie.... He works in the photocopying room.' He raced up to the dressing table and checked his reflection in the mirror. 'I look nothing like him.... And he's got a gammy eye.'

She really wanted to yell at him that she thought he was called 'Fuckin' Quasimodo's twin brother,' but she refrained. She was in enough of a tricky situation already without making him madder. Instead she went for safer ground. 'Look I don't know... I can't remember what your name is.' She began to cry. Most of the tears were just for effect; she was hoping for the sympathy vote.

He paced back and forth before adding, 'Well that just won't do.... If you don't know my name... it's going to make the ceremony awkward.... I don't know what the priest will think.' He shook his head; his few remaining hairs fell away from his crown like Bobby Charlton waltzing about the football field. 'It's Colin.... Colin Liverstone.'

'What ceremony?' Her voice was inquisitive as well as strained. 'What are you talking about?'

'Our ceremony... me and you.' He repeated his bad smile.

She looked at him and couldn't help but contemplate how the hell this man in front of her had the gall, and balls, to snigger at Ernie from photocopying because of his gammy eye. This oddball had a gammy face and definitely a twisted personality. She started to cry, this time the tears were real.

'Look, whatever your name is ...'

'I just told you....Colin.... It's Colin.'

'Ok....Colin.... I don't know if you are on drugs or medication... but I really need to go home now... it's getting late.' She suddenly became aware of the dress she was wearing. The sight of it really should have sent her into a roaring panic, but the image in front of her hadn't had time to penetrate through to her mind quite yet.

She stopped him before purposely asking, 'Why the hell am I wearing a wedding dress?' She looked at him for an instant answer to probably the most important and oddest question she had ever asked someone.

'Because you told me two years ago next Tuesday, that if your husband left you, you would marry me.' He held up an old calendar with a date circled in red pen.

If Amanda had an Adam's apple she would have gulped it hard at that precise moment. She thought about the words he had just spoken, trying to rewind her mind back to the occasion in question. The only time she could recall was just before Christmas a long time ago. The weird bloke had shuffled up to her and shyly placed a lovely card and a box of milk chocolates on the edge of her desk. He had muttered something about her being the best looking woman in the town and she felt sorry for him, so, messing about, she told him that it was a pity she was married or they could go and get hitched and live happily every after.

'But it was a joke.... I was messing with you.... I was being nice.... because I felt sorry for you... you looked like a little boy lost in a department store,' she pleaded.

The look on his face had mystification written all over it. Furrow-lines on his forehead appeared from nowhere. The unfortunate twitch in his left eye spiralled out of control; he stuttered; he shook; spittle rolled down his chin. The anger in his frown was evident and it sent a cold chill all the way down her spine.

She thought she needed to say some more, so she continued. 'Look you are lovely,' she lied through her back teeth; she was glad she wasn't the wooden boy in the Pinocchio story or her nose would have shot across the room and probably smashed the window. 'But I didn't know my husband was going to jump off that viaduct... I didn't mean you any harm... I was just trying to be nice to you because of the present you had bought me.'

He had a harder edge to his voice. 'Well, I didn't think he was going to jump either.'

'What do you mean?' It was her turn to look baffled.

'Like I said.... I didn't think he was going to go.... so that's why I gave him a helping hand.... Timbeeeeerrrrrrrrrrrr!' he whistled, motioning his fingers in a downward ark.

She felt cold. Goose-pimples danced on her skin like wild red Indians in front of a raging fire. She went all dizzy. She needed to lie down; problem was she was already lying down. She thought it essential to find out a little more. 'What did you just say about Daryl?'

'Amanda… sweet Amanda… Daryl doesn't matter now…. I love you… I've always loved you and I'm going to marry you…. Today in fact… in two hours when the vicar turns up.' He sprayed some cheap body spray underneath his armpits then down the front of his pants. 'I can't wait until tonight…I'm going to make you feel very special.' He proceeded to poke his tongue out and flick it about.

'Colin… I still don't fully understand,' that was all Amanda could think of saying, her mind was vacant.

'Hope you like the dress,' he muttered quietly. 'I realise that technically it shouldn't be white… but what the hell…you're still a virgin in my eyes.'

Amanda could suddenly hear the distinctive voice of the pop star, Madonna, singing

'Like a Virgin… fucked by a weirdo for the very first time.'

Amanda now understood she was in grave danger. She struggled to release herself from the straps. She didn't think it could get any worse… astonishingly she was wrong.

The next sentence really belonged in the uncut version of the Exorcists movie. He moved in close and whispered, 'my mother picked the dress out for you…she's dead good at stuff like that.' He turned his eyes towards the corner of the room.

Amanda didn't want to follow his line of sight, she didn't quite know where it would lead, but she sensed it wouldn't be to a picture of a rosy English garden, covered in lovely flowers with a little rope-swing balancing between two old trees. Unfortunately for her, her eyeballs dragged her vision, kicking and screaming, towards the dark corner of the room.

What she saw was too outrageous to comprehend. The silent scream Amanda released sounded extremely loud inside the confines of her own head, but it didn't register a decibel. Her mouth dried up, her eyes bulged from their sockets. She went all queasy.

She only then realised the seriousness of the situation to which she was exposed.

'This must be a dream.' She used the words to try and console herself. 'For fuck's sake this can't be real, this can't be happening to me.' Again, she recognised that what she was witnessing didn't make any sense, but then nothing in the last fifteen-minutes had. It was close to being in the front row watching a David Lynch film whilst on acid, as her parents made-out in the seat next to her.

'I haven't introduced my mother... have I?' The weird bloke swung his arm warmly towards his deceased mother, who sat in a white padded chair; a large silver floor lamp shone light onto the dead woman's face.

'You are a psycho... I can't marry you.... you should be locked up with the rest of the loonies,' she yelled at the top of her voice.

He hadn't heard a word she had said. He was just over the border from listening, and far away from caring. In his warped mind, they were the sweetest set of peas in the pod, the grooviest pair of chicks in the basket. He beamed at her.

He sauntered over to the corpse, and picked it up before carefully slinging it over his shoulders. 'Come on Ma... let's go and get you showered and dressed for the big occasion.' As he walked through the door, he looked at the carcass and muttered, 'What did you say...? She looks beautiful... thanks Ma... I think so too... what's that.... can you sit next to Amanda during the reception?' He rotated around to stare at his wife-to-be on the bed before replying, 'Of course you can.... And if you're good.... You can even sleep with us tonight.'

Just before Amanda fainted she happened to notice a handful of sofa-stuffing and sand falling away from a hole in the dead woman's back.

Chapter 14

Confetti

Lois could hear voices and other peculiar noises coming from somewhere in the house. She was still imprisoned in the basement room and was still unsure why. Her captor had refused to get drawn into any type of conversation, instead, he was just content to turn up a couple of times a day to push food through the flap and empty out the red bucket.

'Hey.... Anyone there?' She banged on the thick wooden panel. It hardly made a sound.

She listened again, burying her ear tightly up against the door. She was sure she could make out furniture being dragged across the floor and someone merrily singing away to some awful tune. Then she heard footsteps coming closer to where she was. She backed away, waiting for the flap to open. She presumed it must have been around lunch time by now.

To her surprise the person on the other side began to unlock the door. She didn't know what to think; didn't know if she should laugh or cry. Was she in danger or not? Was it someone here to rescue her? Had the maniac finally decided that this was the day he was going to skin her? He had fed her well over the last ten days, but, maybe he was just trying to make her a bit chubbier.

The questions spun around in her mind, just as a man entered carrying a large bread-knife and an envelope. There was something about him that was unusual, but she couldn't explain exactly what. She had seen much uglier people in her life, but this one had something demented about him. He looked irregular; out of proportion.

'Oh fuck...,' she sighed. She was now totally convinced she would end up as an overcoat for the lunatic. For the first time in her life she was scared. She cowered in the corner, clutching tightly onto the red bucket.

The man walked slowly towards her. She was shaking. It now dawned on her that he was wearing a morning-suit, but without the top hat. He leant over her and handed her the envelope with a card inside. He backed away, a vacant expression across his features.

After a minute, she realised he was waiting for her to read it. She opened it and examined the contents of the card. She looked at him bewildered, unsure as to what to say. She finally spoke through tight lips, 'Are... are you having a joke?'

He looked back, just as bemused. He shook his head violently to make it clear that he wasn't pulling her leg.

'So does this mean you are not going to skin me?' She was straight to the point.

'Excuse me?' he stopped her from going back down that now boring avenue of mutilation. 'What is this fascination you have with getting skinned...? I think you are weird.... You need to see a shrink.'

'Me...? A shrink? You're the 'King of Kookiness' himself.... with fuckin' bells on.' She clambered to her feet kicking the bucket and its contents to the ground. She read the note again, this time out loud.

'Lois... you are cordially invited to the wedding of Colin and Amanda. It starts at 1pm today in the front room.'

He smiled at her, exposing his beaten-up teeth.
'Look, whoever you are ...'
'I'm Colin,' he interrupted her, pointing at himself.
'Ok... so you're Colin... I still don't understand... why have you locked me in this stinking basement for the last few days and, now, you are inviting me to your wedding? .... It just doesn't make sense.... You could have just sent me an invitation in the post.'
He snatched the card out of her hand. 'I haven't got time to stand here talking to you... I'm marrying your friend Amanda in twenty minutes time,' he announced proudly, but, in contrast, his body language suggested he was becoming very agitated.
'Hang on there just a minute, cowboy.' She held her hand up. 'What the hell do you mean you're marrying Amanda...? It's the first I've heard of it.'
'It's been our secret.... Now get walking.' He poked her in her back with his finger. 'The priest is ready and Amanda and I can't wait for our honeymoon.'
'Where the fuck are you taking her...? The Bates Motel?' She spat the words at him, little realising their significance.
He reacted by pushing her hard towards the stairs and crying, 'Shut up, clever-clogs...! Keep moving.'

He led her into a large room which had been decorated with flowers, freshly nicked from the cemetery that very morning. The entire house smelt of decay and dust; it irritatingly tickled Lois's nostrils.

He forcibly sat her down on an old wooden chair, and then tied her to the uprights of the piece of furniture with nylon string. The thin, blue twine cut into her wrists. Lois tuned her head through ninety degrees. Out of the corner of her eye she could just make out an old woman sitting about ten feet from her in a similar type of chair.

'Hope you don't mind me telling you, love,' Lois whispered to her through clenched teeth. 'You look fuckin' awful...! Has he had you here long?'

The person on the receiving end of her remarks didn't bother to comment. She just sat motionless, staring ahead towards the far end of the room which appeared to have been turned into some kind of temporary altar. She balanced a box of pink, heart shaped confetti on her lap.

Lois could hear people talking behind her. She watched as Colin and another woman strolled passed her sight of vision.

'Hey.... What the hell are you doing here?' Lois yelled in the woman's direction.

'Oh no... it's not you... is it?' the fortune-telling gypsy from the caravan site replied back. 'You're not marrying her, are you?' the woman asked Colin 'Her fanny's seen more cock than I've had hot dinners.'

'Argghh... well you can fuck off wrinkled face.... least I'm not a fake fortune-teller. The only balls you've seen for decades are crystal ones' Lois eyeballed her menacingly.

Colin stepped between the women before they attempted to tear each other to bits with insults. 'Please, ladies, this is my wedding day. And no, I'm not marrying her,' he commented. 'Now, are you ready to perform the ceremony and behave decently?'

'She's not a priest.... She's just a second-hand gyppo, with a dodgy set of cards and a half-bred son.'

The woman physically went for Lois. Colin managed to grab hold of her arm before they made contact.

The pikey straightened her clothes and added, 'I am a sort of priest, and anyhow, anything is better than being a common whore... with a good for nothing junkie for a son.' The old hag's words knocked Lois back on her chair. It was then that the full force of the naked truth of her life smacked her right between the eyes. It really hurt; it was painful, and scarred Lois badly. She went silent and looked the other way, unable to think of anything in return. A tear welled up in the corner of her eye, and then trickled down her cheek.

The smirking and victorious gypsy woman took her position in the archway to the dining room. The sliding glass-doors had been pushed as far apart as possible. A small, white bath rug lay on the floor in front of her feet. This was intended to be the place to stand in front of the altar. Colin depressed the play button on an old-style cassette player and, after a short pause, the strains of Handel's Wedding March danced out of the little dusty speaker.

In another part of the house, Amanda was feeling extremely peculiar. She could hardly keep her eyes open. Somewhere off in the distance she could hear music drifting in and out of her groggy mind. Had she been dreaming all along about the weird bloke from her office? Did his mother really have stuffing escaping out of a gaping hole in her back? And why was she wearing a wedding dress?

She couldn't concentrate hard enough to put together a sensible answer to any of her questions. She decided to relax her eyelids once again. The opening of the door focused her attention to the man entering in his suit, top hat and unpolished shoes.

'Come on, my darling,' his words were sickeningly patronising. 'It won't be long now until we become one. All you have to do is say 'I DO'.'

'I do,' she automatically repeated the words without understanding her actions.

He smiled at her as he helped her up on her feet. She was very unsteady. He knew the drugs he'd given her would make her a little dozy, but he may have regretted giving her twice the prescribed dose. But, on second thoughts, it would make the honeymoon night so much easier to fulfil. And his mother could watch.

He eventually got her to stand up straight. He attached a bouquet to her head. It was made from plastic flowers and rubber bands. The old gypsy's strange-looking son took hold of Amanda's arms and walked her slowly into the front room. Meanwhile Colin rushed down the hallway and through the adjoining door to take his position next to the make-shift altar.

'Amanda…. Amanda,' Lois yelled on seeing her mate floating down the aisle leaning on the gypsy boy.

Amanda turned, smiled, and made a feeble attempt to wave. Lois switched her attention towards the groom. 'Hey…. You…. What have you done to her?'

'Nothing.' He shrugged his shoulders.

'Nothing…. She looks as high as a kite…. Amanda… Amanda…. It's me Lois,' she tried to move, but the bindings secured her firmly to the chair.

The gypsy woman grinned at Lois and said, 'I told you she would meet a dark-haired, handsome man.' Colin tried to hide his blushes and bowed his head in embarrassment.

'Fuckin' handsome,' Lois searched for some other words or phases to complete her sentence. She was too mad to think, so instead she just blurted out the first thing that popped into her head. 'He looks like a deformed garden gnome.'

Amanda giggled out loud. Colin had been used to being called names all his life, but never had somebody called him a garden gnome before, and especially on his wedding day. He steamed over to where Lois was sitting. His fist connected squarely with her jaw. Her head slumped to the side, her eyes closed.

'Shut your dirty mouth....Piggy woman,' he hissed, before spinning in one movement and saying to the other woman in the chair, 'Mam.... what do you think? Doesn't she look beautiful.... the prettiest bride in the world.' He gave his dead mother a kiss on her cheek.

Amanda still wasn't sure if what she had just witnessed had been real or not. Deep inside her the drugs must have been wearing off slightly, because the fog that clouded her mind was beginning to become clearer, less murky.

'Ok.... Ok... let's start,' Colin motioned towards the gypsy woman.

'Right.... We are gathered here today for the wedding of Colin and Amanda.'

Amanda stared at the man's face. She concentrated hard on the woman's mouth, trying to work out what she was actually saying. Her body still felt lifeless, her arms heavy; she swayed back and forth nearly toppling over, the strange-looking kid propping her up.

Before the old hag could continue there was an unexpected, loud knock on the front door, which seemed to rattle the entire house. It caused them all to jump, except, of course, the old, dead woman situated at the back, holding the box of heart-shaped paper.

'Bloody hell,' whispered Colin, 'probably bloody Jehovah's Witnesses…. they'll leave in a minute.'

They all stared at each other as footsteps could be heard meandering towards the side of the house, near to the bay window. Everyone held their breath as they saw someone trying desperately to see through the thick, net curtains that shrouded the glass.

A gentle tap on the window was followed by the sound of the same footsteps travelling back towards the front door. Suddenly the door handle opened.

'Shit!' Colin looked cross. 'I must have forgotten to bolt the door when I went to get the flowers.'

'Who is it?' the fortune teller's voice was almost inaudible.

'Schhhh.' Colin held his fingers to his lips, while sneaking quietly behind the living-room door.

'Hello…. Hello,' a man's voice broke the silence. 'Colin… are you there?'

Amanda thought she recognised the voice. She turned towards the door, she was still light headed.

'Amanda?' Jacob was shocked on seeing her standing there in a white wedding-dress. 'What are you doing here...? Where's my step-brother Colin?'

Sadly, before he had time to realise the seriousness of the situation, a heavy, sharp object bounced off the back of his skull, knocking him out cold.

'He's always interfering.' Colin dropped the blood-stained ashtray onto the floor. He hurried back to where Amanda was standing and grabbed her hand tightly.

'Carry on… carry on,' he quickly indicated to the make-shift priest.

'Do you Colin take this woman to be your lawful wedded wife?'

'Yes…. Hurry up… ask her….. Ask her.'

She turned to face Amanda. 'Hey you… do you take Colin to be your husband?'

It was as if a mist had suddenly cleared from every corner of her mind. Her senses became sharp again. Her vision not blurred; she wasn't moving in slow motion anymore. She looked around the room. She shook the last remains of the drugs from her brain. She saw Lois slumped in a chair; on the floor Jacob lay with blood slaloming down from a head wound.

'Well, do you take this man?' the gyppo asked again, impatiently.

'Don't be so stupid.' Amanda pushed out, sending Colin crashing over a table, 'He's the weird bloke from the office… I'd rather marry Ernie with the gammy eye from photocopying.'

This was the signal Lois needed to spring into action. All along she had been faking being knocked out. She'd been hit a lot harder than that down the years and by bigger men (and women) than Colin. So, while she pretended to play unconscious, she had unpicked the line bonding her to the chair. She jumped up, reached over and grabbed Colin's dead mother in a headlock. The box of confetti fell to the floor.

'Amanda…. over here… quick.'

Colin scrambled up off the floor. He saw Lois holding his mother by the neck in front of her body. 'MOTHER….' He screamed out, his eyes piercing, his chest throbbing. He stepped towards Lois.

'Not so fast…weirdo…! One more step and I'll snap her neck in two.' She tightened her grip on the deceased woman's throat.

'Lois!' Amanda tried to interrupt her mate from making a complete fool of herself.

'Amanda, don't interfere…. Leave this to me…. I'll get us out of here.' She turned back to face Colin, who had stopped dead in his tracks. Lois added 'So… if you don't leave us go…. I'll… I'll strangle her to death.' This time she positioned her fingers around the corpse's throat.

'Lois,' Amanda cried again.

Lois rolled her eyes to the ceiling before giving her the 'Look'. 'Amanda…. For fuck's sake…. Shut up.'

Amanda spoke loudly, 'But she's already dead.'

'Who's already dead?'

'The dead woman in your arms…. is already dead.'

Lois couldn't take this information in. It refused to register in her brain. 'What are you talking about?'

'Lois she's dead… his mother…. she's been stuffed''

Lois turned the corpse to face her. She looked into her fake marble eyes. 'Fuckin' hell… no wonder she didn't talk to me… I thought she was just being ignorant.'

Colin took a step forward. 'Don't you harm my mother!' He was almost in tears.

Amanda had an idea. 'Look you… if you don't let us go… I'll break her face up… smash it to bits…. you'll never be able to repair it.'

'You wouldn't do that….. She's nearly your new mother-in-law.'

Amanda hated the words mother-in-law at the best of times. She bounded up to where Lois, who was standing in stunned silence, was still holding the dead woman in her arms. She then turned the woman back around and without blinking she poked one of the woman's marble eyes into the back of its socket.

'Urrrgggg…. Mother!' Colin went to run at her.

'You come any closer.... And I'll bite her nose off.' She opened her mouth exposing her teeth. 'She'll make Michael Jackson look like Jimmy Durante by the time I'm finished with her.'

'Who's Jimmy Durante?' asked Lois.

'He's a bloke with a big nose.... it doesn't matter,' explained Amanda.

Colin was beside himself. 'Ok.... Ok.... But don't bite her.... She hates people biting her.'

Lois glanced at Amanda in disbelief. 'What a fuckin' loon,' she whispered under her breath, searching around the room for a way out. The two women, plus the corpse, inched their way towards the kitchen door behind them.

'Be a doll and hold this for a minute.' Lois handed the body to Amanda. 'I have something important to do.'

Amanda took hold of the body. Lois strutted casually up to the gypsy woman and without a moment's hesitation head-butted the old hag right on the nose. The sound of bone breaking and the sight of blood gushing like a waterfall was enough to brighten up Lois's day. 'Put that in your crystal ball.' She ambled back feeling like she was the Queen of the Carnival on the 4th of July.

'What about Jacob?' Amanda asked, seeing him flat out on the floor.

'He's too heavy.... We'll send someone back for him.'

They slowly manoeuvred their way through the kitchen, carefully lugging the dead body around the large wooden table. They could see Colin poking his head around the living room door.

'Get back.... or another eyeball goes.' Amanda was sick of pussy-footing around; it was time to take control.

Colin obeyed and backed away. Lois opened what she thought was the back door. Unfortunately, it was the door leading to the pantry. They both stepped back in horror on seeing the naked, decaying body of Desmond propped up amongst the shelves which were full of jam, cans of pineapple chunks and a large jar of formaldehyde.

'What the hell?' Lois went to add some more, but both women's eyes were dragged down towards the groin area of the dead transvestite. Even Lois screamed as they saw that his manhood had been cut off. Dried blood stained his shaven legs; a blood stained pocket pen-knife lay open on the floor.

'So, it was Desmond's cock that was delivered in the post,' Amanda muttered to herself.

'Excuse me.... what cock in the post?' Lois fell into some sort of trance.

'It was when Ramone came over to find out where you had gone,' Amanda replied.

'What cock in the post?' Lois repeated, like a robot with a faulty circuit-board.

'Someone sent it to me.... and your love eggs.'

'A cock in the post?'

Finally, Amanda slapped her mate lightly across the face. 'Lois it wasn't a sexual thing... it was a warning... snap out of it.'

'MOTHER.... MOTHER,' the cry from the other room brought them back to reality. They gathered up the dead mother and began to head into the daylight.

'She'll slow us up.... We will have to leave her.' Lois was correct in her assessment of the bizarre situation.

Amanda thought for a few seconds. 'But with her we are safe. Hang on, I have an idea!' She rummaged around in the cutlery drawer. Her hand emerged holding a large kitchen knife. 'Hold her still,' she instructed her friend.

'What do you mean hold her still.... she ain't going to boogie about.... is she?' Lois was not joking.

'You know what I mean.' Amanda then proceeded to hack off the woman's head. It came away quite easily. Straw and sand exploded out from the neck, similar to lava escaping from a volcano. Clouds of dust hang over the kitchen.

'Ok…. that will be enough.' Amanda placed the head under her arm and raced out of the door, reminiscent of a rugby player, with a ball tucked under his arm.

The sudden blast of daylight hurt their eyes.

Chapter 15

Gravestone

Once outside the house of horrors, the two women scanned their surroundings, searching for an escape route. They knew it wouldn't take long before Colin would build up enough emotional courage and rage to come after them in search of revenge. They knew he would be furious, especially when he discovered the headless body of his already dead mother, laid out perfectly on the kitchen table. Amanda assumed that lunatics' often reacted quite badly in situations where roles were reversed and they become the poor victims. Amanda wondered how he would react when he discovered that Lois had placed an iceberg lettuce where the dead woman's head should have been. She had even taken the time to draw eyes and a nose with lipstick. Even in the land of wicked people Lois was truly one of the wickedest.

'What are we going to do now?' Amanda was exhausted, both mentally and physically.

Lois beamed leisurely, 'Yes, I know... we'll take the pikey's car.' She nodded towards the yellow Volvo parked in the street.

'How do you know it belongs to the gypsy?' Amanda asked, checking that the weird bloke wasn't closing in behind them.

'Because it's got a fuckin' big carpet attached to the roof.... Whose do you think it is? Ali fucking Baba's?' The sign of strain was beginning to become evident.

Amanda let go a nervous laugh. She still found Lois funny, even under the grimmest of pressure. They sprinted directly towards the car.

'OH NO.... MOTHER.... What have they done to you?' His piercing outburst sent birds flapping high into the sky. A second later, a lettuce, with a lipstick face, sailed out of the kitchen window, landing at the girls' feet.

Luckily for them, the door to the car was open. Sadly, the keys' weren't in the ignition.

'It's never like this in the flaming movies,' Amanda cursed their state of affairs.

'It is in a horror movie,' Lois motioned behind her.

They both turned back to see Colin appearing through the back door, armed with an axe, and with an expression on his face that would have burned a hole in an asbestos glove, from ten paces.

'What the hell do we do now?' Amanda asked, unintentionally clutching onto the dead woman's head. A green powder substance puffed out from the damaged eyeball of the corpse. The rotting dust caused Amanda to cough.

'No problem,' Lois replied coolly. 'You don't grow up in a family of criminal brothers without learning some of the tricks of their trade.' In one movement, she kicked a piece of plastic off the dash board with her heel, then searched expertly about underneath for the right wires to connect together.

Outside, Colin was only several feet away and advancing with huge steps. His eyes bulged out of their sockets; the veins on the side of his neck pulsed like a lighthouse sending a distress signal on a misty night; the axe swung savagely about his head.

'MOTHERRRRRRRRRR,' he screamed louder.

'Quick Lois, hurry up.... He's fuckin' coming,' Amanda's words were direct and to the point.

'Two seconds.... give me two seconds.'

Amanda ducked down by the glove compartment. 'We haven't got two sec.....'

The axe connected with the exposed passenger window; glass-splinters shattered all over Amanda. Colin poked his head into the now open window, just as the sound of the engine started up. Lois was quick to put the car into gear, and even quicker at accelerating out onto the road, leaving Colin to tumble backwards onto the tarmac, his face cut and bleeding from where the jagged glass of the broken side screen had ripped into his flesh. The car smashed into a parked car, denting it across the entire wing.

'Yesssssss!' yelled Amanda when they had reached the relative safety of the adjoining street. Lois swerved and clipped the wing-mirror of an innocent, on-coming vehicle.

'Amanda,' Lois said calmly, checking to see if there were any fags in the side pocket.

'What?'

'Will you please stop inviting me to any more of your bizarre functions? If it's not transvestites going bonkers in funerals... it's weird fuckers swinging axes at your wedding.... And by the way, you'd better join a different dating agency…. the type of admirers you attract needs to improve….. Fuck me… I thought I could pick them, but you take the biscuit!'

The laughter which filled the car was a mixture of relief, joy and a hint of tension. It had been a long time coming.

'I wonder if anyone will believe us when we tell them about all this.' Amanda asked, strapping herself in with her seat belt.

'Believe it… I bet you someone makes it into a book or a blockbuster movie.'

'Do you think?'

Lois turned the car into the small road which ran parallel with the cemetery wall. She added, 'Of course they'll make it into a film…. and I bet they cast Julia Roberts to play me.'

Amanda was dying to laugh again. She tried hard to keep a straight face. 'Why Julia Roberts?'

'Maybe 'cos I look the spitting image of her… that's why.' A deep scowl ran across her face.

Amanda looked her mate up and down. 'Lois, you don't look anything like her.'

'Ok… she's not as pretty as me, and my tits are bigger… but they can do wonders with make-up these days…. Anyway, who would you want to play you?'

Amanda hadn't thought about such an unusual query. She tried to picture herself on a big cinema screen, while the audience sat below, silent, watching the plot unfold. 'I'm not sure…. What about someone like Meg Ryan?'

'Don't make me laugh…. You'll never get her to agree to play you,' Lois changed gear and added, 'I was thinking more on the lines of Kathy Burke.'

'Thanks Lois…. You get Julia and I get some fat woman.' Lois winked and smirked at her.

Just then a car sped past them going in the opposite direction. Lois caught a glimpse of the driver.

'Hey! I'm sure that was my Ramone.' She checked over her shoulder and nearly crashed into a yellow skip. 'He looked different.' She shrugged her shoulders 'Anyway, never mind, where were we? Film stars.... Who would play Jacob then?'

Amanda didn't have to think long. 'Someone tall, dark and handsome.... George Clooney would be perfect.'

'What about that weirdo?' Lois frowned.

'Maybe Marty Feldman..... No wait,' Amanda thought. 'Ain't he dead?'

Lois laughed. 'He would be perfect, then.' Amanda nodded. Lois continued. 'And, last of all... what about her?' She pointed to the head in Amanda's lap; she changed down to neutral gear as they stopped at a set of temporary traffic lights.

'Her!' Amanda stared at the features on the stuffed head. 'No idea.'

'I know.... Joan Rivers! Or better still, Davina McCall.'

Their fresh bout of laughter was short-lived, as they were suddenly jerked violently forward in their seats. Lois smacked into the steering wheel, the impact knocking her out (this time she wasn't faking it). Amanda's seat belt had saved her from a similar fate.

The silence which followed the crash was eerie. Amanda slowly lifted her head to try to make out what had happened. She looked at her mate; blood trickled down from her forehead. Amanda could see she was breathing but she looked quite badly hurt. She turned her head to look behind her. It was painful. It took her several takes before she let go a scream. She couldn't believe what her eyes were telling her. There was Colin clambering out of the car that had just smashed into them. Tears rolled down his face, the axe handle clenched firmly between his teeth.

Amanda automatically shook her friend. Lois didn't respond. She realised she was left alone to face the music with the weird bloke from the office. She reached for the door handle. She fell out of the car; unwittingly she still had hold of the stuffed head.

Colin pointed at her, removing the axe from his mouth. He ran towards her. Amanda took off. She sprinted through the old, rusty gates of the local cemetery and onto the grass. She swerved in and out of the gravestones which obstructed her route.

The insane man stopped and looked about in the car the girls had been driving. He was hoping to find the remains of his mother. His blood was boiling. He couldn't believe how Amanda had betrayed him. The girl, whom he loved, had turned into the woman who had broken his heart, sawed off the head of his mother, and replaced it with an iceberg lettuce.

He stared angrily at Lois as she lay slumped against the steering wheel. A mist of hatred descended on him. He dragged the unconscious woman out of the car. She fell like a stone onto the pavement, face up to the sky. He positioned the axe above his head.

'A head for a head, Miss Piggy,' he hissed. He started counting to ten, and the sweat on his hands interfered with his grip.

Suddenly the loud beeping of a car horn from behind him broke his intense and evil concentration. A red Fiesta screeched to a halt next to him.

'That's my mother… you bastard,' Ramone yelled through the window.

Colin didn't hang about; he dismissed his decapitation plan and switched his focus back towards his fugitive bride. He glared insanely at the boy, before heading off through the cemetery gates.

Back in the graveyard, Amanda was short of breath. Her legs hurt, her arms felt heavy. It was then she realised that she was still carrying the head. Without thinking of the consequences, she toe-punted it with all her might at a head stone. The head disintegrated into a thousand pieces; bits of straw, sand, skin and two eyeballs shot all over the grave of a woman called Ethel Candy, who had been beheaded in 1863 for crimes against the crown.

'Isn't life ironic?' considered Amanda.

Now free of the spare baggage, Amanda continued running as fast as her legs could carry her. She could see Colin gaining on her with every stride. She felt like curling up into a ball and letting fate take over. She was sick of all this; sick of all the madness; she wanted it all to stop and go away.

She hid down low behind a gravestone, peering over the top. She watched as the mad-man hunted for her. She could see the manic look on his face.

'Amanda!' He bellowed at the top of his voice. All of a sudden, a loud blast of thunder from the skies was closely followed by a downpour of rain. The droplets bounced off the tarmac walkways, soaking the heads of the flowers which littered the gravesides.

'*Amaaaaaannnnddddddddaaaaa*!' Colin's lunatic scream sent a shiver down her backbone.

She crouched down further; her heart beat high up in her chest. It was then she noticed the name engraved on the marble headstone. She had been too scared to take in any details before that.

'Daryl Peter Grey.... Born 1964 – Died 2004'

It made her think just how cynical life could be, with all its twists and turns. Less than six months ago she was married to the man who was now six feet below her. Now she was getting chased by a mad-man, who not only wanted to marry her, but had killed her husband, and had ended up butchering her ex-husband's transvestite lover. Not even Hollywood could have made up a more bizarre storyline. She then thought back to some of the episodes of Dallas that she used to love in the seventies and realised Hollywood could do anything they wanted to, and get away with it.

'Amanda.... I love you.' The rain washed down Colin's distorted face as he yelled out to her.

Her fingers gently traced the words on the headstone; a million images raced through her mind; the good times and the bad times. It was as though she was dying and her life was flashing before her very eyes. She kissed the spot where Daryl's name appeared, wiping the tears and raindrops away from her face.

It was then she became aware of a large shadow looming over her. She was afraid to look up; scared to come face to face with her fate.

'Amanda... where's my mother's head?' His voice was strangely calm.

Amanda rarely, if ever, lied in her life. She believed nothing good would ever come of not telling the truth, but as he stood above her, balancing on the edge of what was left of his insanity, gripping an axe, she thought that maybe on this occasion God would forgive her for the odd porky pie.

'It's still in your kitchen... we hid it in the bread basket.'

An uncertain expression covered his face. He stared at her with suspicion for a minute, his eyes burned into hers, looking for a hint of a lie.

'What did you do with the bread then?' He knew he had just purchased a large, sliced from the bakery.

Without thinking she replied, 'We put it in the bin.'

He put his finger on his chin and asked. 'Why didn't you put the head straight into the rubbish bin?'

He stepped towards her. 'Out of respect.... It's true... believe me.... Please Colin don't hurt me.' She hugged the gravestone, her body shook. She envisaged the axe cutting deep into her skin.

'You betrayed me.... You and your slutty, piggy friend down there.' He pointed out towards the gates.

'I didn't mean to betray you.... I was just scared.... It was all too much, the wedding, the ceremony.' She looked at the ground. What she was also thinking, but was too afraid to mention, was she was also scared stiff because of all the dead people in his house, the cock in the post, and the gypsy woman with the odd-looking son. She had to concentrate hard to stop herself going to pieces.

He knelt by her side, touching her face. 'Why...? Why would I want to hurt you...? I love you!'

His next sentence caused goose pimples to rollerblade across her skin. 'Amanda.... I forgive you.... Let's just go and get my mother's head from the breadbin, the bread from the rubbish bin, and finish off the ceremony.'

'But Colin.... I don't want to rush into a thing like that.' She could feel his mood changing back towards aggression. His knuckles turned white. She carried on, changing her tack, 'But... I do find you attractive.'

In the background she could see a red Fiesta slowly edging its way in their direction. She did her best to distract his attention and stop him from turning around. 'It's just that I need a little time.' Again, she could sense him tensing up. 'Time to get to know you a little better… we need to spend time together.' She smiled at him, praying that he wouldn't look over his shoulder.

He held out his hand to help her off the ground. 'Ok… but this had better not be a trick.'

Behind his back she watched as the car closed in. Lois was hanging out of the passenger window holding a shovel; Ramone steered the car steadily.

Amanda wrestled the conversation back. 'How about going out for a nice romantic meal tonight?' She watched his face change back, the muscles relaxing around his forehead. 'Just me, you and maybe your mother.'

She smiled, he smiled. The thud from the impact of the shovel caused birds to scatter from the trees. Colin's head jerked to one side. He looked at Amanda before collapsing, stone-cold dead, on the next grave.

'Yessssss,' Lois screamed, racing from the car. 'Fuckin' chew on that, you fuckin' weirdo.' She strolled up and whacked him on the head for good measure and booted him in the balls.

'Amanda… I need a drink and then a damn good shag.'

Chapter 16

Tickle

Amanda sat alone, sipping a cup of milky coffee in the quaint English village café. She continued to stare anxiously out onto the high street. People ambled about. It was obvious to her that the residents who lived in this part of the country didn't walk about carrying the weight of the world on their shoulders; they weren't bursting to the seams with stress, or full up to their eyelids with anger. It was in stark contrast to the hustle and bustle of the town where she had grown up. Here everyone seemed so pleasant to each other. There was a smile here, a wave there, and even a couple of hugs and kisses being handed out for good measure.

It reminded her of a scene from Trumpton. She was half-expecting Huw, Drew and Barney McGrew, and the rest of the toy firemen to come shuffling down the street in search of a black cat to rescue from a plastic tree.

Amanda checked her watch. She was waiting for Lois to turn up. As usual, her best mate was late. It had been over nine-months since the insane incident, which eventually led to the weird bloke's death in the cemetery. For a short while, Lois had been charged with manslaughter, but she was later released without any further action being taken.

Oddly enough, the two girls had become national celebrities after the bizarre tale of abduction, murder, stuffed mothers and arranged marriages were splashed all over the major red-top newspapers. From that day, their lives had never been the same. For a while, they were hounded by the paparazzi and even invited onto daytime chat-shows. Lois had also been asked to pose for an advert promoting hard-wearing shovels on the Sky TV Gardening Channel.

Amanda mainly shunned the limelight. She was trying her best to get her shattered life back on track. It hadn't been easy, but at least Jacob was there by her side. Of course, he had survived the ash-tray attack, although he had a sore head for a few days. When the time was right he had told her all about Colin, his step-brother, from Jacob's father's second marriage. The matrimony had ended around the time that Jacob and his sister were taken away to South Africa. He recalled that Colin had always been an odd child, a bit of a loner, who had an unhealthy obsession with murder magazines, and had always wanted to be a taxidermist.

He hadn't seen or heard from Colin, until, out of the blue, the weirdo had phoned him up to mention that he was getting married to a girl from his works.

When the dust finally settled in Amanda's life, she and Jacob had decided to move away from the area for good. He had sold up his business and with that money, and the cash from the newspaper interviews, they had enough to live reasonably comfortably in a cottage just outside a small village in Cornwall.

It was here that they had fallen in love as it should be. They started to really enjoy themselves, and got to know each other well. It did take a while for Amanda to get over the ordeal and even after all this time, she found it hard to sleep. When she did manage to grab some shut-eye, her vivid nightmares would often wake her up in a cold sweat. But now, at least, there was Jacob there to protect her, to cuddle her in his strong arms and kiss her back to sleep.

The police findings after investigating Colin's house had been shocking. Not only had they found a cock-less man, and a headless woman, they also discovered a room which had been dedicated as a shrine to Amanda. The walls were littered with Polaroids of her, in all situations, stretching back over three years. This had proved his unnatural infatuation for her. It was spooky.

The police had confirmed, after examination, that the rogue 'cock-in-the-post' had belonged to Desmond. Amanda wasn't sure if they had finger-printed it, or just matched it up with the aperture in Desmond's groin area. She didn't bother to ask. The cops had concluded that Colin had probably seen Desmond standing outside Amanda's house and this had led him to dole out his own particular type of vicious revenge. There were signs that torture using matchsticks and a nut cracker had taken place, before the mutilation had been carried out.

Amanda checked her watch for the thousandth time. She couldn't wait to see her mate again. To be fair to Lois, she had made the most of her fifteen minutes of notoriety. After appearing on a game show, Lois had made such an impression on the TV producers that they had given her a programme of her own. The TV industry rumour mill suggested that Lois' popularity with the producers was a result of copious blow jobs in the editing suite. Predictably, the topic was centred on sex and people's problems. Overnight, she became Dr Lois, and

Amanda and millions of others switched on to hear the common woman, who could put any sexual problem to rights without mincing her words, enlightening the nation. She became an instant hit; a national hero and a household name.

Eventually, Lois turned up at the café 45 minutes late. She was dressed like an old Hollywood film-actress, in her fake-fur coat and dark shades, a cheap imitation of Elizabeth Taylor. As they sat talking, someone came up and asked her for her autograph. Amanda was amazed how relaxed Lois was with the entire fame thing. She grinned, and ordered a latté, then pulled out a long, slim cigarette from a silver case.

'How's Ramone?' Amanda asked.

'He's fantastic…. he's off the drugs completely.' The smile on her face was evident to see. 'He's going back to night-school to become a painter.'

Amanda was impressed. 'That's a good trade….painting and decorating…. lots of money in it.'

'No…. not that type of painting. He wants to paint like that guy who had his ear sliced off….you know, painting portraits and all that shit. He wants to specialise in nudes and I am going to be his first commission'

Now Amanda was really impressed. 'I didn't realise he had a flare for the arts?'

'He hasn't…. but anything to keep him off the fuckin' smack is good with me.'

Amanda ordered another coffee and a piece of carrot cake. 'And how are you, Lois?'

Lois was lapping the froth off the top of her drink. The white substance stuck to her top lip and she licked it suggestively as she caught the attention of a young lad. 'Me? I'm great as well. They've offered me a new contract; this time on the prime daytime slot. Imagine that… what a turn up for the books….. Me, the new white Oprah.'

Amanda giggled. She loved Lois. She dug a little deeper. 'Still got a stream of lovers chasing after you?'

'No… I'm a one-man-woman these days.'

Amanda's jaw dropped to the table. 'What…? No way.'

'I'm in looooove… finally…. It's serious….. Honest.' Lois's face was stern. 'Don't look so bastard shocked.'

'No…. no, I'm happy for you…. Who's the lucky man?' Amanda reached out and held her friends hand tightly.

'His name is Toby. He's a sound-engineer on the set. You should see him in jeans… saying that… you should see him out of them.' Lois closed in. 'And best of all… he's got a tongue on him that could tickle a star-fish from five hundred paces and he breathes through his ears. He's got a C.O.C.K. on him that's like a baby's arm holding an orange. I've had my fanny tightened, so what with my new tits, my designer vagina and my labia piercing he thinks I'm dead fit.'

The nosey old woman on the next table nearly choked on her toasted sandwich. Amanda was embarrassed for all of them. As usual, Lois didn't flinch.

'Lois…. Could you leave out some of the graphic detail, please?'

There was a brief silence between the women. Lois broke it. 'Anyway, enough of me… how are you and Jacob doing?'

Amanda looked up from the table, before slowly responding. 'That's why I asked you to meet me…. I've got something to tell you?'

'Oh…. Fuck me…. Don't tell me he's having an affair with a transvestite as well,' Lois slammed her mug down hard on the wooden surface. 'I thought he looked a bit fruity.'

This time the old woman on the next table did actually choke. The waitress had to slap her on the back to dislodge a piece of ham and cheese from the back of her throat.

'No Lois…. nothing like that,' Amanda snapped back.

'Thank God…. I couldn't be doing with another adventure with you… It's like being friends with Mr Ben….. So what have you got to tell me then?'

Amanda was slow to retort. She looked her mate in the eye. 'I'm…. I'm pregnant.'

'Pregnant…. Are you sure…. I thought you couldn't have any rug rats?'

'I know…! I know!' Tears streamed down Amanda's face.

Lois held up her palm. 'Hang on…. who's the father?'

'WHAT?' Amanda shrieked back.

'Only messing!' Lois leapt up, launching the coffee cups into the air and grabbed her mate. The water-works started to flow. Both women cried unashamedly. Even the old woman on the next table joined in, and so did the waitress as she bent over on all fours, clearing up the broken china and mess.

Lois jumped up and announced. 'That's great news…. Lattés all round.' Everyone in the café clapped and cheered.

Amanda held her friends hand. 'Lois…. We would like you to be the godmother.'

Lois was speechless for the second time in her life.

'It was Jacob's idea…. Well, what do you think?'

'Are you serious?' Lois was physically shaking; her hands trembled.

'Of course I'm serious…. will you?'

'Well I'll S.H.I.T. a brick….. Me a godmother...? Does that mean I can drive around in a black car and get people killed…? like Al Pacino?'

Amanda just went with it. 'If you like.'

'I would be honoured…. And I will be the best godmother in the whole, wide world…. I promise. I'll have the little cherub drinking cider and on the fags by the time he reaches short trousers,' she joked.

Amanda smiled through the tears of joy. 'I know you will…. I know you will.'

Lois sat back down. 'Are you two getting married then, or what?'

'Not for a while…. I couldn't go through another ceremony at the moment.'

'When you decide… I know a great, gyppo woman priest with a broken nose…. She'll do it cheap and predict your future into the bargain!'

They laughed out loud and continued giggling for most of the afternoon. They spent another four hours enjoying their own company. Eventually a big, chauffeur driven, black Mercedes pulled up. It was time for Lois to go. She kissed her mate and said goodbye for now. As she got in the car she made sure the young, black driver got a good look up her skirt.

Amanda felt good about herself. Things were on the up; things were going to change forever. To celebrate she decided to go to her local shop and try out a bit of Blind-shopping to kill some time. She was positive she could set a new department store record and make it all the way through the checkouts before opening her eyes. She smiled at the waitress and walked out into the high street.

THE END

Unlimited thanks to:-

- Vince Kerr and Phil Shelley for proof-reading
- Bernard Canniffe for front cover photo / design
- Lyn Williams for cover design (opaldesign.co.uk)
- Nigel Roberts for listening and the red wine
- Greg Charles for the software stuff
- Ralph Coates for the hair styles
- Rasputin for the advice on Butcher shops and women

I'll leave you with:-

"Have you ever been to Love-street
Have you tried on all the shoes
They're for walking on the clouds with
And not for down here in the blues"

World Party

Go Easy….. Step Lightly….. Stay Free

Bunko

www.anthonybunko.co.uk
Email:- anthony@bunko.freeserve.co.uk